HER MIND SCREAMED FIGHT, BUT HER BODY REFUSED TO ANSWER.

Arms scooped her up, lifting her as if she weighed nothing. With effort, she forced her eyelids open and stared up at the man who held her. Not the one who'd attacked her. A little older, maybe. Not oily. A nice face.

"Zack?" The name barely formed on her lips.

"Your companion is gone."

"*Dead*?" She stopped breathing, her vision narrowing dangerously.

"Taken."

A flash of yellow caught in her peripheral vision and then she felt herself dropped bonelessly into the front passenger seat of a vehicle. The Jeep. She struggled without success to sit up. She couldn't even find the energy to reach for the door latch. "Have . . . to find him. Have to . . . escape."

"There's no escaping V.C., *cara*."

She tried to look at him, but couldn't manage to turn her head. "*V . . . C.*?"

"Washington, V.C.," he replied. "Vamp City. Your new home."

By Pamela Palmer

Vamp City Novels

A BLOOD SEDUCTION

Feral Warriors Novels

ECSTASY UNTAMED
HUNGER UNTAMED
RAPTURE UNTAMED
PASSION UNTAMED
OBSESSION UNTAMED
DESIRE UNTAMED

Coming Soon

A LOVE UNTAMED

PAMELA PALMER

A BLOOD SEDUCTION

A VAMP CITY NOVEL

AVON

An Imprint of HarperCollinsPublishers

AVON BOOKS
An Imprint of HarperCollins*Publishers*
10 East 53rd Street
New York, New York 10022-5299

Copyright © 2012 by Pamela Palmer
ISBN 978-0-06-210749-7
www.avonbooks.com

First Avon Books mass market printing: June 2012

Avon Trademark Reg. U.S. Pat. Off. and in Other Countries, Marca Registrada, Hecho en U.S.A.
HarperCollins® is a registered trademark of HarperCollins Publishers.

Printed in the U.S.A.

10 9 8 7 6 5 4 3 2 1

For Keith. My hero.

ACKNOWLEDGMENTS

A huge thank-you to Kelly Poulsen and Kyle Poulsen for their help in brainstorming the world of Vamp City. And to Shannon Silkensen for assistance with the NIH details. Any mistakes are my own.

Many, many thanks to my editor, May Chen, who is a dream to work with; Laurin Wittig and Anne Shaw Moran, my critique partners, soul sisters, and best friends; and the wonderful team at Avon Books, including Pamela Spengler-Jaffee, Jessie Edwards, Amanda Bergeron, and Art Director Tom Egner (for my fabulous cover).

Thanks also to Robin Rue, Emily Cotler, and Kim Castillo for all their efforts on my behalf.

And a huge thank-you to you, my readers. You delight and inspire me.

A Blood
Seduction

CHAPTER ONE

Perched on her stool in the chilly lab of the Clinical Center of the National Institutes of Health in Bethesda, Maryland, Quinn Lennox studied the lab results on the desk in front of her. Dammit. Just like all the others, this one revealed nothing out of the ordinary. Nothing. She'd run every blood test known to science, and they all claimed that the patient was disgustingly healthy. Utterly normal.

They lied.

The patient wasn't normal and never had been, and she wanted to know why. She wanted to be able to point to some crazy number on one of the myriad blood tests, and say, "There. That's it. That's the reason my life is so screwed up."

Because those lab tests were hers.

"Quinn."

At the sound of her boss's voice in the lab doorway, Quinn jumped guiltily. If anyone found out that she'd been using the lab's equipment to run blood tests on herself, she'd be fired on the spot. She set the lab report on her desk, resisting the urge to turn the paper over or slip it in her desk, and forced herself to meet Jennifer's gaze with a questioning one of her own.

"Did you have time to run the McCluny tests?" Jennifer was a round woman, over forty, with a big heart and a driving need to save the world.

"Of course," Quinn replied with a smile. "They're on your desk." She might be running tests she shouldn't be, but never, ever at the expense of someone else's.

"Excellent." Jennifer grinned. "I wish I could clone you, Quinn."

Quinn stifled a groan at the thought. "One of me is more than enough." Certainly more than *she* could handle.

"Hey, you two." Clarice, in a T-shirt and shorts, a fleece hoodie tied around her waist, stopped in the doorway beside Jennifer. It was after 6:00 P.M., and most of the techs had already left for the day. Clarice was clearly on her way out since she'd taken off her white lab coat. But she should be, considering she was getting married in two days. A curvy redhead, Clarice had been one of Quinn's best friends in her first couple of years at the NIH. Before everything had started to go wonky, and Quinn had been forced to retreat from virtually all social events.

Clarice clapped her hands together, the excitement radiating from her so palpable that Quinn could feel it halfway across the lab. The woman practically had the words *bride-to-be* dancing in fizzy champagne bubbles over her head. "Are you two going to meet us at my apartment tomorrow night or down in Georgetown? Larry and two of his groomsmen are available to drive anyone who needs a ride home afterward."

The bachelorette party. Bar-hopping in Georgetown. Quinn nearly swallowed her tongue, forcing down the quick denial. No, she would not be going. Absolutely not. "It's easier for me to meet you there," Quinn replied. No excuse was good enough short of sudden illness. And it was too soon for that.

"I'll meet you at your apartment." Jennifer patted the younger woman on the shoulder. "You look radiant and happy, Clarice. Exactly how a bride-to-be should look. Not a bit the stressed-out crazy person so many brides turn into these days."

"Oh, I'm a crazy person, don't worry. I'm just happy-crazy."

"Stay that way. See you ladies tomorrow," Jennifer said with a wave, and disappeared down the hall.

Clarice came into the lab, now empty but for Quinn, and perched on the lab stool beside Quinn's. "I have a *million* things to do. Two million."

Quinn gave her a half-sympathetic, half-disbelieving look. "Then what are you doing here?"

"Procrastinating. The moment I walk out the door, I'll be moving a hundred miles an hour until I go to bed. If I ever get there tonight."

Quinn grabbed Clarice's hand. "I'm happy for you."

"Thanks." Clarice squeezed hers back. "I'm so glad you're going out with us tomorrow night, Quinn."

"Me, too," Quinn replied weakly, hating that she wouldn't be going. It had been so long since she'd enjoyed a night out, and this one promised to be a lot of fun. And she hated to disappoint Clarice. But she didn't dare go. Not to Georgetown. "I wouldn't miss it."

Clarice slipped her hand from Quinn's and hopped off the lab stool. "Enough procrastinating. I've got to get going."

"Get some sleep tonight."

Clarice rolled her eyes. "I'll sleep on the honeymoon."

"Larry might have other ideas."

With a laugh, Clarice disappeared around the corner.

Quinn turned back to her desk, folded the lab report, and stuck it in her purse, then pulled off her lab coat and glanced down at her clothes, her stomach knotting with tension. On the surface, she was dressed normally for the lab—jeans (purple), T-shirt (red), and tennis shoes (bright blue). The problem was, when she'd dressed this morning, the jeans had been blue, the tee yellow, the shoes white. The Shimmer had struck on her way to work this morning, as it did almost every day now. Why? Why did these things keep happening to her and no one else?

Heading out of the building, she began the long trek across the NIH campus to her car, not looking forward to the long slog through D.C. traffic to get home. Traveling to and from work on the Metro had been so much easier. But public transportation of any kind was out of the question now. What if they passed through a Shimmer? How in the hell would she explain such a color transformation to her fellow passengers?

By the time she reached her car, a ten-year-old Ford Taurus, she was sweating in the late August heat. Opening the car door, she stared at the pink interior, which was supposed to be slate gray, the knot in her stomach growing. With a resigned huff, she slid into the hot car and headed back into Washington, D.C., and home.

Her life had always been a little odd. Now it was starting to come unhinged.

Strange things had happened as far back as she could remember, though rarely. Only twice had they been scary-strange rather than silly-strange, like the color changes. And nothing had happened at all after that second bad incident, in high school. Not until a couple of years ago, when the Shimmers had begun playing with her.

A couple of weeks ago, the visions started.

Yes, her life was becoming seriously unhinged.

As she neared the Naval Observatory on Massachusetts Ave., she saw one of the Shimmers up ahead, like a faint sheen in the sunlight, almost like the rainbow that sometimes appeared in water mist. They were always in the same spots, never moving, never wavering—nearly invisible walls in various parts of D.C. that she'd always been able to see, always been able to drive or walk through without incident. Until recently. Now she avoided them like the plague, when she could. But there wasn't a single route to work that didn't pass through one.

Unfortunately, one cut right through the heart of Georgetown, which was why she couldn't possibly meet Clarice, Jennifer, and the others tomorrow. How drunk would they have to be to not notice her clothes changing color right before their eyes? Too drunk. It was far too great a risk.

As she drove through the Shimmer, the hair rose on her arms, as it always did, her car interior returning to gray, and her clothes and shoes returning to normal.

In some ways, she'd gotten used to the strangeness, but in a bigger way, she was scared. Because the changes were escalating in frequency, and she had a bad feeling that it was just the beginning.

She couldn't help but wonder . . .

What comes next?

Quinn unlocked the door of her apartment on the edge of the George Washington University campus and pushed it open. The warm smell of pepperoni pizza and the comforting sound of a computer gun battle greeted her.

"Oh, nice kill." Zack's voice carried from the living room, low and even. When had his voice gotten so deep? He was only twenty-two, for heaven's sake. A man, now. A computer geek who'd long ago found his passion in game design and, more than likely, the love of his life in his best friend, if he ever woke up to the fact that he and Lily were meant to be more than programmer buddies.

Quinn locked the front door behind her, set her purse and keys on the hall table, then strode into the living room, a room she'd furnished slowly and carefully, choosing just the right shades of tans and moss greens and splashes of eggplant to please her senses. But it was the room's occupants who pleased her far more. Zack and Lily sat side by side at the long table against the far wall, each in front of a computer. Behind them, the television news flashed on the flatscreen, the volume a low hum in the room. But neither of the kids paid the television any attention. Each fiendishly tapped away at a computer mouse, staring fixedly at his monitor. Beside Lily sat a plate with a single thick slice of greasy pizza. Beside Zack, two large pizza boxes. The kid never quit eating.

Lily glanced over her shoulder. "Hi, Quinn." A sweet smile lit pretty features framed by long, sleek, black hair.

"Hi, Lily."

Without glancing away from the computer screen, Zack grabbed a slice of pizza out of the top box. Overlong curly red hair framed an engaging face as he wolfed down half of it in one bite and appeared to swallow it just as quickly.

"Hey, sis," he greeted absently. Though only half siblings, they resembled one another rather markedly, except for the hair. They'd both inherited their dad's lanky height, green eyes, wide mouth, and straight nose. But while Zack had that mass of curly red hair, her own was as blond and straight as her late mother's. Their personalities, too, were nothing alike, which was probably why they got along so well. Zack personified laidback serenity, while Quinn couldn't stay still to save her life. Something had to be in motion—her mind, her body—preferably, both.

Only two things truly mattered to her. Zack and her work. In that order. She liked her job, and she was damned good at it. But if Zack gave her the slightest hint that he'd like her to follow him to California after he graduated, she'd move. Just like that.

But he wouldn't. Zack had Lily, now, if he didn't blow it with her. He didn't need his sister. He'd never really needed her. Not the way she needed him.

"Whoa!" he exclaimed around a bite of pizza as some kind of bomb went off in the middle of the game. "Did you see that, Lily? Awesome."

Quinn grabbed a slice of pizza, then turned up the volume on the television and switched the channel to the local news.

"Another person has been reported missing in downtown D.C. in a string of disappearances that has police baffled. This brings the total number reported missing in the past six weeks to twelve. This last incident is believed to have occurred near George Washington University."

"G.W.?" Lily asked.

But when Quinn glanced at her, the girl had already returned to her game, her lack of concern mired in the youthful belief that bad things only ever happen to other people. A view Quinn had never shared. Unlike most young adults, she'd never believed her world to be a safe, secure place. Never.

Quinn finished her pizza, then carried her laptop back to her bedroom and got online. Sometime later, she heard the front door close and glanced at the time. She'd been on the computer nearly two hours. Was Zack going out or coming back? Closing her laptop, she went to find out.

She found her brother in the kitchen, his head in the fridge.

"Did you walk Lily home, Zack?"

"Uhm-hm."

She grabbed a glass and filled it with water from the sink. "Want me to fix you something?"

"No, thanks."

Zack and Lily, both computer science majors at George Washington, had met their freshman year and become instant friends. They'd interned together this summer at a small Silicon Valley gaming company—a company who'd offered them both jobs upon graduation. Zack had mentioned that they might be doing some testing for the company over the school year.

"Were you guys playing or testing tonight?"

"Both."

Zack wasn't the world's greatest conversationalist. Nine times out of ten, she had trouble getting more than one or two words out of him, though every now and then she asked the right question, usually about gaming, and he talked her ear off.

He straightened, holding a small bottle of Gatorade. "Want one?" Her brother's eyes crinkled at the corners, the unspoken love they felt for one another sparkling in his eyes.

She smiled. "No thanks."

With that, he left the kitchen, his mind wholly engaged by whatever thoughts forever zinged around his head. He'd always been that way, seemingly unaware of anything around him. And yet he'd always been there for her. Always. Zack's love was the one constant, the one absolute, in her life. And always had been.

Quinn downed her water, then poured herself a glass of wine and followed him into the living room, curling up on the sofa, utterly content to listen to Zack's tapping at the computer keyboard as she read. She tried to give Zack some privacy when Lily was here, though she was pretty sure he'd never taken advantage of it in any way. As far as she could tell, Zack considered Lily a friend and nothing more. One of these days, he was going to wake up to the fact that his best friend was a beautiful young woman who happened to be in love with him. And when that day . . .

Quinn froze as a familiar chill skated over her skin. Her breath caught, the hair lifting on her arms. Oh, hell. She'd felt this same chill more than half a dozen times over the past few weeks. Only recently had she connected it to the visions.

She set her wineglass down so fast, it splashed onto the lamp table, then she lunged off the chair and crossed to the window with long, quick strides. But as she approached, she slowed, hesitating, her pulse kicking hard and fast. She knew what she *should* see, looking out the window— the dorms across the street, two dozen windows glowing with light and life, cars lining the street below. Her heart thrummed with anticipation and dread at what she *would* see instead.

Dammit, why does this stuff always have to happen to me?

With a quick breath, she stepped forward and lifted shaking hands to the windowpane, curving her hands around her eyes to close out the light from the room. And, just as she'd feared, she stared at an impossible sight. A line of two-story row houses, decrepit and crumbling, lit only by the moonlight falling from above, stood where the dorms should be. This street, unlike the real one, was unlit, unpaved. Uninhabited?

Three other times over the past weeks, after she'd felt that odd chill, she'd looked out the window to find this exact same scene. *Why?* If it weren't for all the other strangeness in her life, she might think she was hallucinating. Or going insane.

Maybe I am.

The sound of a horse's whinny carried over the sound of the real traffic, for the normal sounds had never died away despite the change in scenery. Her eyes widened. Maybe her imaginary street wasn't quite so uninhabited after all. She pushed up the window and leaned forward, as close to the screen as she could get without actually pressing her nose against it.

"Zack, turn off the light and come here." As soon as the words were out of her mouth, she wanted to pull them back. She'd spoken without thinking. Then again, if he saw it, too . . .

Zack never did anything quickly, but the tone of her voice must have gotten through to him because he doused the light, except for one computer monitor, and joined her a handful of seconds later.

"What?" He folded his long length and peered through the screen beside her.

Quinn swallowed. "I thought I heard a horse. Do you see one?"

His shoulder brushed hers as he turned and looked in one direction, then the other. "Nope. Probably just one of the mounted cops." He straightened and returned to his computer.

Quinn pressed a fist against her chest and her racing heart. Just once, she'd like not to be the only freak on the planet.

The distinctive sound of a horse's clip-clop grew louder, overlaying the true traffic sounds. And then she saw it, pulling a buggy down that empty dirt street, a dark-cloaked figure holding the reins. A moment later, incongruously, a yellow Jeep Wrangler burst onto the scene, swerving around the carriage, causing the horse to sidestep with agitation. The buggy driver shouted with anger. And then the strange sounds and sights were gone, and Quinn once more stared at the dorms and cars that were really there.

"Lily's missing."

At the sound of Zack's frantic voice through the cell phone the next morning, Quinn leaped from her lab bench, her free hand pressing against her head. "Are you sure?" *God.* The disappearances!

"We were going to meet out front and walk to class together like we always do. But she never showed up. And I can't find her."

"She's not picking up her phone?"

"No. She texted me to say she'd be here in five minutes, but that was fifteen minutes ago, and she's not here. She's not anywhere, Quinn. I've been walking around looking for her."

"Zack." She'd never heard him sound so frantic—she'd never heard him sound frantic at all. She scrambled to think of a logical, safe explanation for Lily's disappearance and couldn't come up with a single one that fit Lily's serious, responsible nature. "Have you called her mom?" Lily lived with her parents about six blocks away.

"I don't know her mom's number."

Crap. "Do you know either of her parents' names?"

"Mr. and Mrs. Wang."

"Zack. There have to be hundreds of Wangs in D.C."

"I know."

"Where are you?"

"Starbucks on Penn."

A couple of blocks from their apartment. "Stay there. Inside. I'm on my way."

Thirty minutes later, after handing off her work to a fellow technician, racing to her car, and flying through more nearly red lights than she cared to admit, she found Zack right where he'd said he'd be, his body rigid with tension as he paced. He looked up and saw her, the devastation in his expression lifting with relief. As if she could fix it. *Oh, Zack.* His T-shirt was plastered to his body, his face flushed and soaked with sweat. He loved that girl, she could see it in his eyes, even if he didn't know it, yet. If Lily was really gone, her loss was going to slay him.

And his grief was going to slay Quinn.

She took his hand, squeezing his damp fist. "Where have you looked?"

"Around." His eyes misted, his mouth tightening painfully. "She's not here, Quinn."

"We'll find her."

But he wasn't buying her optimism any more than she was. The cops hadn't found a single one of the missing people, yet. Not one.

"Do you know where she was when you last heard from her?"

"She was close. Within a block or two of our apartment."

Quinn cocked her head at him. "Doesn't she usually buy coffee on her way to class?"

"Yeah."

"Where?"

He blinked. "Here."

"Have you asked if they saw her?"

His face scrunched in embarrassment. "No." He pulled out his cell phone as he walked up to the counter, stepping in front of the line and holding out his phone and, she assumed, Lily's picture, to the barista. "I'm looking for my friend. Did she get coffee here a little while ago?"

The man peered at the picture. "Yeah. Lily, right? She ordered her usual mocha latte no-whip."

Zack turned away, and Quinn fell into step beside him as they pushed through the morning-coffee crowd and left the shop. She squinted against the glare of the summer sun. "She went missing between here and the street in front of our apartment. It's just two blocks, Zack." And the chances they'd find her, after Zack had already looked, were slim to none.

Together, they walked down the busy sidewalk, dodging college kids, locals, and tourists as they searched for any sign of Lily or what might have happened to her. Quinn's chest ached, as much for Lily as it did for Zack. His anguish, thick and palpable, hung in the steamy air.

When that familiar chill rippled over her skin, it startled her. *Oh, hell. Not here. Not now.*

They were nearly to the block their apartment sat on, the street where, just last night, she'd seen an old-fashioned horse and buggy. In the dark. Surely she wouldn't see it in bright daylight.

Her pulse began to race in both anticipation and dread. What if she saw that strange scene again? What if, as always happened when she peered out the window, she suddenly couldn't see the real world? Would she start running into people? Maybe walk in front of a car?

She grabbed Zack, curling her fingers around his upper arm.

His gaze swung to her, hope wreathing his face. "Do you see her?"

"No. I just . . . I don't feel well."

His brows drew down, and he pulled her hand off his arm and engulfed it in his larger one, closing his fingers tightly around hers.

Hand in hand, they crossed the street, pushing through a throng of backpacked college kids, and walked around the construction barricade that was blocking her view of her building. As they cleared the barricade, Quinn swallowed a gasp at the sight that met her gaze. Superimposed upon a small section of her apartment building, to the left of the entrance, was what appeared to be a house of some sort. Or row house. It was set back and partially illuminated as if by a spotlight, surrounded by shadows. A crumbling, haunted-looking house that wasn't really there.

Holy shit. She pulled up short.

"You see something."

Zack's words barely registered, and she answered without thinking. "Yes."

"What?"

His excitement penetrated her focus. "I'm not sure." But she started forward, her gaze remaining glued on that impossible sight. The shadows fully blocked the sidewalk, extending almost to the street, as if the vision were three-dimensional, as if a slice had been cut from another world, a square column, and dropped into the middle of hers. But the house didn't appear to actually stand within that column. In fact, the column didn't appear to quite reach the front of her apartment building at all. It was as if the shadows acted as a window into the world where the house sat, alone and abandoned.

She frowned, trying to make sense of it. Why, when the scene appeared at night, was she able to see what appeared to be the entire landscape of . . . what? Was it another world? Another time? No, it couldn't be another time. Not with a Jeep Wrangler racing across the landscape.

Why could she see it when no one else could? And, clearly, no one else could. People were walking right through those shadows as if they weren't there.

She had no intention of doing the same. With her luck, her face and hair would turn purple.

Zack squeezed her hand. "What do you see, Quinn? Something to do with Lily?"

"I'm not sure. Probably not," she replied out of habit, not about to admit to her weirdness. If Zack knew about it, he'd never said a word. And if he didn't, if he'd remained happily clueless all these years, well, there was no need for him to find out now. "Just give me a moment, Zack." She let go of his hand. "Wait here."

Quinn eased forward, dodging a couple of college kids as she neared that strange column of spotlight and shadows. It wasn't a spotlight, she realized, but sunlight illuminating the front stoop of a house that stood only about twelve feet away. Mold and mud splattered the ancient brick; glass, long since broken, left gaping holes for windows; and the front door hung askew, dangling on one hinge. On that door, a tarnished lion's-head door-knocker sat cockeyed and snarling at unwary visitors. Visitors long gone.

It looked so *real*.

The column itself was only about six feet wide, yet the house sat farther back than those six feet. To either side of the spotlighted front stoop, shadows and darkness lingered, like a nightscape cut by a beacon of sunlight. Yet people continued to flow through that shadowy column, oblivious. Unaffected.

"Lily's pen."

Quinn hadn't even realized Zack had followed her until she saw him reach for the bright green ballpoint pen lying on the sidewalk just inside the shadows.

"Zack, no."

Instinctively, she grabbed his bare forearm just as his arm . . . and her clutching hand . . . dipped into the shadows. Energy leaped at her through the hand that held him, attacking her with an electrical shock that raced over her body like crawling ants, shooting every hair on her arms and head straight up.

Her breath caught, her eyes widened. Her brain screamed, *Let go of him!* But her fingers couldn't react in time, and, suddenly, they were both flying forward.

Into nothingness.

CHAPTER TWO

Quinn landed on her hands and knees, scraping her hands on . . . on . . . *The pavers beneath her hands were not the sidewalk in front of her apartment.* Looking up, the blood rushed from her face.

"Quinn?" The note of fear and confusion that rang in Zack's voice clanged in her head.

She didn't answer him. *Couldn't* answer him through her heart pounding in her throat. She was on her hands and knees beneath a wide, bright spotlight. And all around that single shaft was darkness.

Just like the column.

Head thudding, she pushed to her feet to find Zack standing close by, his stunned expression mirroring her own.

"What the fuck, Quinn?"

"I don't know."

The darkness swallowed everything outside the spotlight, but she sensed that far more was there. Turning, her jaw dropped as she stared at the door she'd seen through the shadows. As before, it hung from one hinge, its lion's-head doorknocker hanging cockeyed and abandoned. Stepping forward, she climbed the two brick steps and lifted her hand to touch the cool, pitted metal.

Real.

How in the hell did this happen?

She turned, her gaze fighting to spear the darkness that surrounded them on every other side. Looking up, she squinted into the sun. Okay, not a spotlight. Sunlight. *But how . . . ?* The sun shone in this spot—and nowhere else.

Thoughts and questions collided against one another in her head, crashing and tangling as she met Zack's wide-eyed gaze.

"Where'd everyone go?" he asked.

"I don't know." The people, the traffic. Her apartment building. All gone. She was starting to shake. Weird stuff was a normal part of her life, but nothing *ever* like this. God, had she *done* this? Had she somehow brought them here . . . wherever here was?

Did I make the whole of Washington, D.C. disappear? Or is it Zack and I who disappeared? Just like the others.

Just like Lily.

Without warning, the spotlight . . . sunlight . . . went out as if an angel had turned off the sun with a flick of a switch, throwing them into darkness.

The bottom of Quinn's stomach fell out. She reached for Zack as he reached for her, their arms colliding, their hands finding and gripping one another's.

"I don't think we're in D.C. anymore," Zack

whispered, as if the darkness were a living thing around them.

"Then where are we?" The air swirled strangely, with currents both sun-heated and moist-cool, and smelled of mildew and mold and something more pleasant—an exotic spiciness she couldn't place.

"I don't know. How can the sun just be gone like that?"

"How could it just shine in one spot?" she countered.

"We must be inside something with a roof. They must have closed the roof." His words sounded logical, but his voice was beginning to quaver. "Do you think this is where Lily went?"

"Maybe." She'd dropped her pen in this exact spot. At least, the exact spot where they'd been standing in front of Quinn's apartment. "But where *are* we?"

Slowly, her eyes began to adjust to the darkness. A darkness that wasn't quite complete, she realized with bone-melting relief. It was only dusk at the moment, not yet full night. But as her vision cleared, and she could see beyond, she felt no relief. All sign of the world they'd left behind was gone—the people, the cars, the city noises. The only thing familiar was the layout of the streets, the way they intersected, their width. But these roads were dirt, not paved. Buildings lined the roads, though nothing like the modern apartment and office buildings of her own neighborhood. These buildings were old-fashioned-looking and crumbling, as if they hadn't been occupied in decades.

Across the street . . . *what the hell?* Her brows drew down as she stared at the same strip of abandoned row houses she'd seen over and over again from her living-room window. So this was it. *This* was the place she'd been seeing.

Somehow, they'd walked right into that world. Which meant there were people here. Horses, buggies, yellow Jeep Wranglers. A frisson of excitement leaped within her, warring with a bone-deep need to escape. She'd love to explore this place, to find out what it was. *Where* it was. But her need to keep her brother out of danger overrode her natural curiosity. And her instincts told her there was danger here.

"We've got to get out of here." The question was, how? But she thought she knew. The column had pulled them in. If it reappeared—in the form of light, apparently—why couldn't they escape the same way?

"We can't leave without Lily." Zack's hand spasmed around hers, then let go. "Lily!" His voice echoed over the ruined landscape.

"Zack, shh! There are people here."

He gazed around with quick, jerky movements. "Where?"

"I don't see them, yet. I just . . . I think they're here."

As if to prove her point, a shout sounded in the distance, a man's shout. Of warning? Of fear? She shivered. Yeah, definitely danger. She needed to get them home. Now. Her stomach was cramping, her chest aching because she kept forgetting to breathe.

The shout died, and no sound followed. No horses, no car engines, no voices. Not even a bird. Silence blanketed everything.

"Come on." Zack motioned her with his head. "We need to find Lily."

"We don't even know if she's here."

"It makes sense, doesn't it? People keep disappearing. Lily disappeared. We've disappeared, now, too. And I know that was her pen. She stood in that exact spot not thirty minutes before us."

Thirty minutes was a long time for the vision to linger, in her experience. Though she'd once watched one out her window for nearly twenty. And she couldn't argue with the evidence.

Quinn swallowed. "We don't even know where we are."

"It doesn't matter. We'll find Lily, then figure it out."

She really wanted to argue for staying put until the column of light appeared again. But she knew Zack too well. If he thought there was a chance of finding Lily, she wasn't going to keep him here. And, honestly, a part of her was dying to explore.

"All right."

Zack started off, his long strides eating up the sidewalk as she hurried to keep up with him. "You act like you know where you're going."

"I want to walk down Penn."

fr...
di...
D.C...

"...

"T...
jaw di...

"'Co...
town. E...

He wa... right. ...
tween th...
twisted, w...
no grass. N...
a desolate, r... Except for
that shout. A... she'd seen a buggy
in one of her ... And, incongruously, that
Jeep Wrangler. There were definitely people here
somewhere.

"There's an easy way to find out if this is some
weird version of the city," Zack said.

She knew exactly what he had in mind, and
they might as well find out. They crossed the
next two streets, reached the corner of Pennsylvania Avenue, and turned onto it without hesitation. She wondered if this was a good idea, if the
smarter option might be to try to find a place to
hide. But hide from what? And for how long? If
Lily was here, they needed to find her, though
God only knew how. Sooner or later, they were
going to need food. And water.

26

[Folded corner text, partially obscured:]
Side by side, they strode down Pe...
Avenue, or this empty, or...
blocks, three." Zack mur...
"Jesus Christ," Zack dropped...
Quinn's jaw ... or what...
House ... once-beautiful...
as everything...
manicure...
dles...

nsylvania
version. Two
it.
...ured beside her.
...s she stared at the White
...ssed for it in this place. The
...esident's mansion was as ruined
...g else she'd seen so far. The once-
...d lawns were nothing but dirt and pud-
...early the size of ponds, dead trees sprouting
...domly from the swampy ground.

She frowned as she stared at the building. Something was off. It wasn't as big as the version she knew. "The East and West Wings are missing. It doesn't look like they were ever there." Even the east portico was gone although there appeared to be some kind of decrepit shell of a structure where the west portico should have been. The roof had partially collapsed on one side, and the white sandstone walls appeared gray in the near darkness, as if the sandstone had begun to melt and run.

Zack's shoulder brushed hers as they pressed together. "That's what the White House used to look like, back at the time of the Civil War. At least it's what the structure looked like. The East and West Wings were added later. My history professor had a print of it hanging on the wall."

"So we're in the D.C. of the past? But the past was alive, and this place is dead, and appears to have been for a long, long time."

"Maybe we're in an alternate universe."

"There's no such thing as an alternate universe." The words came out before she considered their absurdity in light of the current situation.

Zack grunted. "Do you have a better explanation?"

"Not a one."

"Lily's here. I know it. And we're going to find her. Then she and I are going to create the most kick-ass game ever invented because it's going to be based on a place that actually exists."

Quinn had to hand it to him. Even in the face of *insanity*, he was keeping his cool.

"Assuming we can find our way back out of here." What if returning the way they'd come didn't work? Somehow, she wasn't holding out much hope for clicking her heels, and whispering, "There's no place like home."

"We'll figure that out later."

Why worry about level seventeen when you've just entered the game? Except, this was no game.

In the distance, another scream slashed the unnatural silence, this one female.

Zack flinched. "Lily."

Quinn grabbed his arm. "No. The voice was too deep." But it was clear there were dangers in that place, dangers they didn't want to stumble upon. "I think we'd better find someplace to hide until we figure out what's going on."

She glanced at the crumbling White House. Was it stable enough to walk into if they dodged the puddles?

"Do you hear that?" Zack whispered.

Quinn stilled, stiffening at the sound of a horse and carriage. The one she'd seen from her apartment window? Perspiration broke out on the back of her neck. Maybe whoever was in that carriage would help them. Her gut instinct screamed *hide*, but the decision was taken out of her hands as the carriage drove into sight on the cross street a block up, and they were left standing squarely in the open. This conveyance was slightly larger than the one she'd seen in her vision, and even in the low light, she could tell that the couple driving it were dressed as if they'd stepped off the soundstage of *Gone With the Wind*.

Did this mean they *were* in the past, or some postapocalyptic version of it?

"*Whoa.*" The carriage pulled up in the middle of the street half a block away.

"Should we run?" Zack asked.

"One of them is a woman. Maybe they'll help us." As Quinn watched, the couple alighted from the carriage with a strange ease, even the woman, as if all that voluminous material weighed nothing at all. And then, suddenly, they were gone.

"What the . . . ?" Zack exclaimed.

Quinn's heart missed a beat, then took off in a crazy flight, nearly stopping altogether when, seconds later, the pair materialized directly in front of them, not ten feet away. No way in hell had a woman in a full Scarlett O'Hara skirt run faster than the eye could follow down a dirt road.

Her head pounded. Her instincts continued to scream, *Run!* even as her logical mind knew there would be no outrunning this pair. There would be no escape.

She faced them squarely, lifting her chin. Both were young and attractive, the woman as blond as Quinn herself but far more beautiful, her ringlets swept up beneath an elaborate hat, the bodice of her fancy dress cut dangerously low. A deep breath, and she'd be showing nipple.

Her companion was a good fit for her—young and handsome and dressed like Abraham Lincoln. But his smile as he stared at them was as oily as a mechanic's rag, setting off all Quinn's creep alarms. What in the hell kind of world was this?

Zack sucked in a breath. "This isn't good."

"You think?"

The rev of an engine broke the ominous silence. She glanced behind her, praying her own world had decided to make a reappearance, but no. Nothing had changed.

"And where did you come from?" the woman asked, her tone more delighted than curious.

Quinn took a step forward, placing herself between them and her brother. Zack's hands gripped her shoulders from behind as if he meant to pull her behind him at the first sign of trouble. As if he was too much of a man to let his big sister protect him any longer.

"What is this place?" she demanded.

The man's smile widened. "You don't know?"

"They must have entered through the last sunbeam." The woman stepped away from her companion, eyeing Zack hungrily.

It had been years since Quinn had practiced martial arts, but she still remembered a thing or two. Which might be helpful against opponents who weren't *so damned fast*. "Stay back," Quinn warned, shrugging away Zack's hands as she went into her fighting stance, her right leg back, her hands forming fists in front of her.

"And why would I step back, sweet one?" The man smiled, his incisors looking more like fangs than teeth. "I've just found dinner."

Quinn gaped. *Those fangs were growing.*

"No fucking way." Zack's tone sounded more awestruck than horrified. "Vampires."

Quinn scowled. "That's ridiculous."

The man chuckled, his eyes changing, the black pupils turning a milky, startling white as the fangs lengthened, thickened. *Sharpened.* "Is it?"

The woman lunged first, though *lunged* wasn't the right word. She flew at Zack. By the time Quinn could move, the woman had Zack on the sidewalk six feet away, straddling him as she struck, burying her own fangs deep into Zack's neck. She'd kill him!

Quinn roared. But before she could even take a full step toward them, the man was on her, whirling her around as if she weighed nothing, slamming her back against him, his arms pinning her to him like bands of steel. She fought against his hold, kicking back, slamming her head back, but he avoided every blow.

And, suddenly, she felt the stab in the side of her neck. Fangs. *Pain.* This was not happening!

There was no such thing as a vampire, no such thing as an alternate universe.

No.

Such.

Thing.

She tried to fight but couldn't budge. He was drinking from her. Drinking! She could feel the rush of blood through her veins and into his mouth, and it felt . . . nice. *God. This is all so wrong!*

Movement caught her eye, and she watched as Zack's attacker lifted her head, staring at Zack, then rose gracefully to her feet.

Zack followed, his eyes unfocused, clearly stunned. The kid was in shock.

"Zack," she cried out.

A strange lassitude began to flow through her body, leaching the fight out of her. Making her sleepy.

A car engine penetrated her deepening lethargy, and she wondered briefly if the yellow Jeep she'd seen in her vision lived in this world, too.

"Frederick? We need to go." The woman wiped her bloody mouth on a black handkerchief. "You're going to drain her, sugar."

The man only made a sound of enjoyment against Quinn's throat.

Quinn's eyes drifted closed.

"Let her go," a man's voice said. Not the oily one's. "You do not wish to kill her."

But the vampire continued to drink.

"You wish to let her go," the man said, his voice calm, almost hypnotic.

And, suddenly, she was free, sinking to the ground, crumpling onto the hard sidewalk.

"She's mine!" said the oily one. "I found her."

She heard the sound of a scuffle, a shout of pain, then the clink of horse tackle and the fast clip-clop of a retreating carriage.

Then silence.

Arms scooped her up, lifting her as if she weighed nothing. Her mind screamed *fight*, but her body refused to answer. With effort, she forced her eyelids open and stared up at the man who held her. Not the one who'd attacked her. A little older, maybe. Not oily. A nice face.

"Zack?" The name barely formed on her lips.

"Your companion is gone."

"Dead?" She stopped breathing, her vision narrowing dangerously.

"Taken."

A flash of yellow caught in her peripheral vision, then she felt herself dropped bonelessly into the front passenger seat of a vehicle. The Jeep. She struggled without success to sit up. She couldn't even find the energy to reach for the door latch. "Have . . . to find him. Have to . . . escape."

"There's no escaping V.C., *cara*."

She tried to look at him but couldn't manage to turn her head. "*V . . . C.?*"

"Washington, V.C.," he replied. "Vamp City. Your new home."

CHAPTER THREE

Quinn walked down the busy, sunny sidewalk, her arms swinging, low heels clicking on the pavement as she hurried to get . . . where? She slowed, disoriented. Where was it she needed to go? Stopping in the middle of the sidewalk, she looked around, suddenly confused. Nothing looked familiar.

Someone bumped into her, making her stumble. "Move!" he shouted.

A woman strode directly toward her as if she didn't see her, as if she'd walk right through her.

Quinn lifted her hands to keep the woman from running into her, but the woman flew backward, arms and legs trailing her body as she zoomed out of sight.

Around her, everything went still. Every person turned to stare at her, terror on their faces.

"Devil's spawn!" they hissed, making the sign of the cross, backing away.

And that was when she saw Zack, sitting on the sidewalk, his back against the brick wall of a nearby building, his head down as he played his GameBoy. He was younger than she remembered. Twelve, maybe thirteen.

"Don't look up," she whispered to him. "Don't look up."

Slowly, the others turned and fled, the sidewalk and the streets emptying and turning ominously silent. The only sound remaining was the cheery, tinny music of the GameBoy.

"It's time to go home, Zack."

Her brother nodded, rose to his feet, and fell into step beside her, without once looking up.

Quinn tried to roll over and failed, startling awake. Sleepily, she fought to close her legs, spread awkwardly apart, and failed that, too, feeling the same tug on her ankles she had on her wrist.

The last vestiges of sleep fled in a stark wave of fear.

Ropes. *She'd been tied.*

Her eyes shot open, and she blinked at the floral canopy overhead, framed by plain maple bedposts. Her heart pounded in her chest, her mind darting through memories as she tried to remember what happened.

Where am I?

Shifting slightly on the far-too-soft mattress, she felt the press of clothes against her skin. At least she was still dressed.

How did I get here?

The place smelled unfamiliar—musty, like an old house. The chime of a grandfather clock echoed somewhere below, cut by the laugh track of an old television show. Rolling her head to her left, she spied an old-fashioned washstand complete with porcelain water pitcher. In the small mirror above it . . . the reflection of a man.

She jerked her head the other way . . . and froze. He stood in the doorway, dressed all in black, one broad shoulder propped against the frame. He was tall and lean, well built, his skin possessing a hint of the Mediterranean, his hair a dark brown cut short, framing an arresting, strong-boned face. His cheekbones were high and pronounced, his jaw well-defined, his nose long and straight. His mouth, intriguingly sculpted, was tipped up at one corner, a match for the devilish gleam in his dark eyes.

He looked familiar. He was the one who'd picked her up and deposited her in the front seat of his Jeep. After the . . .

Memory returned with a frontal assault. The *Gone With the Wind* couple's attacking them, *biting* them. *Vampires.* She turned rigid with shock. No. It hadn't happened. It couldn't have happened.

"Zack." Her voice cracked with disuse as she stared at the man. "Where is he?"

He pushed away from the doorframe and started toward her, his eyes turning flat. Cold. "I suggest, *cara*, you worry about yourself."

"We were attacked." Was that part right? Or had it all been a hallucination? Well, it couldn't have *all* been a hallucination, or she wouldn't be tied to the bed of one of the players. Unless she was still hallucinating. "I need to know where he is. Did they kill him?"

"You worry about another when you're tied to *my* bed?" He smiled, revealing sharp, twin incisors. "At *my* mercy."

Oh God, this is not happening. He is not a vampire. But whatever . . . whoever . . . he was, she was in deep trouble. Her heart thudded like it meant to fight its way out of her chest. "What do you want?" *Don't say blood, don't say blood. Vampires don't exist. They don't exist!*

"You know what I want." He closed his eyes, tilting his head back as if he were in the throes of great pleasure.

Oh, Zack. What have I done? I never should have let you get near that column.

The man opened his eyes again and sat on the bed beside her, watching her with a piercing intensity . . . *a hunger* . . . that had panic clawing at her mind. She was utterly at his mercy. Tied. Spread-eagled.

He reached for her, and she flinched, her heart thundering in her ears as his cool fingers curled lightly around her throat. Her breaths came quick and shallow, fear a living thing inside her as she watched him, as she waited for him to . . . what? Strangle her? Rape her? Or, God help her, dip his head and bite her, sucking the blood from her body?

He's not a vampire!

She shook, in a fever of dread, yet he drew out her torment, sliding those fingers up and down her throat as he watched her with that expression, at once rapturous and hungry. And very, very sexual.

"Are you going to kill me?" she gasped.

A small, cold smile lifted the corners of his mouth. "Of course."

Of course. Her stomach cramped. Tears burned her eyes.

His look of intense pleasure only grew. "Eventually." His hand slid down, pressing against her chest, sliding lower to cover one of her breasts. "But not until I've had my fill of you." As her pulse raced like a runaway freight train, his fingers found her nipple, plucking at it, striking a discordant note of pleasure against the terror screaming in her head.

Still, he watched her with that dangerous intensity. He reached for her arm, the one tied to the bedpost closest to him. His cool hand curled around her forearm, his thumb tracing the vein from her inner elbow to her wrist, slowly, as if savoring the feel of the blood pumping beneath her skin. He dipped his head.

"No," she gasped, her heart ratcheting.

But he didn't stop. His nose teased the crook of her arm. His mouth tasted her skin as she lay, tense as a steel rod, dreading the stab of his fangs.

Instead, he slowly rose again, a dangerous smile in his eyes as if he enjoyed her fear most of all. The sadist.

He stood and moved to the foot of the bed, kneeling between her spread legs.

What are you doing? She refused to give voice to the question that burned in her throat. He enjoyed her fear, she could see it in his eyes. And she would give him no more satisfaction than she had to.

When his hands found her waist, her breath

caught on a gasp. Pushing up her T-shirt hem, he unbuttoned her jeans, unzipping her fly with deft fingers.

"Don't," she breathed.

But he ignored her, yanking her pants down over her hips, where they got hung up on her spread thighs. But not before he'd revealed her black satin panties.

His hand shot between her legs, sliding along her most private flesh, stroking her through the satin. In the blink of an eye, he turned to the post where her right foot was bound and untied it.

The moment her foot was loose, she struggled to kick free, to knock him aside, but his grip was like iron as he forced her legs together long enough to push her pants down past her knees and off her right leg altogether. Then he was yanking her legs apart, tying her ankle again.

"Damn you!" She fought him, but there was nothing she could do to stop him.

He smiled, a darkly satisfied look on his face as he stared at her spread before him, only the small black panties barring his way.

Her breath trembled into her lungs, her body flushing hot, then cold, then hot again as he reached for her, this time stroking her inner thigh, watching her. "Do you have any idea how fast the blood flows out of the body when the femoral artery is breached?" As he spoke, his unusually sharp incisors began to lengthen and thicken. His pupils slowly turned white, surrounded by a sea of near black. Just as the other vampires' had. *Vampires. Oh, God, how can they be real?*

Slowly, he leaned forward, his face and those awful, sharp fangs dipping between her legs. Quinn bucked in panic, terror pulling at her mind as she struggled against the ropes tying her to the bed. Cool hands gripped her thighs roughly, holding her still. Teeth grazed the sensitive flesh of her inner thigh, and she quaked with terror over the fangs that were about to steal her life.

Tears blurred her vision. She should have kept Zack safe. If only she'd ignored that strange sight in front of her apartment. If only she'd turned and gone the other way.

Without warning, the vampire rose from between her legs and came to stand beside the bed, looking down at her. He leaned over, grabbing her jaw. "Look at me."

"I thought you were going to drain me."

One dark brow lifted. "Disappointed?"

"No," she gasped, her pulse pounding so hard she could barely breathe, let alone form words. "Of course not."

"I do not kill my slaves." He squeezed her jaw. "Nor do I wish them to fear me."

"I'm not your slave. And you love my fear. You love it!"

"Yes. But I've had my fill. And now you will forget."

She met his gaze stonily. "I'm not your slave."

A smile lifted his mouth. "Oh, but you are, *pic-*

cola." He stared deeply into her eyes as if he were trying to hypnotize her or something, and slowly began to frown. His eyes narrowed. His grip tightened. "What *are* you?"

She scowled. "A woman. What in the hell do you think I am?"

True anger flashed in his eyes, reigniting her fear all over again. He leaned forward, crowding her, scaring her. "*What are you?*"

A freak. I'm a freak. A soon-to-be-dead freak, at the rate things are going.

The vampire attacked her without warning, turning her head, baring her neck, biting her. Like before, the puncture hurt for only a minute. And then he reared back, licking the blood off his lips as he stared at her.

"*Mio Dio.*"

Without explanation, he released her and strode out of the bedroom, slamming the door closed behind him. "Blood!" His voice rattled the windows.

Quinn stared at the closed door, her mouth open with disbelief. *What in the* hell *just happened?*

She tipped her head back as her heartbeat slowly returned to something approximating normal, even as her mind whirled, a suffocating mass of confusion, questions, and dread.

A half hour later, maybe—it had felt like twenty years—the door opened, and a pleasingly round woman bustled into the room, carrying a tray. Eggs, by the smell of them. And coffee.

What was the vampire doing, fattening her for slaughter? Quinn's muscles bunched, an instinctive reaction as she fought against pulling on her ropes. Her wrists were raw and abraded from where she'd done just that too many times already. But she hated being so vulnerable. *Hated it.*

"I am Ernesta."

Quinn's pulse, which had begun to jackhammer at the first rattle of the doorknob, slowly began to calm. How, she wondered, was she supposed to eat or drink when she was still tied to the bedposts?

"The master wishes you fed," the woman, clearly Latino, said in accented English. She had the broad face of a South American Indian and wore a drab, plain servant's dress. "I have brought you eggs and toast. You must eat."

"How?"

The woman set the tray on the washstand, then turned to Quinn and began digging at the knot that held one of Quinn's wrists.

"Thank you, Ernesta. Are you . . . a vampire . . . too?" Her mouth didn't want to form the word any more than her mind wanted to accept that such a creature could possibly be real.

But the woman didn't laugh or smile or correct her in any way.

"No. I am one of his slaves."

Quinn really wished she'd laughed. "How long have I been here? It's still dark."

"It is always dark in Vamp City." The woman looked at her as if she were a moron. "Vampires shun sunlight. Even through clouds they can burn."

So, what, they'd figured out a way to enthrall the sun? "I thought vampires were a myth," she muttered.

"That is what we want humans to think."

"We?" Quinn looked at her in surprise. "I thought you said you weren't a vampire."

"I am something else." The rope came loose, freeing Quinn's wrist. As Quinn bent her arm, the blood rushing through it in a swift ache, Ernesta moved to her foot and the knot there. "Something equally impossible for a human to accept."

"May I ask what?"

The woman's smile didn't reach her eyes. "No." Moments later, one ankle was free.

Quinn lifted her knee slowly, easing the stiffness in her leg. "Can you at least tell me how this place exists?"

The woman glanced at her, her dark eyes enigmatic. "In 1870, the sorcerer Phineas Blackstone created a city just for vampires. A city where the sun never shines."

In 1870. And that's exactly what it looked like, wasn't it? A world created in 1870 . . . a duplicate of Washington at that time . . . left to rot and decay for over 140 years.

"But . . . where is it? Another planet or something?"

"No, no, no. It exists precisely where the original lies. One on top of the other, duplicate worlds. Duplicates at first. No more. The outside world has changed. And this one has moldered."

"Can the vampires get out? Into the real world?"

"Of course. At least, they could. They traveled freely between the two worlds, living here, hunting there when they chose. Until the magic began to fail." As she talked, Ernesta moved to Quinn's other ankle, freeing it, too.

Quinn moved her legs, closing them, groaning at the stiffness. Why was Ernesta untying her? The vampire must not believe she'd try to escape. Which was his mistake. Or maybe he was simply convinced she wouldn't be successful if she tried.

"Now the vampires are trapped by the failing magic," Ernesta continued. "If another sorcerer is not found soon, one to renew the magic, all those caught in Vamp City will die." She shook her head sadly. "But there are no more sorcerers. They are all gone."

All would die? Quinn's breath trembled. She had to find Zack and get out of here before that happened. She frowned as a thought occurred to her. Was Vamp City's failing the reason she'd started to see it outside her window at home? Were the two worlds starting to bleed together?

"Do you sometimes see the real world from here?"

Ernesta looked at her with surprise as she moved to untie her second wrist. "No. But the sunbeams break through sometimes. A vampire died out front just a few days before your arrival. None use the front door now."

So they must expect the sunbeam to break through in the same spot again. Is that what the beams do? Of course it is. She knew that from her own experience—the vision that kept appearing right in front of her apartment window.

When the rope at Quinn's wrist came free, Ernesta stepped back. Quinn slowly sat up, easing stiff muscles, then reached for her jeans. "Can humans ever leave Vamp City?"

A shadow crossed the threshold, freezing her in place. Ernesta glanced at the door. "Master."

The vampire. Her heart shot to her throat. Was he back for another bite?

Quinn struggled into her jeans with shaking hands, then slid off the bed on the side farthest from the door, fumbling to pull the jeans up over her hips as her captor stepped back to let Ernesta exit the room. Slowly, casually, he propped his shoulder against the doorframe and watched her.

She met his gaze, lifting her chin, trying to hide the quaking fear that was threatening to sweep over her again. She hated this place. Hated it!

His gaze slid leisurely over her like a predator assessing his next meal. "You ask if humans ever leave Vamp City, *cara.* The answer is no. A vampire may play with his food, but he never sets it free."

But what did she expect him to say? If humans did manage to escape, he'd never admit it. And it didn't matter. She'd find a way. Even if she had to be the first, she'd find Zack and get them both out of here.

He didn't move, just stood there leaning against the doorjamb. At least he looked normal again.

No fangs, no white-centered eyes. Dressed all in black, he looked like a dark angel, the collar of his shirt open, revealing a vee of gold-dusted skin. He was good-looking, she'd give him that. Really good-looking. Too bad he was an evil monster.

His eyes drifting closed in visible pleasure, he tipped his head back. "Do not fear me, *cara*." Slowly, his lashes lifted, and he pinned her with a gaze that, thankfully, was still dark, still normal. "I have come to make amends."

Those certainly weren't the words she'd expected to hear. *What game is he playing, now?* She watched him warily, every muscle tensed to fight him if he flew at her again, even as she knew he'd move too fast for her to do a damn thing to protect herself. If only she'd known that vampires were real. If she ever got out of this mess, she'd never again go out without a silver cross and garlic bulbs in her pocket. And a wooden stake. Definitely a wooden stake.

Her fingers curled around the bedpost, and she wondered if she could break it.

His dark eyes softened as he watched her, his mouth kicking up on one side again. "How much do you know of vampires, *cara*? The real ones, not the myth."

Good question. Maybe garlic didn't really work. "I know you bite."

He gave her a nod that was almost gallant. "We do indeed. What the legends fail to reveal is that not all vampires feed entirely on blood."

"You eat food, too?"

"I do, though not for sustenance. Only for pleasure." He pushed away from the door and took a step into the room. Her grip on the bedpost tightened. "I was not speaking of food."

Quinn's shoulders hunched reflexively. "What else do you need, then?" Dammit . . . if he said sex . . .

"Fear."

The word reverberated in her head, sending chills rippling over her skin. "What do you mean?"

"Vampires are not all the same. I am an Emora vamp, as are most within Vamp City. Emoras, like the name would suggest, feed on emotion as well as blood. And require both to survive."

"Fear."

"For me, yes. Each is different. My master, Cristoff, feeds on pain."

Her stomach clenched.

"A good friend of mine feeds on pleasure."

That would be better. Probably. "And you feed on fear."

He gave her another of those slow nods just short of a bow. "I do. I scared you intentionally, *piccola*. And I fed quite well. But I did so with the full belief I would soon glamour you and steal your memory of it. And that is where I failed."

She frowned at him. "Why steal my memory of it? Why not keep me afraid if you need fear to survive?" And was she an idiot? Was she *trying* to talk him into scaring the crap out of her again?

"Terrified slaves make poor servants. Quaking

hands drop things." He shrugged. "I had believed I could take your memory. Hence my apology for terrifying you when I had no ability to remove that terror."

His regret rang true. Which was . . . startling.

Quinn shrugged. "You weren't *that* scary." Which was an out-and-out lie, but she had her pride.

To her surprise, the vampire grinned, transforming his face, giving it a boyish charm that did funny things to her insides. Things that had nothing to do with fear. "Now you insult me."

She found herself almost smiling in return, which was extraordinary. "Don't get me wrong, it was a damn good effort."

He nodded. "My thanks." But his amusement remained.

"So . . ." Her fingers lost their death grip on the bedpost. "You're not going to bite me again?"

His smile darkened. "I most certainly will bite you. But I will bring you pleasure when I do so, *cara*. I have no intention of hurting you."

A cool shiver trembled down her spine as she remembered a still from a movie, Dracula holding a scantily clad woman in rapturous thrall as he drained the life from her. *Is that to be my fate? Why toy with me if he's only going to kill me in the end?*

She released the bedpost, crossing her arms over her chest, refusing to show her fear even if he seemed to be able to sense it. Feed off of it. Her gaze traveled the room, noting the simple old-fashioned furnishings—a plain maple dresser with an oil lamp, an overstuffed chair upholstered in faded yellow-and-white stripes, the ivory walls dotted with framed floral needlework, and a hardwood floor without rugs.

"What did you taste when you bit me?" she asked, turning back to him. "Why were you surprised?"

His amusement faded. "Your blood is nectar. Your taste exquisite, a rare sweetness that laces the blood of far too few humans and makes them particularly desirable to vampires. It is why your attacker nearly drained you."

Quinn frowned. "How could he have almost drained me? I feel fine. It takes weeks to recover from that kind of blood loss."

"Not if you've been bitten by a vampire. A few days. Four at most."

Her eyes widened. "How long have I been asleep?"

"Nearly three days."

"Three . . ." She gaped at him, the words sticking in her throat. *Three days?* Zack. He could be anywhere. He could be dead. No. No, he wasn't dead. She'd know. Somehow she'd know. She started around the bed. "I have to find my brother."

Impatience flashed in his eyes, all humor fleeing, and she pulled up short.

He nodded toward the washstand. "Eat the food Ernesta prepared for you. Your body needs the sustenance to fully replenish the blood you've lost." He turned to go.

"Wait."

He whipped back around, a dangerous light gleaming in his eyes. "You will address me as Master."

"I'm not your slave." The words came out reflexively and were the wrong thing to say. Suddenly, he was at her side, pushing her back against the bedpost.

A low, startled squeak escaped her throat. "Quit *doing* that!" Her heart was pounding like a tom-tom. "You're going to give me a heart attack."

Those dark eyes stared into hers, sharp with annoyance, as his cool palm brushed her throat, lifting until she was forced to raise her chin. She was above average height, but he was taller by a good four or five inches.

"I have apologized for terrorizing you needlessly," he said coldly. He was so close, she could see tiny flecks of gold in his near-black irises, and the tiny lines radiating out from the corners of his eyes as he frowned at her. "But I am your master, and you will both address me and treat me as such."

She began to tremble. Not since she was a little girl had she felt this helpless. "Will you at least answer a question?"

He lifted a brow.

"Please? *Master.*"

His mouth twitched as he stroked her, his fingers barely touching the sides of her neck, setting off ripples of dark pleasure. "That's better." Slowly, he began to dip his head toward the juncture of her neck and shoulder.

She grabbed his shoulders. "Don't." But her strength was useless against him. She tensed for the pinch of fangs, yet felt only his cool lips and the brush of his nose. "What are you doing?" she gasped.

"You smell of the same sweetness that I tasted in your blood. You tempt me." His lips moved up her neck, his hair brushing her jaw, soft as silk. His scent rose to engulf her senses. He smelled like rich, dark liqueur—almonds in moonlight—seductive, intoxicating, and very, very male.

She struggled not to be affected by the languorous warmth of his mouth and failed. Her body began to melt, her chest rising and falling with increasing frequency as the pleasure of his touch, of his scent, wove a lush net of desire around her senses.

How could she be attracted to this . . . this creature? But it was classic, wasn't it? A vampire's power of seduction.

"I'm not fully recovered," she reminded him, her voice breathless.

He kissed her jaw. "If you were, you would be beneath me, and we would be one."

His words shocked. A rush of damp heat followed as she imagined him on top of her, entering her. Her breath turned ragged. Without intending to, she reached for him, her fingers sliding through his soft, thick hair.

What's the matter with me? He's doing this to me!

"Tell me your name," she murmured against his temple.

"Master," he replied, his warm breath tickling her neck.

She snorted. "No, it's not."

He lifted his head, his eyes hot and amused. "It is to you." His steel-like arm curved around her waist, pulling her hips into contact with his . . . and with the very thick ridge that rose between them.

Quinn gasped. *"Vampire . . ."* Her body was on fire for him, but she didn't want this. The memory of those fangs between her legs rose. A shudder coursed through her, dousing the fire he'd fanned. She pulled her fingers from his hair, pushed at his shoulders. "My question."

"You've asked it." His mouth grazed her temple, making her shiver all over again.

"Your name was hardly my question. And you didn't answer it. I have to find my brother."

The vampire tensed. "Your brother?"

"The young man who was with me. Please . . . *Master* . . . please, help me find him."

His mouth moved, and she felt the flick of his damp tongue along the edge of her ear. She gasped, accidentally rocking forward, pressing her hips against that thick erection. The groan that escaped her throat sounded embarrassingly happy.

"Will you help me find Zack?"

"No." One long-fingered hand rose to cover her breast.

Her head tipped back, her eyes drifting shut at the wicked pleasure. This was wrong. So wrong. "Please. You must."

His lips returned to her jaw. "You are magnificent, *tessoro*. Built like the sleekest racehorse, all long limbs and lean strength." He released her, his fingers suddenly at her waist, unzipping her jeans. "There is nothing I *must* do. Except have you."

Quinn grasped his wrists. "You said I wasn't fully recovered." But, oh he smelled decadent. It would feel so good to let him finish, to feel his hands on her, his body over hers, inside hers. It was so tempting to push one of the wrists she held down, forcing his hand lower, between her legs. How could she be so hot for him? For *him*?

As he nuzzled her jaw, he nicked it, the sharp prick of pain making her rear back.

The vampire lifted his face, and the blood drained from her own. His eyes once more had those awful white centers, and his fangs were growing, thickening. Her desire fled on a rush of panic.

He went still, his eyes drifting closed, that look of intense pleasure returning to his face. "You're afraid of me."

Her breath trembled out. "I don't want this. You. Sex." Her eyes started to burn. "I don't—"

His finger lifted to her lips, silencing her panicked plea as his eyes returned to normal, his fangs retracting. "Then we will not."

She stared at him. Just like that?

To her amazement, he stepped back, his expression unreadable. "Eat, *cara*. Rest." He turned and started for the door.

Quinn launched herself after him. "Wait! At

least tell me where Zack is. Tell me if he's still alive."

The vampire turned back. She half expected to feel the sting of his anger, but the look on his face remained closed and enigmatic. "I know not, nor does it matter. The life you led before is over, *piccola*. You belong to me now. And your brother is no longer your concern. The sooner you accept that, the longer you will last."

"As long as I draw breath, he's my concern."

But the vampire left without replying, closing the door behind him.

Quinn stared at the door, lifting shaking hands to her head as she wondered if she was going to implode from the emotional whiplash of the past minutes. Raging desire, crippling fear. And the desperation to find Zack. He'd been gone for three days. *Three days.* "Dammit!" She sank back against the bed, tears burning her eyes.

Zack was still alive. He had to be. And she had to find him soon.

Brushing at the tears that were starting to fall, she took a deep, unsteady breath.

It was time to start hunting a way to escape.

CHAPTER FOUR

Zack Lennox strained to push the full wheel-barrow, his teeth clenched so hard he feared he was going to crack his molars. His hands were blistered, his muscles screaming, but he didn't make a sound. He'd learned that lesson on the first day. If you shouted, if you groaned, if you did the unthinkable and actually spoke—meet Mr. Whip. And fuck did that guy sting.

Rivulets of sweat ran into his eyes, making sight next to impossible, but he'd traveled this path a hundred times, at least, over the course of the past couple of days, wheeling load after load of bricks back to the wall. Several of the other slaves were actually building the wall, while still others stirred the mortar.

He was sweaty and grimy and sore, but the worst of the misery was the constant, excruciating hunger. How the fuck did they expect him to keep working his ass off with no food? Well, some food, but not nearly enough.

Are they feeding Quinn better than me? God, I hope so. He hoped she was okay. All he remembered was their being attacked, that vampire bitch knocking him to the ground and sitting on him as she bit him and sucked blood from his neck. At first, he'd been too stunned to think, let alone react. Who would've guessed vampires were real? But then he'd seen Quinn with that vamp's arms around her and her struggling, and all he'd wanted to do was tear that guy off her, grab her, and run. But he hadn't been able to move. The vamp bitch might have been female, but she'd held him down like she was fucking Xena, and then she'd hypnotized him or something, and the next thing he knew, he was waking up in a basement with a dozen other guys, and he'd been working ever since.

A slave. To vampires. *What the* fuck?

He'd spent the first day plotting and planning escape, imagining stealing one of the long knives all the vamps wore at their waists and chopping their heads off. Then one of the slaves actually tried it. He might as well have been moving in slow motion—to the vamps, all humans apparently did—because one moment the guy was reaching for the vampire's blade, and the next, that blade was sticking out the back of the guy's throat.

Zack's vision swam as he remembered the horror of watching one of his companion's die. The vamp who'd attacked him had pulled his sword out of the man's throat and drank his fill, the blood pouring down his chin and over his clothes, but he hadn't seemed to care. Other vamps had joined him, and they'd gorged while still another told the rest of the slaves, "You may dream of escape. If you attempt to act on it, you will die. I promise you."

His hope of getting away had been destroyed in that moment. His hope of ever seeing his sister or Lily again. Of ever seeing the sun again. His life was over.

Struggling with the full load, he tipped the wheelbarrow and dumped the bricks, then turned back for another. He paused, lifting a hand to push his damp hair off his face, his gaze catching sight of someone standing in a window of the second floor of the mansion, a stack of towels or something in her arms. A woman. He couldn't see her face, only her silhouette, the light shining behind her. But she had the same slender form, the same long, sleek hair as Lily. His heart stuttered. *Could it be?* He'd never been inside, except for the basement dungeon, where the slaves slept. In the three days he'd been here, he'd never seen any women except for the two girls who brought them their meals. Could Lily be here, too?

He heard the whistle of the lash a second before he felt the fire down his back.

"Move!"

Sorry, fucking vampire. Zack tore his gaze from the woman, grabbed the wheelbarrow, and moved.

Even if it was Lily, what difference did it make? He couldn't rescue her. He couldn't escape. He couldn't even take a piss unless a vampire said so.

So, no, it didn't matter. Lily was lost to him, either way.

* * *

Quinn glanced at the bedroom door, then strode lightly to the window, her pulse lifting on a rush of adrenaline. If she could get it open, she might just stand a chance of escape.

Solid beige curtains hung, ceiling to floor, blocking the windows entirely. There was little need to let in the light in a place where the sun never shone. She slipped in between the curtains, letting the fabric hang down her back as she reached for the latch on the double-hung. She turned it, then tried to push up the lower sash. Nothing. Not so much as a creak. It was stuck tight.

Rubbing her palms on her jeans, she tried again, bracing her legs for maximum leverage, and pushed with all her might. Unlike at home, she didn't dare pound on the frames. The last thing she wanted was for the vampire to realize what she was up to. Her muscles strained, her palms ached, her teeth clenched, but still she pushed.

Come on.

Finally, she felt it give, just a little, and she backed off with a relieved exhale. Brushing her damp, aching palms on her jeans, she took a deep breath and tried again. Another, louder, groan of wood, and the window slid open. *Finally.*

There was no screen, and she leaned out, peering with surprise at the tight crowd of structures, all of which appeared to be in good repair, unlike those she'd seen west of the White House. She could even see lights glowing here and there in some of the large structures back behind. Her eyes narrowed. It was a city block, she realized. Houses, or row houses, along the street fronts. While behind . . . what would they have had in the 1870s? Stables, probably. Maybe a cookhouse or washhouse? Servants' quarters? Whatever they were, this part of Vamp City was apparently occupied. Unfortunately, the occupants were almost certainly vampires.

Her fists clenched at the prospect of trying to escape when vampires could be anywhere. *Do they sleep?* She had no idea. And if they did, she couldn't begin to guess when. She'd yet to figure out the difference between day and night.

Peering down, she saw what appeared to be a large generator. Over the hum, she could make out other sounds—the cheering of a crowd in the distance that reminded her of the high-school football stadium about a mile from her home when she was growing up.

A shout sounded closer, followed by laughter. A moment later, a man's scream of agony cut the night, stopping Quinn's breath.

Did she really want to venture out into this place alone? No. If she were perfectly honest, the answer was no. The thought of what awaited her terrified her. The vampire had said her blood tasted sweet. If another vamp caught her, she might not survive. But staying here wasn't an alternative. She had to find Zack.

Slipping back between the curtains, Quinn headed for the bed, intending to pull off the linens, then glanced at the dresser and decided to do a quick search of the room first. Pulling open the bottom dresser drawer, she smiled. Sheets, blankets, towels. She grabbed several white, crisp, cotton sheets, opened them wide, then twisted them into ropes as she'd done too many times as a girl. Her stepmother, Angela, used to ground her for anything and everything. Most of the time, Quinn had taken the punishment and retired to her bedroom to do homework or read, but sometimes, especially as she got older, she'd slipped out of the house after her dad and Angela were asleep.

If not for Zack, she'd probably have run away and never returned. What would she have done without him? He'd been the keeper of her heart and the protector of her soul when they were growing up, the only one who'd stood by her, even if it was only to sneak into her room and play GameBoy on the rug while she did her homework after she'd been grounded. It used to drive Angela crazy that she couldn't keep the son she adored away from the stepdaughter she loathed. But she'd never succeeded. Zack had always known when Quinn was angry or hurting, which had been all too often. He'd always come. Always. A silent presence offering unquestioning love.

When it was time to choose a college, he'd told his parents he was moving to D.C. to live with his sister. The years apart had been hard on them both. Angela had been livid, but in the end, she'd been unable to deny her beloved son even that. And when Zack got accepted to George Washington University, Quinn, who'd been living near work in Bethesda, promptly rented an apartment in the heart of G.W.'s main campus. And they'd been living together ever since. Three years.

Now she'd lost him. Maybe even gotten him killed.

The thought twisted like a blade.

No, she couldn't think like that.

With the sheets knotted, she tied one end around the dresser leg and gave a hard tug. The heavy dresser didn't budge. Perfect. Nervously, she glanced at the window, then strode to the washstand and the tray of food. Quickly, she shoveled down a few bites of eggs and ate half of one of the rolls, then slid the knife into her back pocket. It was an eating utensil, not a weapon, but it was better than nothing.

She pulled on her socks and tennis shoes, which were sitting neatly against the wall, then grabbed the sheet rope and carried it to the window. Peering into the dim light, spying no one, she dropped it. The sheets hit the top of the generator with a thump.

Okay. She shook her hands at her side. Nerves were about to crawl out of her skin. *I can do this.*

Climbing over the sill, she gripped the rope between her legs, then lowered herself slowly and carefully. Sweat broke out all over her body. She began to shake, not with fear, but weakness. Since when was she too weak to climb down a sheet rope? She'd been doing it since she was thirteen!

But she knew the answer to that. Since she'd

nearly been sucked dry three days ago. She'd felt fine, but clearly she wasn't fully recovered. Not at all. Holy hell, her muscles were turning to rubber. She started to slip, her arms beginning to shake so badly she feared she might not be able to hold on. Even her legs were beginning to feel nearly useless.

Sliding the rest of the way, uncontrolled, she landed on the generator with a dull thud, then sat there, out of breath, stunned, and dismayed. If she'd had the strength, she might have tried to climb back into the room and try again later, but there was no way in hell that was going to happen. She was committed, now. She was just going to have to go a little slower than she'd anticipated, that was all.

Pushing herself off the generator, she landed on her feet and swayed, her face feeling cold and clammy as she reached for the wall to steady herself. In a minute, she'd be fine.

The sound of footsteps coming at a hard, fast run had her pressing back against the brick. A moment later, a man rounded the corner and dashed across the vampire's backyard without a glance her way. He was shirtless, his hair long and dirty, his body gleaming with sweat and blood from the lash marks striping his back. Terror radiated from him with every movement, every racing step.

Quinn's heart pounded from exertion, from indecision, from the need to get out of there before the vampires found her. The thought had barely formed when a strange vamp male materialized not ten feet in front of her, his fangs long and sharp, his eyes gleaming with white centers, his gaze fixed firmly on her.

Her heart clogged her throat.

A second later, a second vamp, a female, appeared beside the first. "Did you find him?"

"No. I found another. A sweeter one."

Quinn shook her head with disbelief. This escape attempt was a flaming bust. If she didn't do something quick, she was going to die right here, right now. Pulling the knife from her back pocket, she opened her mouth to call for her vampire. Better the devil she knew . . .

He appeared beside her as suddenly and unexpectedly as the others had, startling a gasp from her.

"Arturo!" the male vamp called in greeting. "I didn't know she was yours."

Arturo's arm snaked around Quinn's waist, pulling her close. "She is mine, Salazar. How goes your hunt?" he asked the pair affably.

The woman smiled, her eyes dancing with excitement. "This one is clever, Arturo. He eludes us well. Come join us!"

The vampire's cheek brushed Quinn's temple, and he chuckled. "My breakfast awaits, don't you, *cara*?"

Quinn stiffened in his hold. Was he toying with her even as he plotted retribution for her escape attempt? Or simply making his excuses?

"While *your* breakfast gets away," he added.

The other two vamps looked at one another,

laughed, and were gone faster than her eyes could track.

Quinn tried to pull out of the vampire's hold, but her strength was nothing compared to his, even when she wasn't clammy and shaking.

"Were you going somewhere?" he asked coolly, the friendliness gone from his voice as if it had never been.

There was no sense in lying. Or telling the truth, for that matter. They both knew exactly what she'd been up to. Her sheet rope hung from the window, the end lying on the generator, where she'd left it.

He released her, took her elbow, and steered her toward the door, the threat of punishment thick in the air. The question was, what form would it take? Would he tie her to the bed again? Or worse? Cold fingers of dread crawled along the back of her neck.

Opening the door, he ushered her into a kitchen oddly incongruous to the times—either the one in which Vamp City had been created or her own. With its olive green fridge and range and the big butcher-block-topped island, it looked more 1970s than 1870s. Over the island hung a rack laden with pots and pans of every shape and size. Recessed lighting on the ceiling and undercounter lights lit the room admirably.

The smell of frying hash brown potatoes filled the room as a girl of perhaps twenty served up a plate. She was cute, with a pert nose and fine features. Unlike Ernesta, she wore modern clothes—a

worn sixties retro dress with faded splashes of
pink and green. Her light brown hair hung long
and straight, parted down the middle and high-
lighted with a strange, phosphorescent glow.

"Your breakfast is ready, Master."

The hand on her arm tightened. "Did you eat
the eggs brought to you earlier?"

"I'm not hungry."

"Two plates, Susie. And have Horace close the
window upstairs." He steered Quinn through the
doorway on the other side of the kitchen and into
a formal dining room complete with gold-and-
crystal chandelier, dark red wallpaper, and what
appeared to be large golden candelabras casting
flickering light on the gilt-framed paintings lining
the walls.

Ernesta bustled in, setting a place for Quinn
with gold-toned . . . maybe real gold . . . flatware
and a linen napkin. Susie followed, setting plates
before each of them. Eggs Benedict, broiled toma-
toes, and hash browns.

Did he really expect her to eat? Her stomach
was in knots.

"Thank you, *cara mia*," Arturo said kindly to the
girl. But when Susie and Ernesta had left, his voice
turned cool once more. "Dispense with your fear
and eat. I will not punish you for your escape."

She looked at him warily. "Why not?"

"Every slave attempts escape at least once. Now
you know what will happen. You will be caught."

Maybe. Maybe not.

He gripped her wrist. "Oh, I will catch you, *cara*. Every time."

"You can read my mind now?" she snapped.

He smiled and released her. "I can read your expression. Now eat. The food is exceptional, but it will not remain so once it is cold."

The food did smell good. And she *was* hungry. Cutting a small bite of the eggs Benedict, she lifted it to her mouth and nearly moaned. Perfect. The English muffin was neither too crisp nor too soft, the Canadian bacon perfectly cooked and flavorful, and the hollandaise sauce the best she'd tasted.

She glanced at the vampire, who sat watching her, making no move to join her. "I thought you said you ate."

"At the moment, all I can taste is your fear. I will not be able to enjoy my meal until you calm."

She stared at him. "You're really not going to hurt me?"

"I am not. It would be counterproductive, would it not, when my goal is for you to lose your fear of me?"

The tension slowly fled her body. "I suppose."

"Yet still you tremble."

"I'm exhausted."

He straightened, picking up his knife and fork. "I did warn you that you've not yet recovered from the blood loss."

Quinn cut another bite. "Apparently, you were right." Upstairs she heard pounding, as if someone were doing some construction in the house. She chewed the bite, then cut another.

The vampire began to eat as well, but he continued to watch her. Disconcerted, she turned to study the nearest painting on the wall as she chewed. It was a painting of a child that she'd seen dozens of times in prints, but this one looked . . .

"Is that *real*?" she asked.

"Quite real. They all are, though not quite original."

She turned back to him. "What do you mean?"

"They're duplicates, in a manner of speaking. Vamp City is an exact copy of Washington, D.C. Or at least it was at the time of its creation 140 years ago. Not everything replicated, of course. Almost nothing living—people, animals, even the plants and grass failed to reproduce."

"But you have trees."

"Dead trees. Oddly, they grow that way, which makes them ideal for firewood. V.C. is a world devoid of life but for the vampires and their slaves who soon moved in. But the wealth of D.C.'s citizens did replicate. The money in the banks, the silver in the silver chests, the artwork."

Quinn stared at the landscape on the opposite wall. "They must be worth a fortune."

The vampire grunted. "How do you sell an original of a painting that already exists?"

"I see your point. So you keep them and enjoy them."

"I do, yes. Others have sold paintings as forgeries. Extraordinarily good forgeries. The amount they get is far less than they would for the originals, of course. But there is little chance of giving ourselves away."

Quinn took a bite of hash browns, which melted in her mouth. Susie was an excellent cook, there was no doubt about it. Already, Quinn felt her strength returning.

"Where do you get the food if you can't grow it here?" She stabbed a bite of tomato.

"Traders—nonvampires—can still come and go. They make weekly deliveries to each of the vampire strongholds, truckloads of goods and foods from the real world, though I fear the shipments may stop as the magic continues to fail."

"What are Traders? Are they human?"

"They are not your concern, *cara*. Finish your meal." He took another large bite of eggs Benedict, clearly enjoying the taste. As he cut another, he glanced at her. "You will tell me about yourself."

She bristled slightly at the command, then sighed. "My name is Quinn Lennox, twenty-seven, born and raised in Lancaster, Pennsylvania, and I'm a research technician." She looked at him curiously, wondering if she needed to explain, but he appeared to understand.

"And your people? Do you know your family history?"

She almost smirked. "Are you wondering if you've known any of my ancestors?"

"I am."

"How old are you, anyway?"

He peered at her. "Six hundred, give or take."

Six hundred. Holy shit. "You were born *in the 1400s?*"

"I was. Your family . . . ?" he prompted.

The 1400s. My God, the things he's seen. She shook her head, trying to clear it enough to answer his question. "I don't know much about my mom's family. Her parents died when she was a teenager, and she died when I was a toddler. I've never met any of my relatives from that side."

"Her name?"

"Jillian Minor. I don't know what her parents' names were. My dad is Darrell Lennox. His mom was a Markham, I think. Beyond that, I don't know."

"You know little about your own flesh and blood."

"My ties with my family have never been strong. Except with my brother."

"Tell me about Zack."

"Why?"

"I wish to know."

Was he finally going to help her? She tried to quell the flutter of hope and couldn't quite manage it. "He's actually my half brother, born to my stepmother three years after my mother died. He's twenty-two and looks kind of like me except he has curly red hair."

"A half brother," he murmured. As if that mattered.

They lapsed into silence as the vampire finished his meal. Ernesta cleared their plates, then

poured them each a cup of coffee. So . . . civilized.
As if she were his guest and not his captive.

"What are you going to do with me?" she
blurted.

He watched her as he took a sip of the steaming
liquid, then looked away. "I will keep you."

"As your slave."

"Yes."

Still he didn't meet her gaze, and her instincts
began to ring a low warning. He wasn't being
honest, and she wasn't sure what it meant. Did it
matter? She was at his mercy either way.

"You will help Ernesta with the housecleaning
and the laundry."

She looked at him warily. "That's all?"

"No. You will feed me. But I will not do what
was done to you before. I will never take enough
to weaken you." He reached for her, his cool hand
covering hers, drawing her gaze to his. "I promise
you, *cara*, when I draw from your vein, you will
feel pleasure." His eyes turned smoky, his smile
breaking slowly and turning very, very carnal.
"When I slide my fangs into your neck, I will slide
my cock into your body, and you will scream with
pleasure, I promise you."

His words turned her at once hot. And cold.

"Every fourth day, I will visit your bed to drink
from you."

"Every *fourth* day?"

"When I add you to my household, I will have
four slaves."

Quinn jerked her arm away from his hand, realizing what he was saying. "You have sex with *all* of them?"

His mouth twitched. "Not Horace."

She'd seen nothing intimate between him and Ernesta. A servant/master relationship and nothing more. Was that the way it would be with her? A quick feed and fuck every fourth day, then back to work cleaning his house? Was this to be her life?

No, she couldn't accept that. *Wouldn't* accept it.

"*Cara*," the vampire said quietly, drawing her gaze back to his. "Do not attempt to escape me again. If you become too difficult, I will sell you to one of the Traders for the slave auction, and your fate will be far worse than here with me." His fingers closed around her wrist in a cool vise. "There is no escape for you. Humans never escape Vamp City. If they did, you would have heard of it, yes? The missing would have returned. Yet none ever have." He squeezed her wrist lightly. "Accept your fate, and you will be content here. I will see it so."

She didn't argue with him, didn't reply at all. Perhaps the best thing to do was let him think she'd given up.

Heavy footsteps approached, and, a moment later, a man appeared in the doorway, a broad-chested, stocky man, with little hair on top of his head but a thick, bushy, graying beard that shimmered just like Susie's hair. "It's done, Master."

The vampire nodded once, released her, and rose. "See Quinn to her room, Horace."

"Yes, sir."

As Quinn rose, the vampire met her gaze again. "Rest today. Tomorrow, you will begin your duties. All of them." Then he turned and walked out of the room, leaving her to stare after him.

All of them. She shivered even as her body warmed.

"Come along, girl," Horace said gruffly.

With a frustrated sigh, she followed Horace into a compact entry hall and up the hardwood stairs to the bedroom she'd left less than an hour before.

"You were a fool to try to escape, girl," Horace said, as they reached the door. "The master's the best of the lot of them. He don't hurt his slaves like the others do. And he don't give us over to other vamps."

"But he feeds from you."

"'Course he do. Feeds from my wrist. It don't hurt none."

"What about your family?"

"Family's long dead, young'un. Been dead for more 'n a century. Now git you in there and forget everything that came before. Don't none of it matter no more. This is your home, now."

Feeling stronger than she had earlier, but still more tired than she should, she walked into the room, allowing Horace to close and lock the door behind her.

The linen rope was no longer tied to the dresser leg. She couldn't see it at all. And the curtains made no movement, making it clear that the window had been closed.

Suddenly, she remembered the hammering. Her

eyes widened, and she ran to the window, pushed
the curtains aside, and stared at the boards that
had been nailed across it. He'd boarded up the
window!

Gripping the boards, she pulled, the wood digging into her fingertips, refusing to budge.

"Shit!" *How in the hell am I supposed to get out of
here, now?* She wasn't, which was precisely why
the vampire had done this. Spinning away from
the window, she paced across the room, her fingers digging hard into her hair. *I'll never get out of
here, never reach Zack. I'll never see him again, never
know if he's alive or dead.*

Despair slowly got the better of her. She climbed
onto the bed and curled into a ball of misery as
the tears began to roll.

Hours later, Arturo stood at the foot of the bed,
watching the woman sleep. Quinn Lennox. An in-
teresting name though not the one he'd expected.

She lay atop the covers on her side, both hands
balled tight against her chest. A lock of sun gold
hair caressed her chin, making his fingers itch to
move it, to feel the satin softness once more beneath his fingertips. Her eyes were puffy, dried
tears streaking satin cheeks. Despite the tears, her
skin was lovely, a flawless lightly tanned cream
with a spattering of freckles across the bridge of
her slender nose.

Her lips, a ripe, natural pink, were parted, her
mouth lush and lovely. Soon, he'd taste those lips,

when her fear of him had abated. Soon, he'd taste far more than her lips.

Very soon, or it would be too late.

Even in sleep, she intrigued him. There was a freshness about her, a natural beauty untainted by feminine guile or vanity. And a stubbornness he understood all too well.

If not for the brother, she might do fine here. But that deep vein of devotion for the one she loved would cost her. She wasn't likely to give up easily or quickly, which ensured she would suffer. He wasn't without compassion, but compassion would do her little good. Both her fate and her brother's had been sealed the moment they'd walked into that sunbeam.

Why couldn't she have simply been like any other slave, easily glamoured, easily controlled? Then again, would she interest him this greatly if she were? Unlikely. Perversely, he liked that he couldn't control her thoughts. He liked her tartness, the way she spoke freely to him, often sarcastically, despite her fear. A fear she was remarkably adept at hiding though he could taste it all too well.

Sun-kissed lashes fluttered up, her head turning as if she'd sensed his presence in her sleep. Green eyes found him in the shadows, and the rich taste of fear caressed his tongue, feeding him. Vexing him.

Quinn shot up, scooting back toward the headboard. Her hair was sleep-tousled, one cheek rosy from the pillow, her T-shirt slightly askew. The thought of running his fingers through that fall of golden hair, of straightening her shirt and running his fingers over her sweet, sweet breasts, had the heat building in his body to pool thickly between his legs. It was all he could do not to join her on that soft bed and pull her beneath him, to push inside her.

But nothing doused his ardor like the fear of his partner. He wouldn't take a woman who feared him. He couldn't.

"I'll not harm you, *cara*."

"What are you doing here?" She raked one hand through that golden hair, pushing it off her face.

"Watching you."

His words made her visibly shudder. At least her fear didn't spike though it continued to feed him, continued to annoy him. "You were staring at me as I slept?"

"You are a beautiful woman."

Her eyes narrowed. "You're not helping your case."

"I have no case. I own you, *tessoro*. I can watch you whenever I like." *Cristo!* The wrong thing to say to a woman he wished to calm. "Someday, you will trust me, Quinn Lennox." Though that was probably a lie. And not his first. "Someday, you will not fear me."

"Bring me my brother, Vampire, and I'll trust you."

Stubborn, intriguing, *desirable* female. "Go back to sleep, *cara*."

He left her there, sliding the outside bolt on her door before he was tempted to try to seduce her again. If he pushed her too fast, he'd only frighten her more. Or earn her hatred.

Though her hatred, unfortunately, was sure to come.

After the vampire left, Quinn sat on the bed, staring into the room as her heart rate slowly leveled off. An oil lamp glowed dimly on the dresser, its light dancing with the shadows on the ceiling. Damn the vampire for waking her from a sound sleep. At least in sleep, she could escape the terrible pressure on her chest, the grief and the helpless frustration.

A distant scream sounded outside. A male scream, a horrible one, which made her forehead turn hot and throbbing. *Please, God, don't let it be Zack.* Then again, at least it would mean he was still alive.

The sound of the door's opening had her stiffening, but it was only Ernesta with another tray. How long had she slept? Long enough to be hungry again.

As the woman cleared the door, Horace pulled it shut behind her, leaving the women alone. They weren't taking chances, were they? At least the vampire hadn't ordered her tied again.

"Your lunch." The woman carried the tray

around the bed to the washstand without looking Quinn's way.

"Thank you, Ernesta."

Quinn glanced at the door. In a moment, Horace would open it again to let Ernesta out. Could she possibly shove her way past them? Unlikely. If the vampire thought she could escape Horace, he'd never have sent her with him last night. She wasn't even sure the man was human, not with that shimmery beard.

No, she'd find a better opportunity. Better to wait until . . .

The bed beneath Quinn lurched suddenly, nearly knocking her over. Ernesta screamed and clutched the nearest bedpost.

What the hell?

The entire house began to rattle. Was this an honest-to-goodness earthquake or something else?

Ernesta clutched the bedpost, her eyes squeezed shut. And Quinn realized that this was the opportunity she'd been waiting for. If she had the nerve to take it.

For Zack? Hell yes. She'd do anything.

Not giving herself a chance to think about it too fully, she slipped off the bed, grabbed the ceramic water pitcher off the washstand and, with a stab of guilt, swung it at the back of the shorter woman's head. She hit her hard, remembering too well Ernesta's assertion that she wasn't human. To Quinn's relief and sick dismay, the woman sank to the floor.

Quinn stared at her. *What if I've killed her?* She'd never attacked anyone outside a Tae Kwon Do sparring match. She had no idea how much force was enough, let alone too much.

But it was done. Forcing herself to focus, she slammed the pitcher against the wall, shattering it, then picked up a large, sharp piece and began to yell. "Help! She's injured!" She raced for the door, leaping behind it just as Horace lunged into the room. Quinn slipped out, slamming the door shut, and throwing the bolt.

"Hey!" the shout rumbled from inside, loud enough to bring every member of the household running.

Bright light flooded the small foyer and the stairs in a sudden, startling burst, as if someone had turned on the sun. Screams rang out both inside and out. Energy danced over her skin.

This was it! Another sunbeam. Her pulse pounded. She was finally going to learn if she could leave Vamp City the same way she'd entered.

She flew down the stairs, threw the bolt, and flung open the front door to an extraordinarily welcome sight—a wide sunbeam cutting across the dirt street a yard in front of her. And in that sunbeam, her world, cars zipping past, people walking along the sidewalk.

"Master!" Horace yelled from behind the locked bedroom door. "She's escaping!"

Quinn lunged forward. Just as it had before, the energy caught her, tingling along her arms, raising the hair on her body and head as it pulled her through. This time she was ready and only stumbled onto the sidewalk instead of falling. Her world. *The sun.*

Dodging a trio of businessmen in suits, she whirled, backing away as she stared at the now-sunlit Vamp City house she'd just left, the door she'd flown through still wide open. Arturo's house. From behind the safety of the curtains in one of the front windows, the vampire watched her, his mouth hard, his black eyes squinting against the sunlight, filled with frustration. And anger.

And then he was gone. As suddenly as the sunbeam had appeared, the vision of the dark world ended. The gate between the worlds had closed. She turned back to the welcome sight of a bright, teeming city, sighing with relief at the welcome feel of the sun heating her skin. Looking around, she found her bearings. F Street NW, two blocks from the Treasury Building.

Pressing her fist to her chest, she willed her heart to settle down, turned, and started the long walk home. Euphoria and bone-deep relief twined with despair. She'd done it. She'd escaped Vamp City.

But Zack had not.

CHAPTER FIVE

Quinn slipped an extra package of flashlight batteries into the backpack that sat on her kitchen counter, ready and waiting for her return to the vampire world. And had been for six days. As she'd done more than a dozen times since she escaped, she inventoried the contents—three water bottles, a flashlight, a half dozen breakfast bars, and five wooden stakes.

Her stomach cramped. God help her, she was going back. Assuming, that was, the damn worlds ever opened to one another again. Six days she'd been waiting for that crawling sensation that would tell her she'd see that dark street from her window again. Hours on end she'd stared out the window or paced endlessly in clothing fit for the mission—cargo pants with lots of pockets, thick-soled boots, a tank top, and a lightweight jacket since it had been far cooler in the darkness than it was in the sunlight.

So far, all for nothing. She'd barely left the apartment, instead spending hours on the computer studying everything she could find about vampires. If they were real, then someone knew about them. Some of the myths had to be true. And she needed to know everything she could about how to protect herself. And how to kill them.

When she'd first gotten home, she'd immediately called work. Jennifer had been immensely relieved at first, glad Quinn hadn't become one of the missing. But as Quinn had tried to explain that she was in the middle of a family crisis and would have to take a little time off, her boss's tone had cooled. Especially with Quinn forced to be so vague about what was going on or how much time she needed. Of course, if she'd told her the truth, that her brother had been captured by vampires, and she was preparing a rescue attempt, she'd have been fired on the spot for insanity. She still had a job waiting for her when this was over. For now. But she'd worry about that later. All that mattered was getting back into that world. And getting Zack out.

Some mornings, she awoke feeling like she really was insane, that none of it could have actually happened. Then she'd walk into the living room, see Zack's laptop sitting there, and her chest would cave. It was all real. He was gone. Lost. And she was the only one who could possibly save him though she'd give anything if she weren't.

She left her backpack and walked into the living room, stopping before the window where she'd begun to wear a hole in the carpet. As much as she longed to see that shadowy street appear, she dreaded it more. The last thing, *the last thing* she wanted to do was go back to that place. She still knew virtually nothing about it. A quick google of Vamp City brought up exactly nothing. If people on the outside did know the truth, they weren't sharing.

Staring at the traffic on the street below, she wondered for the umpteenth time if she shouldn't call the FBI. After all, she *knew* where those missing people had gone. She could tell them exactly what had happened to them. She could send *them* in to rescue them all, including Zack.

Except she wasn't an idiot. They'd never believe her, at least not until she pulled one of them through a sunbeam. The bigger problem was that she knew vampires well enough by now to know that no human could possibly be a match for them. No one. Taking others with her into that world was as good as signing their death warrants. Or consigning them to slavery for the rest of their lives. At least she knew how to get in and out. She'd gotten Zack into this mess. It was up to her to get him out. And Lily, too, if she could find her.

If only the damn worlds would open again!

She raked her hair back from her face, frustrated and impatient. Ever since she'd gotten home, she'd been a twisted bundle of nerves. If another sunbeam did break through, what then? She had no real plan other than to get back in, no idea where to start looking for him when she did.

All she knew was that they'd been attacked close to the White House and that the vampire, Arturo, lived on F Street, on the other side of the White House in what had appeared to be a thriving vampire neighborhood. She was almost certainly going to have to head back that way if she wanted to find her brother. Even if the thought gave her nightmares.

Her cell phone rang. She reached for it and glanced at the number. *Shit.* Pressing the answer button, she lifted the phone to her ear, fighting to keep her voice calm and level.

"Hi, Dad."

"Hello, Quinn," her father replied formally. Too formally, as if they barely knew one another. Or as if he didn't know how to breach the chasm he'd long ago allowed to form between them. "Where's Zack? I thought you said he'd be back from that sail two days ago."

Uhn. She'd been dreading this. It was a little hard to explain to one's parent how you'd accidentally led his only son into an alternate universe where he'd been taken prisoner . . . or been killed . . . by vampires. No, not killed.

"The cruise was kind of open-ended, Dad," she lied. "I spoke with the outfit yesterday, and they said the fishing has been really good, so they decided to extend it a few more days. I'll have him call you the minute he gets back, I promise."

"Your mother and I still don't understand why he didn't tell us about this before he left."

"She's not my mother."

Silence. "I'm surprised he didn't call is all."

"He's skipping class, Dad. It's not really something a guy wants to tell his parents. Not until after the fact, at least."

"That's not like him. He's never done anything so irresponsible before."

"One last fling before he enters the real world, I guess."

"And you didn't try to talk him out of it?" There was accusation in his tone. As if none of it would have happened if he hadn't been living with *her*. The worst part was, she knew damn well Zack's being missing was all her fault. She was the one who'd led him to that strange column. She was the one who'd grabbed his arm as he reached for Lily's pen. If she hadn't touched him, he'd probably have picked up the pen without any problem, without ever knowing he'd breached the intersection of two worlds. He'd have passed through the sunbeam unaffected, just like everyone else. But she'd fallen victim to her curiosity—first mistake—and tried to protect him—second mistake. And gotten them both sucked into that world instead. At least her dad didn't know he was missing. Yet. "I made my opinion known, but he's twenty-two, Dad. He's an adult."

Out of nowhere, the hair on her arms began to rise. Her breath caught as she recognized the energy that meant the worlds were once more bleeding together.

"Yes, but you're five years older. Your mother . . . Angela . . . and I think it's high time—"

"I've got to go, Dad. I'll have him call you when he gets home." Without waiting for a reply, she hung up, ran to the kitchen for her backpack, and raced out the door, ignoring the elevator for the stairs. Forty seconds later, she was flying out the front door of the apartment building. There, not ten feet away, stood those odd shadows through which she could see that crumbling house with its cockeyed lion's-head doorknocker.

She started forward, letting the crowd on the sidewalk carry her forward, allowing that now-familiar energy to grab her and suck her back into Hell.

Like before, Quinn landed on her hands and knees on the pavers. The pull was oddly stronger going in than coming out. Unlike before, she knew exactly where she was and why. She'd done it!

The moment's triumph dissolved in a rush of gut-cramping terror. She was back in Vamp City.

The sunbeam lit the street, revealing the same disintegrating house it had the first time. Dust floated in the sunlit air while the sunlight illuminated her like manna from Heaven. Or dinner to a vampire.

With a chill, she pushed to her feet and ran out of the sunbeam. Rounding the nearest corner, she slipped into the shadows, taking care to make as little sound as possible. If only they'd been more careful the first time, maybe she and Zack would still be together. Maybe he'd still be free. The ache of loss had settled beneath her breastbone, a constant dull throb.

Heart pounding, she stopped close to the wall, avoiding the moldy brick as she listened for the sound of a horse or Jeep. Or vampire. No sound met her ears. She and Zack had found nothing and no one between here and the White House the last time. Maybe she'd be lucky again. But she was taking no chances.

With a deep breath, she continued on, cutting between buildings, staying to the shadows until the sun went out, which she suspected could take anywhere from a minute to possibly an hour or more. If Lily really had disappeared through the same sunbeam she and Zack first passed through, an hour wasn't unrealistic.

As she rounded the front of an abandoned building on Nineteenth Street, in the distance she spied a glow in the sky. Another sunbeam? It was north of where the vampire's house would be. They were obviously breaking through in multiple places, which was a good thing to know in case she needed another quick out. Looking both ways, her heart drumming in her chest, she slipped across the street, feeling like she had crosshairs aimed on her forehead, then dove between another pair of buildings on the other side. Halfway through the block, the light from the sunbeam disappeared behind her, blanketing the landscape in the gloom that marked day around here.

In the distance, she heard a shout. And a scream. Sweat broke out on her brow, and she pressed deeper into the shadows, her stomach cramping with fear. Now that she'd finally gotten back into the place, all she wanted to do was run the other way. Find another sunbeam and escape again.

But she had a mission this time. And the sunbeams were gone. She had no choice but to continue forward.

In the distance, the cheer of a crowd lifted into the air, followed by the peal of laughter. It was as if the sunbeams had silenced everything, and with their retreat, the world had come alive again. That was probably exactly what had happened. The sunbeams threatened the vampires' existence. That part of the legend was almost certainly true, or they'd never have created a dark world in the first place.

The pounding of horses hooves carried over the still air.

Quinn pulled one of her wooden stakes out of her backpack and gripped it tight. She'd never before hated the dark. As a kid, she'd been notorious for escaping into the backyard in the evenings, scrambling up the trees, feeling the darkness close around her like a security blanket. Angela would yell and yell for her to come down from the tree as Quinn huddled, shaking with fury and hatred and hurt. But Angela couldn't see her in the dark and couldn't have climbed the tree after her if she had. How many times had Quinn snuck back into the house, long after everyone else had gone to sleep, and slid into bed with bark scratches on her shins and elbows? If she could have slept on a tree branch, she'd never have gone back inside at all.

But there was nothing safe about this dark. Nothing comforting. Because this dark was home to the real monsters.

If only she had a guide. Alice had had the white rabbit. Lucy, Mr. Tumnus. Dorothy hit the jackpot with the scarecrow, tin man, and cowardly lion. Quinn wasn't picky. Even a talking pigeon would do. Anything that could tell her where to go to find her brother.

There was never a fairy godmother around when you needed one. And she needed one, badly.

Reaching Eighteenth Street, she looked both ways, then started across. She was nearly in the middle of the dirt street when she heard the hoof-beats again, stronger. Closer. *Hell.*

She'd barely run three steps when she saw the horses enter the intersection out of the corner of her eye. The sudden shout told her they'd seen her, too. *Dammit.* Her gaze darted, hunting for a way through the wall of row houses that lined the street, but she saw nothing. Did she dare run inside one? It might collapse on top of her. Then again, was that fate so much worse than being caught again?

No, it wasn't.

She ran for the closest door and turned the knob with shaking fingers, but the door was locked tight. And fully on its hinges. *Shit.* Veering away from the riders, she ran for the next doorway, but the horses were too quick. One of her pursuers kicked up a choking cloud of dirt as he passed her, then pulled up, bringing his horse around to face her, blocking her path. The second rider came to a stop behind her, effectively cutting off any means of escape. If she'd ever had one.

"And what have we here?" the one in front asked in an annoyingly nasal, high-pitched voice. As the dust settled, she got a halfway-decent look at him in the low light and had to fight not to gasp. He clearly was not human. His ears were a little too large, his head a little too big for his body. But it was his eyes, glowing bright orange, that gave him away. Oddly, he was dressed in modern clothes, his khakis stained, his polo shirt sporting a good-sized hole in the front. Angling herself so that she could see both of them, she glanced at the second, noting that he looked much like the first, his eyes also glowing orange.

Quinn crossed her arms over her chest, gripping her stake. "Who are you? And what are you doing here?" A good offense was often the best defense.

"We're Traders." The first male cocked his head at an odd angle. "Looking for runaways. Who did you run from, girlie?"

"Who says I'm a runaway?"

"Yer human, aren't ye? Free humans in V.C. are always either runaways, or they've come in through a sunbeam. Is that what ye did then?"

"What about the slayers?"

"Slayers?"

"You said humans are either runaways or accidental visitors. What about the vampire slayers?"

The other one hooted. "Vampire slayers?" A deep-belly chuckle rolled out of his mouth. "Ain't no humans who stand a flea's chance against a vampire, girlie. None."

That stank. "What are you two? You're not vampires."

"Traders," the first one repeated, as if that was supposed to mean something to her. "Come, now. You had a nice little run, I reckon, but you're ours, now."

Like hell. Quinn carefully unfolded her arms. "Do Traders die from a stake through the heart?" she asked quietly, giving each of them her best touch-me-and-I'm-going-to-rip-out-your-eyeballs look.

Grins twisted their faces into masks that looked increasingly inhuman. "Looks like we got us a fun one, Bart," the first Trader crowed.

Damn them both. Cold fear shot down her spine as she got a vision of them having *fun* with her, throwing her to the ground and tearing off her clothes. Well, they were going to have to catch her first.

Pivoting, she took off the way she'd come, her

boots eating up the dirt. Behind her, the Traders shouted, horses leaped. She'd always been a
runner and was damn good at distance. If she
could just get back to the alley she'd just come out
of, she might be able to dodge . . .

One of them grabbed her, hauling her face-first
across his lap with startling strength.

"Troublesome bitch." A second later, something
crashed against the back of her skull.

The lights went out.

CHAPTER SIX

Quinn woke to the sound of chaos.

Screams rent the air, crying, yelling. Someone fell on top of her, twisting Quinn's right leg at a painful, awkward angle. As she opened her eyes to the firelit night, she caught an elbow on the cheekbone.

Eyes stinging with pain, she struggled to sit up, to free herself from the tangle of limp bodies and flailing limbs, trying to make sense of her surroundings, trying to remember . . .

The Traders.

Her heart fell to her stomach. She'd gotten herself caught. Again. *Dammit.*

She looked around and saw what appeared to be a roped-off corner of some kind of open building, the once whitewashed walls dirty and liberally stained with . . . *blood?* Lamplight flickered on the walls as men and women dressed in a weird mix of nineteenth- and twenty-first-century garb stood in a wide circle around them, their heads tipped back, their eyes half-closed as if in a rapture of prayer, or the throes of orgasm.

She knew that look. She'd seen it on Arturo's

face often enough. They were feeding on the fear of their captives.

An elbow caught Quinn in the back as the others struggled to sit up around her, their faces reflecting a terror Quinn understood all too well. Unlike them, she knew where she was this time.

Something pulled at her ankle, yanking her foot hard and fast, making her fall into the person beside her. The loud clank of chains clued her to the problem a moment before she caught sight of the shackle around her ankle, a shackle chained, apparently, to someone else. Two someone elses. No wonder they were so badly tangled.

Pushing herself up, she managed to turn onto her knees. She glanced down, glad to see that she was still fully dressed, boots and all. No backpack, of course. God only knew where that had gone.

She looked around, studying her companions in this dark game of Twister. The best she could figure, there were about twenty of them chained together by one ankle, men and women alike. All looked to be relatively young—late teens to midthirties, though that was where the similarity ended. They were from all walks of life. Black, white, Asian, Middle Eastern, wearing everything from business suits to fraternity T-shirts, fanny packs to saris. Though a couple remained unconscious, most were fighting to get free, shouting, crying, screaming.

A dull haze of smoke filled the air, along with the smell of burning lamp oil and rank, acrid fear.

"He's killing her." The woman on Quinn's left, crouched like a terrified animal, stared at a spot over Quinn's head.

Turning awkwardly, her leg caught under the person next to her, Quinn followed the woman's gaze. *Ah, hell.* One of the people standing around the room . . . were they all vampires? . . . had a young woman caught tight in his arms as he fed from her neck. The victim, dressed in a pair of skimpy shorts and a running bra, whimpered as the vampire lifted his head and handed her to the man beside him as if she were an oversized rag doll. The vamp met Quinn's stare and grinned at her, his fangs gleaming with blood.

Her face paled, and she looked away quickly, not wanting him to think she wanted to be next. Sweat broke out on the back of her neck. She might have come here voluntarily this time, but that didn't mean she intended to die here. And she was going to have to watch her step very carefully, or that was exactly what would happen.

One by one, the circling vamps drank their pint of blood from the young runner, passing her along to the next in line. After the third feeding, she'd fallen unconscious. By the time the seventh vamp sunk his teeth into her neck, he pulled up a moment later, his fangs clean of blood. The young woman was dead.

The disgusted vamp tossed her back into the tangle of humans, raising another round of screams as the body landed on them. The girl's head came to rest near Quinn's knee, her blood-less face a mask of calm repose, before one of the panicked men kicked her away.

Quinn turned, bile rising in her throat. Panic tore at her control. As a bloodcurdling scream rose a short distance outside the circling vamps, she began to shake. She'd thought she understood this place. One vamp had attacked her; the second, Arturo, had nearly seduced her. He'd also treated her like a guest, apologized for scaring her, and left her virtually unmolested.

The screaming continued, a horrifying sound of unendurable pain. Quinn squeezed her eyes shut, wishing she could close it all out. Arturo had treated her like a princess in comparison to these monsters. If only he'd show up and whisk her out of here. She'd happily let him tie her to his bed again. Too late, she realized that she'd understood nothing about this place. Nothing at all. And she was in deep, deep trouble.

Several of those in the tangle cried out in fear. One of the men, one who'd managed to climb to his feet, choked with horror and turned away. "Sweet Virgin Mary. They're tearing her apart."

The crying intensified, the humans huddling together in abject terror, no longer concerned with untangling the chains, no longer worried about the corpse that couldn't hurt them as they trembled from fear of the horrors that awaited them next. The smell of carnage caught Quinn's nose. She gagged and began breathing through her mouth instead.

By the time the bloodcurdling screams fell silent, Quinn was shaking badly. The vamps around the circle began to move away. One strode into the tangle of humans and jerked a sobbing girl in a pair of dirty white shorts and a navy blue GWU T-shirt to her feet, yanking her around to face him. The tears drenching her face gleamed in the firelight.

"Look at me!" The vampire gripped her tanned face between pale fingers. Her crying stopped. Instantly.

The girl straightened, her body relaxing as her expression transformed to one of calm acceptance. No, not acceptance. Blankness. Vampire mind control. The glamour Arturo had tried on her and failed.

"On your feet, all of you!" While the vamp held the arm of the now-silent girl, two others waded in to untangle the rest of them, hauling them, one by one, to their feet. Quinn tried to get up on her own and was knocked down twice, her shackled leg repeatedly jerked out from under her. One of the big vamps grabbed her arm roughly, jerking her upright, until finally, they were all on their feet.

As the vamp led the first girl off at a slow pace, his companions forced the rest of them to follow in chained order. Quinn found herself squarely in the middle of the line, directly behind a slim, dark-skinned cop. Most of the humans were silent, now, or crying only quietly, glad to be standing, Quinn supposed. She certainly felt more in control on her feet again. Though any control was an illusion.

As the line started forward, clanking like any chain gang, Quinn kept her gaze studiously away from the place where all the screaming had come from, terrified of the carnage she'd see. As they crossed the open floor, vampires watched them from either side, dozens of vamps. Maybe a hundred or more. Why? Was this about to turn into some horrific feeding frenzy? An all-you-can-eat buffet, vampire style. A chill slid down her spine.

The first in the chained line began to climb a short series of steps, and Quinn realized that there was a stage up ahead. Perhaps just a dais. What kind of horror would the vampires visit on them this time, just for the sheer entertainment value? Losing her focus, she got out of step with the cop and nearly lost her balance as he stepped before she was ready.

One by one, they climbed the short stairs onto the stage, then lined up, one behind the other, pushed and prodded by their vampire captors. Another vamp, a burly man with a thick black beard, strode to the woman at the front of the line—the one who'd been hysterical—and took her face in his hand, staring into her eyes. At once, she gasped, then began to whimper and cower as he moved behind her and tore off her T-shirt and bra as if they were made of tissue paper, spilling her ample breasts into his waiting hands. The poor woman cried out.

"Well stacked," he called out over the noise,

clearly addressing the watching crowd. He jerked her around to face him, curling his lips back to reveal sharp fangs. The girl's cries turned to shrieks, over and over until Quinn thought her eardrums would burst. Finally, he grabbed the girl's jaw and captured her mind once more, silencing her. "And a bundle of pure terror," he said, turning back to the crowd.

"Four hundred!" shouted someone in the audience.

"Five!" shouted another.

A slave auction. Quinn tasted bile at the back of her throat.

Heart pounding sickly, Quinn watched as one after the other of her companions was paraded before the vamps like so much meat. Most of the women and all of the males were divested of their shirts, most shaking or crying, or rigidly still. Only those who screamed or fought had their minds controlled. The vamps enjoyed their fear too much to quell it with glamour.

As the humans were bought, they were enthralled and unshackled, then led away by their new masters. Quinn watched with increasing tension because when her turn came, they wouldn't be able to enthrall her. Not unless this new vamp had more power than Arturo had.

The cop in front of her was finally pulled to the fore, Quinn right at his elbow as the vamp tore off the stoic man's shirt, revealing a fine six pack.

"Show his cock!" a woman shouted from the audience.

The poor man's face turned a dark cherry.

"Drop your pants, slave, or I'll do it for you," the auctioneer ordered. "And I'll not be careful."

His jaw set hard enough that Quinn thought he might start dropping broken teeth, the man unfastened his belt and did as he was told. Quinn looked away, unable to add to the man's misery. Fury and a deep, quaking fear trembled inside her as she saw the hungry faces in the crowd. She searched for the two she'd recognize—the woman who'd taken Zack, and Arturo. She desperately hoped he was out there somewhere, ready to claim her again. But she saw no sign of him. No sign of either of them.

"Seven hundred!"

"A thousand!"

The cop went for more than any of the others had. Maybe after spending that much money on him, they'd take care to keep him alive.

The woman who'd demanded a look at his cock ultimately bought him, a female with a round, cherubic face and deep dimples. As he pulled up his pants, she leaped onto the short stage, grinning like a girl. "We're going to have so much fun, you and I." She gripped his chin, capturing his mind, then, once his ankle was released, led him away.

It was Quinn's turn, and she was shaking. *Calm down*, she told herself. *Don't fight it. Now's not the time.* But the moment she felt the auctioneer's hands moving around her, ready to rip off her shirt, the instinct to defend herself reared up, eclipsing everything else. She slammed her head back, colliding with his nose.

The vampire roared, and she pressed the advantage, throwing her elbow into his chest. But he didn't budge. He just glared at her with a snarling, bloody fury.

This is when he's going to kill you.

Instead, he hauled her against his chest, one arm binding her to him like a steel bar until she could barely breathe.

"This one's a fighter! Perhaps a good choice for the Games. She hasn't much in the way of tits, but she has good long legs and broad, strong shoulders. An excellent laborer. Do I hear five hundred?"

The crowd was silent.

Seriously?

And how screwed up was it that she was offended that no vampire wanted to bid on her?

"Two hundred," a woman called unenthusiastically, as if she were doing the auctioneer a favor in offering so much. *Jeez Louise.* Unlike the others in the crowd, this vamp looked like she'd stepped out of the 1940s—bright red lipstick, smooth, stylized hair, and a clingy dress that fell to just below her knee.

"Two hundred going once, twice, sold!"

The auctioneer moved in front of Quinn and gripped her chin painfully. At first, she thought he was about to seek his retribution. Almost too late, she realized he was trying to capture her mind. And like Arturo, he was failing.

Her pulse skipped. She had to pretend to be enthralled!

She forced herself to meet his gaze, then let her eyelids droop, her eyes unfocus. As her pulse continued to pound, he knelt to release her shackle. A big, bald, ebony-skinned man strode up onto the stage and took her by the arm. She didn't fight him, didn't even look at him as he steered her down the wooden steps to the woman who'd bought her.

"Hold her with the rest," the woman said with a casual wave of a slender, manicured hand.

"Yes, Mistress." As the auctioneer listed the attributes of the man who'd been chained behind her, the bald man led her through the crowd and out the door into what appeared to be true night. The street was lined with horse-drawn conveyances of every size and shape, the horses nickering softly. Across the street sat a couple of automobiles—a Land Rover SUV and a monster pickup. With disappointment, Quinn saw no sign of a yellow Jeep.

Her captor led her to a small gathering of three men, two of whom she recognized as slaves who'd been bought before her—a skinny man in suit pants and wingtips and an Asian in basketball shorts and high-tops. The third was a big, blond wrestler type with hair that shimmered like Horace's and Susie's had, dressed all in white. A guard, then.

Still fighting to appear mindless, she noted that the other two slaves remained unfettered.

And why would they bother to tie or chain them if they'd been enthralled? They wouldn't. Which was exactly what she'd been counting on. If she planned to make a move, she'd have to do it soon, before her new vampire mistress arrived. If that vamp moved anywhere near as quickly as the ones who'd attacked her and Zack, there'd be no outrunning her. Hopefully, the two guards didn't have that kind of speed, or she was going nowhere.

If she could make it behind the building across the street, perhaps she'd find alleyways to escape through.

She waited until the man who'd fetched her from the stage left again, no doubt returning to his vampire mistress. When the man in white turned away, Quinn took a breath for courage and took off, running as fast as her feet would carry her over the dirt-packed road.

Moments later, she heard the guard's shout and feared her escape was over before it had begun. But the big man didn't come after her, and she wondered if she might just pull this off after all. Her heart pounding in her throat, she darted down the nearest alley. It was lined with barrels and crates, boxes, and metal cylinders of all shapes and sizes. She considered trying to hide, but decided that way would almost certainly lead to capture. Ahead, the alley dead-ended into another. Once she turned the corner, she'd be out of sight of any pursuer. She might just make it!

But as she turned right into the connecting alleyway, she pulled up short at the sight of the woman standing there, as if waiting—the red-lipsticked, now-furious-faced vampire who'd bought her.

Holy hell. There is no outrunning these bastards! Not unless an errant sunbeam kept them at bay. The female stood a few feet away in her slinky dress, looking as if she'd merely run a few feet to catch a taxi instead of zero-to-sixtying it in high heels to catch a runaway slave. The woman moved . . . zoomed—there was no other word for it—closing the distance between them to snap a thick metal slave's collar around Quinn's neck before Quinn even registered the movement. She felt the heavy metal bite into her collarbones. A moment later, her mouth exploded in pain, blood tricking over her tongue. The bitch had slapped her across the mouth. Hard! Though she never saw the vamp's hand move.

The woman grabbed her arm and dragged her back to where the others waited, plus one more. Another female slave, a slender brunette, whom she must have just bought. The two big guards placed collars on all of them and fed a chain through the eyebolts of one collar, then the other, stringing them together. Quinn was last. The female vamp pushed Quinn forward, and she soon felt the clank of steel against her neck as she was chained to the others. Four across, the two men on one side, the two women on the other.

One by one, the female vamp unenthralled Quinn's companions. The woman gasped. The Asian growled. Wingtip remained perfectly silent.

None of these three had been hysterical during the auction, as Quinn remembered. They'd all been stoic and quietly furious.

The two giants left, returning several minutes later, each carrying a brightly-lit lantern and leading three horses between them.

The humans eyed one another, but remained mute as the two giants and the vampire mounted. The bald guard rode around them, coming to a stop before the four slaves. "Follow me and make no sound. The more you cry out, the worse it will be."

His words chilled. With that cryptic statement, he started forward. None of them moved. Not until the first crack of the whip slashed down the farthest man's back, and he stumbled forward, dragging his chained companions with him. The other three hastily caught up, none wishing for a taste of that whip.

But moments later, Quinn heard the crack, felt the lick of stinging fire down her back, and clamped down hard against the cry of pain that clawed to get out. Over and over, the whip cracked, flaying the four of them equally. It didn't seem to matter what they did, whether they walked quickly or slowly, not even if they cried out as Wingtip had begun to do every time he was hit.

Quinn's back blazed, her cheeks growing damp with the tears she tried to hold back. Fury rode her, a need to grab the lash and beat its wielder to a bloody pulp, but she was collared to the others, unable to move except as they did. And even if she could move, she'd seen the vampire's speed for herself. She was helpless against her. They all were.

The bald man turned, something akin to sympathy in his dark eyes. "She's a pain-feeder. When she's sated, she will stop. If you anger her, she will continue regardless."

A pain-feeder.

She hoped to heaven Zack hadn't been taken by such a creature. More than a week he'd been trapped here.

The lash tore through her shirt, burning a strip of fire down her back for the fourth time. Quinn hunched her shoulders against the pain, squeezing her eyes closed against the tears she couldn't control.

Beside her, the other woman cried out as the lash finally broke her composure.

Block after block, they walked, in the heart of downtown. It was true dark, now, and she could see little beyond the light shed by the two lanterns. But twice she'd spied street names on the corners of buildings and knew they walked east on K Street, not far from the Capitol, for whatever good it did her.

The woman beside her glanced at her, then away. "What is this place?" she whispered.

Quinn hesitated, not wishing to draw the vampire's fury, yet feeling incredible sympathy for the woman. "Washington, V.C. Vamp City. Some kind of otherworld for vampires."

"Hell on Earth for humans," the woman muttered.

"Silence!" The lash burned across Quinn's shoulder. A second snap, and the woman beside her groaned. Quinn had to hand it to her, and to their other two companions. Only Wingtip had yelled at the sting of the whip and only the last time or two. The vampire had chosen her slaves well.

At the corner of K and Third, the vampire called for them to stop, and the black man rode back to his mistress.

"Bring me the smaller woman," the vampire commanded. "I don't want the fighter."

The woman beside Quinn gasped. One of the men muttered a low, "*Fuck.*"

Quinn grasped the other woman's hand. "She won't kill you. She paid too much money for you." She prayed she was right.

As the big black guard unlatched her collar, the woman fought, kicking out, clearly done with acting strong and stoic, and Quinn couldn't blame her. The guard slung her over one broad, bare shoulder, carrying her to his mistress as if she weighed nothing.

Quinn glanced over her shoulder, watching as the female vamp took the struggling woman from him and grabbed her against her with the ease of an adult cradling a small child. The vampire's fangs dropped, her pupils turning white as she struck, sinking her fangs deep into the throat of her victim.

Quinn turned away, sickened, terrified the vamp would drain her dry and toss her aside like so much trash.

The sucking, hungry sound of the vampire's feeding had the rest of them edgy and tense. Quinn was certain she wasn't the only one wondering if she'd be next.

Now that they were still, the chains no longer clanking, the sounds from the auction began to drop like pebbles in a pond around them—the clip-clop of retreating horses, the rattle of horse tackle, the low keening of sharp misery punctuated by the occasional shout or scream. And underneath it all, the sound of a vehicle engine. One of the two she'd seen parked across from the auction?

Moments later, a familiar yellow Jeep turned the corner, kicking up a small cloud of dust, Arturo in the driver's seat. Quinn's knees nearly buckled in relief. Then again, did he even know she was here? Would he care? And if he *was* looking for her, it might be only to track her down and torture her for hurting . . . *killing?* . . . Ernesta with the water pitcher.

Her stomach twisted sickeningly at the thought. But she'd still choose him over the pain-feeder who'd just bought her.

With wary eyes, she watched as he slowed the Jeep to a crawl, then pulled to a stop a short distance in front of them, climbing out with a smile she could hardly credit. A bright, boyish, charmer's smile that did strange things to her insides and seemed so out of place on such a dangerous male. And it was firmly directed at her new mistress.

He was dressed, as before, all in black, the sheath of a long knife hanging from his waist. Dangerous *and armed*. His dark hair ruffled by the wind, Arturo was the epitome of rugged handsomeness as he strolled past Quinn, sparing her no glance.

"I see you've been shopping, Francesca." Clearly, they were old friends. "Stopping for lunch on your way home?"

"Arturo Mazza." The female vamp lifted her face from her meal with a look of faint annoyance.

Okay, so maybe they weren't such good friends.

"You look radiant, Francesca. But then you always do."

The female vamp snorted. "And you have a silver tongue, Arturo. And always have."

He glanced at Quinn, only a moment's look, but enough to tell her he was definitely there for her . . . whatever his motives.

"And how fares your kovena?" he asked Francesca.

Do as I tell you if you want to survive the week, cara. Arturo's voice. Quinn jumped. Arturo hadn't moved. He was still facing Francesca. *Pretend you do not hear me!*

My God, he was talking in her head. She struggled to relax, to look away.

Francesca goes through a slave every couple of days. We must get you away from her.

Was he really going to help her?

"My kovena fares well enough," the woman replied. "I'll not share my food with you, Arturo, you old charmer. Though my bed is another matter."

Arturo's laugh, warm and appreciative, was a sound that should have pleased and didn't . . . quite. The tone was off. Forced.

"Just a nip, my dear? From one of the others?"

"Absolutely not. I'm saving them for dinner."

Arturo strolled leisurely toward the remaining chained slaves, studying each in turn, revealing no recognition as he looked Quinn over. "You have a good eye for human flesh, Franny."

"Truly, I have a good ear. I can't stand the screamers."

He looked up, that wicked grin all the more dangerous for the sharp incisors it revealed. "I rather enjoy the screamers."

Francesca groaned. "You should have come to the auction, then. Such wailing. Henri has taken to slaughtering two of every bunch, one in front of the other captives for the fear-feeders. The other in torment for those of us who prefer the pain. Such screaming."

Arturo smiled absently, still looking Quinn over. "Perhaps I'll attend next week." He ran his finger down her cheek. "How much do you want for this one?"

Francesca kicked her horse, easing forward, drawing up again a few yards to Quinn's side. The vamp's victim remained tight in her arms, still alive, though lethargic. "She's not for sale, my

Italian prince. She takes the lash perfectly. I wish to see what else she can endure."

Wingtip released a trembling moan, and Quinn nearly did the same. Arturo's words, that Francesca went through a slave every couple of days, suddenly made a horrible sense. The vampire tortured her slaves to death. And at the moment, Quinn was one of those slaves.

Wiping her mouth on her sleeve, Francesca straightened in her saddle, allowing her food source to do the same. When she lifted her victim's hand, Quinn thought she intended to hand the slave back to her guard. Instead, she took one finger and snapped it like a twig.

The poor woman screamed. Francesca closed her eyes as if experiencing soft rapture.

Quinn thought she was going to be sick.

Make a scene, Arturo spoke in her head. *A cowardly, noisy one.* He gripped her jaw and said out loud, "I want this one, Franny. She may have taken the lash, but she trembles beneath my hand, her terror thick and lush." He stared at her. "What do you say, beauty? Do you want to come home with me? Do you want to scream for me?" *Do it.*

"No!" A decent yell, but hardly a cowardly, noisy scene. She'd never been a screamer. "No, please!" He gripped her shoulder where the lash had cut her. The bolt of pain was exactly what she needed. She released the scream that was bottled up inside her, released the tears she'd been fighting. "No! Let me go. Let me go!" She threw a punch at Arturo's middle, which he easily blocked, then another, fighting, kicking, screaming with the pain that ripped up and down her back with every movement, making as much noise as she could.

"Enough!" the woman cried, but Quinn continued. If the female vamp hated screamers, Quinn was going to scream.

"Double the price I paid for her, Arturo. One thousand."

Quinn gasped.

Keep it up, the voice warned. "Six hundred."

Quinn wailed, starting to get into it now. "No, no! Don't hurt me!"

"Eight hundred, and she's yours, my prince."

"Seven-fifty."

"Done. Manchester, free the slut. Get her out of here, Arturo."

Moments later, she was free, Arturo's long fingers curling coolly around her upper arm. But she knew better than to stop too soon. The female would know she'd been faking. Struggling in her vampire's grasp, Quinn continued to scream, kicking him in the shin. A bit of retribution for his scaring her half to death the first time he'd found her.

As he steered her toward the waiting Jeep, Quinn glanced back at the other slaves, sick with the knowledge they'd likely all be dead before another week passed, dying horrible, painful deaths.

Arturo opened the passenger door of his Jeep and shoved her in, his hand flat on her torn back. The pain tore a scream from her lungs, and she gave in to it, cutting the night with her misery, reveling in the knowledge that Francesca was probably covering her ears. *Take that, you bitch.*

Arturo closed her door, and she grabbed for the roll bar with one hand and the top of the windshield with the other, desperate to keep her bleeding back from banging against the seat as he flew over the pitted road. This ride was going to hurt.

On a roll now, she continued to wail as Arturo climbed into the driver's side, started the vehicle, and took off. The ride was every bit as bad as she'd feared it would be. As hard as she tried to keep her back off the seat, she kept slamming into it with excruciating regularity. Sweat rolled down her temples, unwanted tears down her cheeks as she clenched her teeth against the need to cry out, tired of hearing her own screams and pretty sure they were far enough away now that she didn't have to keep up the pretense. The nausea rose, slow and steadily, until she had no choice but to say something.

"I'm going to be sick." The words were little more than a gasp, but the vampire heard. The car came to a slamming halt, and, for an instant, she thought she was about to fly through the windshield, but his arm braced her before she ever saw him move. Who needed a seat belt when you had a vampire?

She fumbled for the door, but he was already there, opening it, lifting her out, keeping her from stumbling forward as she fell to her knees and retched in the dirt. For long, trembling moments, she stayed there, drenched in sweat, feeling like the world's biggest wuss. Yes, her back was a bloody mess, but this was nothing compared to the pain the others would endure . . . were already beginning to suffer. Her stomach didn't seem to care.

When she was fairly certain she wasn't going to heave again, she looked up to find Arturo standing a few yards in front of her, watching her with cool eyes, the charmer once more gone as if he'd never been.

"You did well," he murmured. "My ears are going to be ringing for hours."

"Thank you for rescuing me. Did you? Rescue me? Or am I going to suffer at your hands, too?"

"Have you suffered at my hands, *cara*?"

"No. But I escaped you. I hit Ernesta." She cringed. "Please tell me I didn't kill her."

His mouth pulled up on one side, but that tiny bit of a smile rose nowhere near his eyes. "You didn't kill her though you gave her a hell of a headache."

Her breath trembled out with relief, and she realized how much that had been weighing on her. "Good. I didn't mean to hurt her. I only meant to get away." She pushed herself to her feet, wincing at the pain that lanced her back with every move.

"Yet here you are."

She shrugged and moaned as that hurt, too, then met his gaze. "I have to find my brother."

He shook his head. "You're a fool to have come back here. He's probably dead by now. Or as good as."

"He's my brother."

For long moments, he studied her, then finally held his hand out to her. "Come."

She hesitated, then started to reach for his hand, only to snatch hers back as she realized his pupils were beginning to turn white, his fangs starting to elongate. "You're hungry."

"You're bleeding."

She shuddered. "Right. Trust me, I'd rather not be."

At his soft snort, she looked at him, surprised to see the smile reach his eyes.

"Do you need to bite me?"

"Wish to? Always. Need to? No. Your blood is far too enticing, and you've been weakened. Again."

Despite the fearsome visage he presented, she placed her hand in his. And held on tight.

CHAPTER SEVEN

As Quinn braced herself, feeling shaken and beaten, Arturo pulled into the alley behind his house. He handed Quinn out of the Jeep and led her into the kitchen as he had when he'd caught her trying to escape him the first time. His hand circled her upper arm to steady her, she supposed. They both knew she wasn't about to try to escape. Not yet, at least. Not after what had just happened. Her back burned from Francesca's lashings, her stomach was still sore and tight from the vomiting, and she felt more than a little lightheaded. Another advantage of having a vampire companion—if she stumbled, he'd be able to grab her before she fell.

"Susie!" Arturo led her to the stairs. They were halfway up the flight when the girl appeared in the hallway below.

"Yes, Master?"

"Quinn is in need of tending. Gather your supplies and meet us upstairs."

"Yes, Master."

Quinn glanced at her companion. "She's kind

of young, isn't she?" He'd already admitted to having sex with her. Every third day.

"She's older than she looks." At the top of the stairs, he ushered her into the room where she'd first found herself tied, spread-eagled, to the bed. "Susie will be up shortly, then I will leave you in her care. I would appreciate it if you would refrain from attacking any more of my servants."

Quinn grimaced. "Sorry. No attacking the other slaves. Promise." She shrugged. "At least, not unless I'm provoked."

"That's what I was afraid of," he murmured.

Susie appeared in the doorway, throwing a sweet smile at Arturo before shifting a wary gaze to Quinn. *Seriously?* In this kid's eyes, she was more scary than a vampire?

"She'll not hurt you," Arturo told the girl. "I have her word."

Quinn felt about two feet tall.

Arturo met Quinn's gaze. "I will not be far. In case you get another urge to sunbathe."

He wouldn't let her escape again. Part of her didn't want to. Horace's words, that Arturo was the best of the lot, had been soundly illustrated today. Yet, trapped was trapped. Only free would she stand any chance of finding Zack.

Arturo left. Susie remained in the doorway, clutching a basket of medical supplies against her abdomen. Good grief, her hands were actually shaking.

"Susie . . ." Quinn lifted her hands, palms out.

"I didn't mean to hurt Ernesta. I mean, I did, but only because I was trying to escape to find my brother, and she'd told me she wasn't human. I figured that meant I needed to hit her hard. But I'm sorry. It wasn't anything against her personally. And I don't want to escape this time." At least not this moment. "I won't hit you, I promise."

The girl stepped forward cautiously. "Where are you hurt?"

"My back. I was lashed."

Taking a deep breath and letting it out slowly, Susie nodded toward the bed. "Take off your shirt and lie down." The girl was suddenly all crisp efficiency. And she no longer sounded so young.

Quinn did as she was told, shrugging out of her jacket, then nearly moaning at the pain of peeling her tank top out of the wounds on her bloody back. If the girl had been looking for a bit of retribution for her friend, she was getting it in spades. Quinn forced herself to yank the top free as tears burned her eyes. With trembling hands, she pulled her running bra over her head, peeling it off, too. Finally free of the garments, she lay on the bed, the cotton bedspread cool and comforting against her sweat-damp skin.

The bed sank at her side as Susie joined her.

"The ointment will heal the wounds, but the application may be uncomfortable. I'm sorry if I hurt you."

She doubted that. "It can't hurt much more than Francesca's whip."

The girl's fingers were surprisingly gentle, the ointment cool to the touch, the sting not nearly as bad as Quinn had expected.

"You were lucky the master saved you," the girl murmured, her voice soft. "They say no slave survives Francesca, not even the immortals."

"Immortals? You mean vampires?" Little by little, the pain began to disappear beneath the ointment.

"Immortal humans. They call us Slavas."

Quinn glanced back at Susie with surprise. "You?"

Susie smiled gently, the oil lamp casting a soft light over her young face. "Yes, me. It happens to all of us who've been here a while. If you live long enough, it will happen to you, too." She lifted a lock of her own light brown hair, holding it up where she could see it. "You know you've become immortal when your hair starts to glow."

"What makes it do that?"

"No one knows, but they think it has something to do with the magic of V.C. because no slaves ever had glowing hair before this place was created. Vampire saliva, shared during feeding, has always had a healing effect on humans. But only the humans in Vamp City have ever actually turned immortal."

The girl's skin was perfect, unlined. "You look like you're twenty."

She grinned. "I was born in 1950. That makes me . . . oh, goodness. Over sixty years old."

Quinn gaped at her.

"I was nineteen when I was caught and sold in a slave auction. Within a couple of years, I stopped aging."

"Arturo bought you?"

"No. I was bought for his master's, Cristoff's, slave hall. I . . ." Her face tightened, shadows darkening her eyes. "I didn't like it there. After a few months, Arturo bought me and brought me here, and I've never left. And never want to. He's not like the others. You're very lucky he's chosen you."

Quinn turned back, resting her chin on her hands. Without a doubt, she owed the vamp for getting her out of Francesca's clutches. And he really didn't seem to be like the others. Still, there was no way she could accept that this was it. That she would spend the rest of her life in this house, serving a vampire. She had a brother to save, a job to get back to, a life to live in *her* world, the real world, where the sun shone and the roads were paved and every man walking down the street wasn't trying to eat her.

It would kill something inside her simply to give up and give in, even if Zack weren't involved. Arturo might not be one of the truly bad guys, but it was highly unlikely he'd simply let her walk away. She was going to have to play this carefully.

"Do you ever leave the house, Susie?"

"No, and I don't want to," she said quickly. "It's safe here. *I'm* safe here. I like it here."

"You might be able to go home. Back to the real world. I did."

Susie shook her head. "It's unlikely I'd survive. A few vampires have tried to take their slaves with them through the Boundary, but the slaves instantly revert to their true age. Even if they weren't too old to live, the shock of aging that quickly usually kills them. No, there is no going back for me, and nothing to go back to."

"Horace is older than you, isn't he?" Suddenly his comment to her before, that his family had been gone more than a century, made sense.

"He's more than a hundred years older than I am, yes. He was one of the first slaves brought in after V.C. was created."

Quinn closed her eyes, trying to absorb Susie's words. This girl was over sixty. Horace, one of the first brought in, was a man of the 1800s. He must have looked and talked just like he did now, back in 1870. Incredible. She hadn't time-traveled. Not exactly. And yet . . .

"Do the vampires ever let their slaves go? Those who haven't turned immortal?"

"No. They don't let any go. But not all vampires live within V.C. Those who live in the real D.C. need slaves, too."

She looked at the girl with surprise. "How many live in the real world?"

"I don't know. With the magic failing—"

"Thank you, Susie. That will be all, *cara mia*." Arturo's rich voice had Quinn's attention whirling to the doorway, her heartbeat jumping.

"Yes, sir." Flashing a quick smile, Susie rose,

picked up her supplies, then grabbed Quinn's discarded clothes.

When Quinn made a sound of objection, Susie met her gaze. "I'll wash and mend them for you."

Chastened, Quinn nodded. "Thank you, Susie."

Arturo closed the door behind her, then moved toward the window, out of Quinn's line of sight. She didn't like having him behind her, but she was bare from the waist up, with nothing to put on.

With a sigh, she levered herself up, amazed that her back no longer hurt. Swinging her feet over the side of the bed, she sat, crossing her arms over her chest. She'd rather be able to see him, all things considered.

She found him watching her from the far side of the room, his body utterly still, his gaze quite active, dropping to her chest, to her legs, then slowly climbing back to her face, a heat in his eyes that made her shiver. Had he come to claim his sexual rights as her slave master?

Slowly, he moved toward the bed, his steps as silent as any predator's. "Stand up."

"Why?"

"You make a terrible slave, *cara*. I wish to see your back."

Turning her back on a vampire hardly seemed like the smartest move. Then again, as fast as he moved, what difference did it make? She did as he asked, keeping her arms crossed over her chest as she rose, which effectively hid all evidence that she had breasts. Lucky her.

His fingers skimmed her shoulder blade, then

her hip, two places untouched by the lash. "Is the pain gone?"

"Yes. Completely." She looked at him over her shoulder. "What's in the ointment Susie used? It has some serious antipain properties."

A gleam of laughter entered his eyes. "Magic." His head dipped, his cool lips pressing against her bare shoulder.

She shivered at the gentle, sensual kiss, her nipples hardening beneath her forearms. "Vampire . . ." Her voice sounded breathy.

His hands came around her, grasping her arms, tugging them lightly as if to open her to his gaze. "No."

The soft, damp stroke of his tongue over her ear sent another tremor through her. "Why do you hide yourself, *cara*? I wish to see you."

Quinn grunted, letting him pull her arms away, dropping them to her sides. "There's not much to see." As an athlete, she'd always had far more of an appreciation for what her body could do than what it looked like. In sports, her lack of curves had been an asset. With guys, not so much.

Cool hands slid over her breasts, covering them completely, which wasn't hard to do. But, oh, it felt good.

He flicked her nipples with his thumbs, sending a rush of hot desire flowing through her veins. Over and over, he rubbed his thumbs back and forth over the tight buds. "You have beautiful breasts." The huskiness of his tone almost made it sound like he meant it.

"If you're into fried eggs."

"They are not fried eggs. Size is not everything."

"Most men would disagree."

"Most men are fools." He turned her to face him, then gripped her waist as he studied one breast with the raptness of a connoisseur, tracing her areola with his thumb. The gentleness of his caress made her tremble. "Soft as silk," he murmured. "The skin flawless. Your nipples are beautifully shaped, perfectly formed pink buds. Among the finest I've seen."

She watched him, torn between pleasure and wariness. "I can't decide if you're playing me."

His gaze flicked up to meet hers. "And what would I be playing you for?"

"Sex."

That ever-present amusement lifted his mouth. "Seduction takes many forms. But my words are true, *cara*. I've seen many a breast." His brow arched wickedly. "Many a breast."

She laughed. For the first time in forever, she didn't feel lacking with her shirt off. Thanks to a vampire.

Without warning, he knelt before her, gripping her waist with long, cool fingers as he pulled her close, and took one of her breasts into his mouth. His tongue took over for his thumb, flicking her nipple. Surprise caught in her throat. Desire shot straight to her core.

"*Vampire.*"

She didn't want this. And yet she did. He

sucked at her, pulling her breast into his mouth. Without thinking, she gripped his head, sliding her fingers into the dark silk of his hair, breathing in the rich, intoxicating scent of him. Almonds. And night. And potent, virile male.

Oh, God, I want this. Her body melted beneath his touch, her legs turning to soft butter.

His mouth released her breast, his lips trailing kisses down one barely there slope and up the other to give equal attention to its twin. Flicking, sucking, his hands sliding up and down her sides, then down to her hips and behind, gripping her rear, sending heat leaping within her.

While she held him to her with one hand, with the other she slid her fingers to the back of his neck, feeling the tendons and rock-hard flesh. His skin wasn't cold to the touch, not at all. Just a little cooler than her own. Wonderfully so. She wanted to press her heated flesh against him and cool the raging fever he caused with his touch, with his mouth.

His hands slid to the front, and he reached for the waistband of her pants.

Instinctively, Quinn grabbed his shoulders. "No."

Arturo released her breast and looked up, meeting her gaze. His mouth was damp and swollen, his eyes hot and questioning. "You want this."

"No. It's too soon." He was a stranger. *A vampire.*

Slowly, he rose until he once more had the height advantage, crowding her. His mouth tightened with . . . displeasure? Frustration? He lifted a lock of her hair, twirling the blond strand around one long finger, studying it.

"What am I going to do with you?" The edge of frustration in his tone told her this was no rhetorical question.

"Let me go? Maybe even help me find my brother?"

His gaze snapped to hers, but he didn't laugh. He didn't scoff. He just watched her as if he were actually contemplating it.

Her pulse, already erratic from his touch, leaped into overdrive, and she held her breath, waiting . . . praying . . .

"And what will you give me in return?"

"Anything." The word shot from her mouth. *"Anything." Please, please, please let him be considering and not just toying with me.*

He grasped her head in both of his hands, staring at her intently. "You, I will not free, *cara*. But your brother, perhaps. If you promise to never escape me again."

She stared at him, her heart thudding, her stomach cramping from the blow. *You, I will not free.* Ever. She'd never go home if she didn't escape him.

But Zack might. If the vampire was telling the truth and not simply placating her. Nothing mattered but getting Zack out of this place. Nothing. She had to make this happen.

"I have to see him. And his friend Lily. I have to know they're safe."

Arturo snorted. "Two of them, now? You ask much."

"*You* ask for my life."

He lifted a dark brow. "I already own your life, *piccola*. I ask for your cooperation."

She was beginning to shake. Tears burned her eyes. After all that had happened, it was this . . . this chance of actually saving Zack . . . that threatened to shatter her control.

"Yes. You have it. But I want them out of V.C."

"That will be difficult until the magic is renewed."

"But not impossible?"

His jaw hardened, then slowly eased again. "No. Not impossible."

The tears began to slide down her cheeks. Arturo watched them, frowning, then brushed one away with his thumb. "Why do you cry? I offer you much."

"I don't know." She swiped self-consciously at her other cheek. "Because I'm relieved. And because, either way, he's going to be lost to me."

He leaned forward and kissed her temple. "You owe me a boon in return, *tessoro*."

"I promised I wouldn't escape you."

"Yes. And now I want you in my bed. I want your body. And your blood."

Her legs turned to rubber at the raw confession, heat liquefying her center. She blinked against the blur of tears and met his gaze.

He stroked her hair. "I'll not hurt you, *piccola*. I will bring you great pleasure. As you will bring me."

And, really, did she have a choice? This was to

be her life, now. This man's slave. The remarkable thing was that he was asking, that he was at least pretending to leave the choice in her hands.

She took a deep, trembling breath. "Okay."

Arturo reached for her, pinching her nipples lightly. Desire shot straight to her core. How could such a simple touch ignite her so thoroughly?

Cool lips grazed her cheek, trailing kisses down to her jaw. Lost in the sensation, she tilted her head, giving him access when his mouth dipped lower, his tongue sliding along the side of her neck. Shivers engulfed her.

The sharp prick of fangs brought her up short. He'd bitten her! Gripping his shoulders, she tried to push him away, but his arm went around her waist, hauling her closer.

"Vampire . . ."

His lips closed around the wound as he took a long pull of her blood, shocking her with the rush of pleasure. Delighting her. The legends were absolutely true. *God.*

Quinn felt cool fingers at her waistband, sliding down into her pants, into her panties. Into her. The intimate invasion, the pull of his mouth on her throat, and she was gasping, melting, shattering. She clung to him, shaking, weak. Utterly overwhelmed.

Arturo pulled his hand from her pants, his fingers shifting to unfasten the button of her fly as he lifted his face from her neck. His visage . . . bloody fangs protruding from his mouth, his eyes gleaming with white centers . . . sent her heart thudding.

Primal terror rose in a blinding rush even as she battled it back. He wasn't a demon. He wasn't going to hurt her.

Probably.

But logic held no sway over primitive fear.

Arturo moaned, as if in rapture, tipping his head back as his fanged, bloody mouth dropped open.

He was feeding on her fear again. Furious with him, furious with the fine panic that had seized her, she pushed at his chest, trying to force him away, but he was as solid as cold steel. So she balled up her fist and delivered a knockout blow to his jaw.

He gripped her wrists so fast, his terrifying, enraged face suddenly inches from her own, that she gasped, her heart thundering in her chest.

"Get away from me," she hissed through clenched teeth.

Slowly, his fury turned into a monster-sized scowl, and he whirled away, propping one fisted hand on the wall as he stared at the floor as if struggling for composure. He stood like that for so long, Quinn wasn't sure what to say, what to do. Had she blown it? Would he renege on his offer to find Zack and Lily? Slowly, her heart rate settled back to normal, and she sat on the bed to wait for him.

Finally, he turned and strode to the door without once glancing her way.

"Get some sleep. We'll leave in the morning."

"We?"

He paused, one hand on the doorknob, his face dipped as if he studied his fingers curling around the knob. "I do not know what they look like, your brother and Lily."

"Thank you, Arturo."

Still, he didn't turn. With a brief nod, he left, closing the door behind him.

She heard no click of a lock. But then she wasn't going anywhere. Not when he'd promised to find Zack and Lily come morning. Not when there was a chance he might actually do it.

And she'd promised to stay here . . . to be his willing slave. Forever.

"We're walking?" Quinn asked the next morning as she accompanied Arturo out the kitchen door and past the Jeep. Adrenaline had her wired, a mix of nerves and wariness as she walked beside this man who had touched her so intimately last night, this male who she'd nearly given her body to. And her body had not forgotten, nor had it forgiven her. Despite the orgasm he'd given her while drinking her blood, she'd lain awake half the night in a fever of need for his touch, for his possession. Long enough to wonder if he'd somehow pulled her under an unnatural sensual spell.

She was hyperaware of him this morning, the strong lines of his body, as he moved with pure, predatory grace beside her. The raw, masculine scent of him that wafted over her as the wind shifted just so. He was dressed in his requisite black, the long knife sheath once more hanging from the belt at his waist.

They walked around the front of the house and to the sidewalk that fronted F Street. The Treasury Building loomed a block ahead, vast, dark, and windowless. A shell of its true glory.

"We shall start with my kovena's stronghold," he told her.

"What's a kovena? A nest of vampires or something?"

The look he threw her chided. "A family, if you will. Many within the kovena were sired by our master, Cristoff, or by one of the other vampires. Many have joined the kovena out of loyalty or for protection."

"And you?"

"I long ago swore an oath of loyalty to Cristoff."

At the corner, they turned right, heading north. "Where exactly is this kovena?"

"Gonzaga Castle is only a few blocks."

"A castle? In D.C.?"

"Not D.C."

"Right." Unlike last night, the light was back, though so dim there was no color anywhere, just shades of gray. Her scientist's brain rejected the possibility that such a thing was possible. When she looked up at the sky, she saw clouds, gray smudges against the grayer sky. It made no sense. *Magic.* "This place shouldn't be possible," she murmured, then turned to him. "Do you really like living someplace so . . . dead?"

He grinned at her, making her stomach flip. "It is the perfect place for vampires, is it not? No sun, no need to hide for fear of detection by the far more numerous human race. Vamp City was promoted as a utopia, *cara*. And in many ways, it still is. Where else can vampires hold horse races and soccer matches, hunts and other games at any time, day or night, free to use our full range of abilities, free to feed on the humans in our midst without fear of reprisal or discovery? Without fear of the sun? We are free to be ourselves here, as we are nowhere else."

"I suppose it does sound kind of perfect from a vampire's point of view. But if it's so great, why do ... did ... some of you live in the real world, too?"

"Personally, I am fond of modern conveniences. And I have many investments to look after."

"You're wealthy."

"Only a fool or a layabout would not be after six hundred years."

As they crossed the next street, the buildings all but disappeared, nothing left but foundations. "What happened here?"

"Fire. We lost several blocks before we were able to contain it. It happened decades ago."

No volunteer all-vampire fire department, she supposed, which was probably too bad. As fast as they moved, with the right equipment, they could probably put out a fire in seconds.

"How many vampires live here?"

He glanced at her with amusement. "You are full of questions this morning, *cara*."

"I'm a scientist. I'm always full of questions. Do you mind answering them?"

His response was a little late in coming and not as enthusiastic as she might have liked. But he shrugged. "There are roughly four hundred vampires divided into nine kovenas. Most prefer to live in the strongholds though some prefer their own abodes."

"Like you."

"Like me." He pulled something out of his pocket and held it out to her. "Would you like one?"

"What is it?" The silvery wrapper shone in the low light. "SweetTarts?" she asked incredulously.

"I have a weakness for them."

She reached for the roll and pulled off the top candy, popping it into her mouth, enjoying the explosion of tart green apple. "Thank you."

"You're welcome." He placed one of the candies into his own mouth and pushed the roll back into his pocket.

When they were past the Treasury Building, Quinn glanced left, drawn to the sight of the White House, standing like a once-beautiful woman, now age-ravaged and graying, and very, very alone. "I'm surprised no one moved into the White House. It would have been fully furnished."

"It was. And we did. For nearly a hundred years it was my master's stronghold."

She looked at him in surprise. "What happened?"

"Time and neglect. The president's mansion, as it was known back then, was built of sandstone.

Without proper maintenance, sandstone slowly turns to mud."

"But the real White House hasn't disintegrated."

"It is painted regularly. And it underwent a full reconstruction in the early 1950s, when it was discovered to be in imminent danger of collapse."

"I didn't know that."

"You weren't around at the time." A lilt of humor lifted his voice.

"So is that when you decided you needed to move?"

"Five years prior, the ceiling over the kitchens in our version collapsed. The deterioration here had been more swift, but then we've never maintained our properties with the same vigilance as the humans."

"Your house seems to be in great shape."

"It is."

"Because you care about it."

"I do."

A distant scream broke the stillness up ahead. Quinn tensed. She could just make out what appeared to be a walled compound beyond the derelict properties making up the next block. The sound of classical piano music carried on the air, along with voices and a peal of laughter.

"Is that where we're going?" she asked warily.

"It is." As they rounded the corner, the compound came into full view. The walls were made of stone and were at least twenty feet high, all but obscuring the large house within. "Is this it, the castle?" She grunted. "Calling it a castle might be pushing it a bit."

They followed the wall, approaching a pair of huge, black, iron gates with a design of intricate swirls. When they were finally upon them, she got her first glimpse of the mansion inside. And it was huge. Maybe *castle* wasn't a bad name for it after all.

Just inside the gates stood two guards, dressed in what appeared to be some kind of eighteenth- or nineteenth-century military uniform, swords strapped to their backs.

"Who do they guard the place from?"

"Everyone." His tone was short.

"Do the kovenas war against one another?"

"Of course," he snapped. He was getting testy. *Why?*

Rather than opening the massive gates, one of the guards opened a small door within the nearby wall for them to enter.

"Arturo," the guard said with a deference that surprised her. Her vampire master must carry some weight around here.

Arturo allowed her to precede him through. As the door clicked shut behind them, they started the long walk to the house. Shouts of laughter and gaiety filled the air as if a party were in full swing. She heard the splash of water. A pool? She'd imagined a vampire castle to be a dark, broody thing, but this one was lit up like an octogenarian's birthday cake.

As they climbed the brick steps, the massive front doors opened, two liveried butlers standing back to let them in.

"Arturo," the two said as one, bowing.

Arturo acknowledged them with a shallow nod. Taking her upper arm in a firm grip, he led her into a massive marble-and-ivory foyer the size of a small ballroom, in the center of which sat a mammoth black lacquer grand piano. There were vampires everywhere, holding drinks, fondling the Slava females who walked among them in what appeared to be a uniform of short skirts and low-cut peasant blouses. Along one of the walls sat a line of velvet benches, where two vampires appeared to be making out. Close by, a silk-robed vamp male grabbed one of the Slavas to him, pulling her back against him, baring and fondling her breasts as he bit her. As Quinn watched in horrified fascination, his lashes swept up, his white-centered eyes spearing her as if imagining his fangs in her neck instead. As if promising her just that.

Quinn shivered and looked hurriedly away, her face flaming, her body flushed with intense discomfort. This place was like a playground for the depraved.

"Ax!" One of the male vamps, in blue jeans and a black silk shirt, strode toward them, a drink the color of whiskey in his hand. He had dark circles under his eyes, lines of strain along either side of his mouth. Despite that, he seemed genuinely glad to see Arturo.

The two vampires greeted one another warmly. "How do you fare, Bram?"

"Not well. I'm going fucking crazy in this place." He lowered his voice. "They lie around doing nothing but drinking and fucking as if there's nothing else to life. If the magic's going to kill me, I wish it would just do it and get it over with. Take me out of my misery."

"I've heard a rumor a solution may have been found."

Bram's eyes widened. "Pray you're right about that." He turned to Quinn. "Who's this?"

"My most recent acquisition," as if that were all she was.

She was tempted to thrust out her hand and introduce herself simply to make them acknowledge her as more than a slave. But an instinct for self-preservation warned her against drawing any more attention to herself in this place than she had to.

"Are you bringing her to Kassius?"

"No," Arturo replied slowly. "She's of Blackstone's ilk."

Bram's brows shot up, and he turned to stare at her as if she were suddenly the most fascinating thing in the room. Quinn turned to Arturo for explanation. But his attention was on the other man.

"Thank, God," Bram murmured, then frowned. "I don't smell it." Without warning, he leaned close to her, sniffing at her hair.

Quinn reared back. "What do you mean *Blackstone's ilk*?"

A bloodcurdling scream sliced the air, raising the hair on the back of Quinn's neck and lifting the heads of several vamps nearby. Bram stiffened, his breath turning suddenly short, and shallow. The screaming continued until Quinn wanted to cover her ears to shut it out. Someone was being tortured mercilessly. Killed. Her breath hitched. Half a dozen vamps disappeared in a blur of silk and velvet, reappearing at the top of the curved stairs.

Bram's expression grew pained, his eyes filling with misery. "I have to go." He shoved his glass into Arturo's hand, then turned and climbed the stairs, human pace, his shoulders bent as if he fought every step, and lost.

Arturo took her arm and steered her away from the stairs and out of the huge foyer, into an even larger room, but the change of rooms did little to dampen that horrible, continual scream. Vampires played billiards on one of the two tables, while others played poker at one of three gaming tables. At the far side of the room, an entire wall of glass doors had been opened to the outside and a swimming pool lit by torches.

None of the vampires appeared to even hear the woman's screams, let alone care. She glanced at Arturo. "How can you all ignore that?"

"Calm yourself, *cara*. Cristoff is a pain-feeder." He said it so matter-of-factly.

"And that makes it okay?"

His dark eyes flashed. "We are vampires, Quinn

Lennox. One way or another, we feed off humans or we die. We're at the top of the food chain."

"So all we are to you is food?"

"To most vampires, yes. I am afraid so."

She wanted to ask if he felt the same and couldn't, afraid she didn't want to know. She had a feeling she wouldn't like his answer, not at all. "The vampires who ran for the stairs. They're pain-feeders, aren't they?"

"Yes. As is Bram, as much as he hates it."

And she'd seen that, Bram's misery, his reluctance to climb those stairs and join the others. She thought of Arturo's words to him. "What did you mean I'm of Blackstone's ilk?"

"Quiet, *piccola*. That was not meant for other ears." He leaned closer, his voice dropping to a bare whisper. "There is danger here."

With that cryptic warning, he steered her through the game room and out onto the pool deck, where several vampires swam in the nude.

Her instincts told her to pursue the question, that she needed to know. But she hardly trusted Arturo to tell her the truth. So she held her tongue. For now. "Is there no other way for Bram to feed?"

"Before the magic began to fail, he worked as a trauma doctor in the emergency room at George Washington Hospital. He has for the past twenty years."

She looked at him with disbelief. "A vampire *doctor*?"

"Bram is an excellent doctor. He genuinely likes

to help humans in pain. He hates that he's forced to feed on that pain, but it has been a good compromise for him."

"And now he can't get to the hospital." She was beginning to understand his misery, though. Were there really vampires who were that moral, that altruistic? Maybe there were. "Do you have an outside job?"

He led her around the pool while she kept her eyes averted from the carnal play going on in the water. "I do not."

"Do you have a house in the real world?"

"No, but a friend of mine does. I have an office in Micah's house, where I work on the computer a couple of nights a week. When I was able to get there."

"Is Micah still in the real world?"

"He is. But I've no way to contact him. He's as locked out as we are locked in. Would you like a drink?" he asked, steering her to the bar.

She would, absolutely, if it might dull the piercing screams that went on and on and on. But she had a feeling she'd better keep her wits about her in this place.

"No, thank you."

Slowly, the screams began to die away. As did, undoubtedly, the screamer. She tried not to think of her, of how she was dying, even now, for fear she'd start screaming herself. And she couldn't. No matter what happened, she had to keep it together. For Zack.

"Come, *piccola*." Arturo steered her back toward the foyer. "We must speak with Cristoff, and this will be a good time, now that he's fed."

She shuddered at the thought of what might happen if they approached a pain-feeder at a bad time. As Arturo led her past the piano, toward the stairs, Quinn was hit with a terrible smell, like something burning. The smell only worsened as they climbed. At the top of the stairs, he ushered her a short way down a wide hallway to a pair of open doors, then inside a huge room. A throne room. There was no other word for it. The ceiling soared, propped up by thick, gilt pillars. The walls were hung with all manner of weapons and tapestries and coats of arms. At the far end, the marble floor rose to a low dais graced by a huge golden chair . . . a throne . . . upholstered in dark red velvet. And upon the throne sat a young man staring with unrestrained pleasure at the naked woman lying in the middle of the room in a shallow puddle of blood, being fed upon by four vampires.

Around them stood half a dozen vampires, including Bram, who appeared to be coming out of the throes of pleasure. Bram's mouth was tight as he raked his fingers through his hair and turned away.

As Arturo led Quinn into the room, she caught sight of the woman's arms and legs, the raw, fresh burn marks, and knew she'd found both the source of the screams and the horrific smell. Burning flesh. Her stomach cramped, her head turning hot, then cold as Arturo steered her toward the man sitting upon the dais.

Cristoff? He looked too young, too strange, to be such a powerful vampire. Then again, vampires didn't age. He could be very, very old, and he'd still look twenty-five, she suspected. He had good bone structure beneath a shoulder-length fall of bleached white hair, his eyebrows and small King Tut beard jet-black in contrast. His mouth was thin and cruel, his pale blue eyes as cold as a killing frost. *A pain-feeder.*

A primal anxiety crawled across Quinn's flesh. She wanted out of here, out of this room, this house, this world. And she wanted out, now! But she swallowed hard, tamping it down. Fear was an emotion she couldn't afford to show, let alone feel. Not in this place, where they fed on such things. There would be no hiding it.

She forced her gaze away from Cristoff, then wished she hadn't as she met the gaze of the bald guard standing at his right, a vampire whose gaze felt like rancid fingers stroking her flesh as he looked her over. His eyes gleamed as if he had every intention of throwing her down and having his way with her. She sidled closer to Arturo even though he still gripped her arm.

"Master." Arturo dipped his head slowly, in a show of deep respect that felt somehow wrong. How could a man with any kind of morals bow to such a monster? "I have found you a sorceress."

Arturo pushed her forward.

Quinn's jaw dropped, her head suddenly ringing with his words. With his *lie*. "I'm not!" She whirled on Arturo. "Why would you say such a thing?" What did he think he was doing?

Out of the corner of her eye, she saw a flash of movement, then shrieked as Cristoff grabbed her and bit her neck with a razor-sharp stab of pain. Tears burned her eyes as she struggled against his impossible vampiric strength.

Cristoff lifted his head, a triumphant look on his face as he stared at her, his mouth bloody and smiling. "You've done well, my snake."

"I'm not a sorceress." But the weirdness she'd lived with all her life raised its ugly head and laughed at her denial.

She turned to Arturo for help, saw the apology swimming in his dark eyes, and understanding crashed. This was why he'd brought her here. This. Not, as he'd told her, to search for Zack.

Arturo turned back to Cristoff. "She has a half brother who was taken by one of Lazzarus's vamps. I have a contact within the kovena. I can find out if the brother possesses any magic, if it please you."

She stared at him, her scalp crawling with his betrayal. He knew exactly where Zack was. He'd known all along.

"Do it, but say nothing of the sister. She is our secret, for now."

Quinn stared at Arturo, willing him to meet her gaze. "Will you bring Zack here?"

He didn't turn. "No. He belongs to another."

"Please!"

He whirled on her, all warmth gone from his eyes. "Forget him," he snapped. "He's lost to you."

"You lied to me."

"I said what I must to keep you from trying to escape." And this time she saw only truth in those hard eyes. This had been his intention all along. To bring her to his master.

Cristoff laughed softly, a sound that formed ice crystals in her veins. "I call Arturo my snake for a reason."

On a burst of fury, she tried to get at the vampire who'd betrayed her, but Cristoff held her fast, binding her against him with an iron arm until she could barely breathe. She trembled with outrage and a deep, quaking terror.

"Go, now," Cristoff ordered his snake.

And Arturo did, walking away without a backward glance.

Arturo's gut twisted with guilt as he descended the brick steps, leaving behind the suffocating confines of Gonzaga Castle. The sorceress hated him for what he'd done. Rightfully so. But they'd needed a sorcerer badly, and she was the first they'd found in more than two years of searching.

He'd known what she was the first time he'd tasted her. As Bram said, she carried no scent of magic, but the taste of it in her blood was strong for those who knew what magic tasted like. And Arturo knew.

Ah, her blood was sweet. But she was Cristoff's now.

The guard opened the front gate, nodding as Arturo passed through onto the paved sidewalk, leaving the lit compound behind with long strides. Letting the darkness embrace him.

Cristoff knew her value. He wouldn't hurt her. At least, he wouldn't injure her unduly. He couldn't risk it. But Arturo knew all too well what Cristoff was capable of, and it chilled him to the bone to leave a fully mortal female in his master's hands.

But he'd had no choice. It mattered not if he'd taken a liking to the woman. Or if his blood heated every time he touched her soft, warm flesh, every time he smelled the sunshine in her hair.

There was far too much at stake for a bit of pleasure to get in the way.

He crossed the dusty, empty road as he made his way back to the sanctuary of his home, remembering the look on Cristoff's face as he'd presented his gift, the sorceress. Cristoff had been pleased. Well pleased, and the notion stroked satisfyingly within him. He'd done well this day even as he knew the furious betrayal in those green eyes would haunt him for a long, long time.

Perhaps an eternity.

CHAPTER EIGHT

elivery! Now!"

Zack set down his hammer atop the roof of the small brick building he and the other slaves had been working on since his arrival in Vamp City. Swiping the sweat out of his eyes, he scrambled for the ladder, fighting and jostling with his companions until they were all in danger of falling off the roof. No one wanted to be the last one down. The last always took the brunt of their master's whip.

He managed to beat two others down the ladder and took off at a run the moment he reached the ground, determined to stay in front. Following the other slaves, he rounded the corner to the wagon that must have pulled up while he'd been hammering, a wagon laden with crates of fruits and vegetables and boxes containing only God knew what. It didn't matter. He and the other slaves were the ones who would carry it inside even though the vampires could lift a hundred times what the humans could.

Most of the guys were grabbing two crates at

a time, but Zack didn't need to prove anything to anyone. He grabbed a single crate of vegetables. But he'd only taken two steps from the wagon when the whip sliced down his back. Fire exploded, and it was all he could do not to lose the crate in his hands.

"More, you ninety-pound weakling!" the vampire yelled.

Gritting his teeth against the mortification as much as the pain of the lash, Zack set down his crate, returned to the wagon for a second, then dropped it on top of the first and struggled to lift them both. *Motherfucker.* His back bowed, his muscles shaking with strain, he made his way after the other slaves, knowing that if the fucking vampire whipped him again, he'd lose both crates. Then he and Mr. Whip would get to know one another way too well.

Sweat rolled down his temples, his face red with strain. He wasn't weak. Not weak. He'd just never seen much sense in spending hours in the gym like the meatheads. Programmers didn't need muscles. Unfortunately, slaves did. But he wouldn't be a slave forever. He'd find a way to escape—when he was stronger, when he'd solved the puzzle of this place. Then he'd rescue Lily and Quinn. He wouldn't let himself even think about whether or not his sister was still alive.

Struggling to move one foot in front of the other, to keep going, he eyed the door the others were entering, held open by a female slave. He'd never been in this part of the house before and was mildly curious. If he made it that far without dumping his crates.

Twenty more feet. Fifteen. Ten.

Finally, he reached the steps to the back door and stumbled inside without losing hold of his load, miracle of miracles.

A woman grabbed the top crate, swinging it away as if it weighed nothing, heating his face even more. She was probably a vampire. Except she was dressed like a slave.

He set down the second crate beside the others, his muscles burning. He turned to go back outside, and that was when he saw her, walking past the doorway, a mop in one hand, a heavy bucket in the other.

"Lily."

At his call, she slowed and turned. Their gazes met, and she paled, her eyes dark with exhaustion, filling with tears. But she didn't stop, and, a moment later, she was past the door and gone again.

"Lily!"

A hand clamped his shoulder. "Shut up, you moron." Reggie, one of the other slaves, leaned in close to his ear. "You have no idea the sadistic games they'll play if they discover two slaves care for one another. Ignore her. *Forget* her."

Zack paled, his breathing ragged, his emotions soaring and crashing all at once as he looked around the kitchen. No vampires had witnessed his outburst. Not that he knew of.

But Lily was here, just like he'd thought. And she was okay . . . maybe. Kind of.

God help him if the vampires came after them both.

Cristoff gripped Quinn's arm hard enough to cause bruises as he led her past the dais, through a doorway at the back of the throne room, and into a narrow passage lined with manacles chained to the walls. Walls badly stained with . . . *blood*?

She was shaking with fury, gritting her teeth to hide it. Damn Arturo. Damn him! She'd believed him. She'd *liked* him. Worse, far worse, she'd begun to almost trust him. Not that she'd had a lot of choice. But she knew better! People couldn't be trusted and, clearly, definitely not vampires.

But she'd trusted him anyway because she'd so badly wanted what he'd offered. To free Zack. Now he'd given her to this pain-feeder, this *monster*, without a second thought. She hated him! Hated them both.

But it was more than anger that had her body quaking. Fear crawled through her, rank and terrible.

At the end of the hall, Cristoff ushered her into another room, one far smaller than the throne room. A room that seemed wholly out of place in this house of horrors.

If the room had been anywhere else, she might have called it warm, inviting, with its walls lined with bookshelves and the glass cases displaying all manner of intriguing artifacts—vases, ivory statues, a jewel-hilted sword. On a thick-piled Persian rug, before the wide, welcoming hearth, sat a worn brown leather recliner.

"You're a reader?" she asked her captor with disbelief.

"All great men are readers," he replied coolly.

She wouldn't exactly lump powerful, sadistic vampires with *great men*, but she wasn't fool enough to offer that opinion out loud. Not to a man who fed on pain. She tried to envision this cruel creature stretched out in his La-Z-Boy, *A Tale of Two Cities* in his hands, and failed completely.

Behind her, he closed the door and threw the bolt. Her racing heart missed a beat.

A sorceress, he'd claimed. He and Arturo both. *A sorceress.*

She wasn't. She was just Quinn. Just . . . weird.

Except, she knew better. As badly as she wanted to deny the claim, part of her knew it to be truth. People . . . humans . . . who were simply *weird* didn't see shimmers in the air and didn't watch their clothes spontaneously change color every time they passed through one.

Was Zach a sorcerer, too? Had she hidden her strangeness from him all these years for nothing?

No. How many times had Angela called Quinn's real mother *the witch*? Goose bumps rose on her arms. *The witch.* For the first time, she realized the term had been literal. Angela must have known. Quinn's father must have told her. Yet he'd never told Quinn. He'd let her believe the weirdness was hers alone. Something to be ashamed of. Something to hide. Something evil.

Cristoff gripped her arm. "Now we'll discover the depth of your power, my dear." He looked too young to be using the term *my dear.* An illusion.

She eyed him warily, trying to remember to breathe through the block of fear that was attempting to wedge itself in her throat. "How are we going to do that?"

Without replying, he steered her to the back wall, to the clear box in which the jeweled sword hung as if suspended on air. He lifted his hand, pressed his palm against the glass, and the top sprung open. As she watched, he lifted the sword as if it really had been floating within that case. How was that possible?

To her surprise, he handed it to her. "Hold it."

She held out her hands, her muscles bunching at the unexpected weight as she took the sword. She considered trying to stab Cristoff with it, but knew she'd never get it lifted before he stopped her. And the thought of what this creature might do in retaliation turned her knees to rubber.

Instead, she studied the beautiful weapon. The steel was etched in intricate vines, the hilt solid gold, inlaid with a row of dime-sized sapphires.

"What is it?" she asked.

"It is the sword Escalla. An old wizard's sword that recognizes great power." His tone turned flat. "Power you do not possess." He took the sword from her hands and replaced it in the case.

"So I'm not going to be of any use to you?" She wasn't sure if that was good news or bad.

He turned so fast that she gasped. Gripping her around the throat, he lifted her off her feet, all but choking her. "A sorcerer's power comes in many forms. You will renew the magic of this city. And whatever else I wish of you." Those black brows, so startling when framed by such white hair, drew together, cruelty leaping into his pale blue eyes. "If you fail, sorceress, I will kill you. Slowly. And very, very painfully."

He released her. "It that clear?"

Quinn stumbled back, coughing, eyes watering, heart pounding like a twenty-person drumline.

"Yes." God help her. She didn't know the first thing about magic, and now her life depended on it? Impossible. She couldn't do this! She didn't know how to do what they wanted. She'd fail, and they'd torture her and kill her, though by then, death would be a blessing.

How could Arturo have done this to her? Damn him to hell. Damn them both. She hoped she *didn't* succeed in saving their godforsaken city. She hoped the magic did fail, and Cristoff and Arturo both died horrible deaths, then spent the rest of eternity in Hell, writhing in fear and pain.

If not for Zack, she'd be sorely tempted to make certain she did fail. But if her failing might endanger Zack, she had no choice but to fight to save Vamp City. At least until she got him out of there. Then again, everything Arturo had told her could be a lie. And how in the hell was she supposed to find the truth when she was trapped in the monster's lair?

Quinn paced the tiny room, four steps from one end to the other. Little bigger than a jail cell, the room had bare white walls, a wood floor, a single bed that looked to be little more than a down-filled comforter over a rope-and-wood frame. A small washstand with an oil lamp sat against one wall, a chamber pot on the floor beside it. And there was space for nothing else. The room certainly wouldn't have passed any fire-code inspection. It had no window at all, and the door was firmly locked from the other side and had been from the moment Cristoff deposited her here after showing her his sword.

How long ago had that been? Three hours? Four? She had no idea. She never wore a watch anymore, and her cell phone was tucked into the backpack that had long since disappeared. Not that either of them would have worked in this place. Not that it really mattered. Five minutes or five hours, it would all feel the same.

So she paced, over and over and over, frustration and anger in every stride. And fear. God, she was scared though she'd never admit that to anyone. Though any fear-feeding vampire within feeding distance probably already knew it.

She'd been an idiot to believe that Arturo would help her find Zack after all the times he'd told her to forget him. Not that it would have made much difference if she hadn't believed him. She might have tried to escape last night, but it was doubtful she'd have succeeded. He'd have just caught her and locked her in her room again, then brought her to Cristoff today anyway as he'd clearly meant to do all along. No, it probably didn't matter, but it hurt, as much as she hated to admit it. After he'd rescued her from Francesca, she'd felt a connection with him, as if they were almost starting to become friends.

She was so damned gullible.

She raked one hand through her hair, holding it back from her face as she tried to pull her thoughts away from that bastard. What she needed to do was find a way out of this castle. They called her a sorceress. Was it true? A *sorceress*? All her life, she'd tried to hide her weirdness. What if she could use it? What if it could help her, for once, instead of ruining her life? She sank down on the side of the bed. And sank until she realized there would be no sitting, so she lay back, propping her hands behind her head, and stared at the lamplight flickering on the ceiling.

If she was really a sorceress, why couldn't she do magic? Only twice had she ever done anything truly extraordinary. The first time was when she was six years old, fighting with her stepmother, mouthing off. Angela had slapped her. Quinn, furious, had pushed Angela back, slamming her against the wall. Without touching her. All she remembered was lifting her hands and wanting Angela to go away. And her stepmother had flown back. She wasn't sure which of them had been more surprised. And she'd never done it again. Not after the spanking her father had given her that night and the threat that if she ever did anything like that again, he'd send her away for good.

At the time, Quinn wasn't sure she cared, except for one thing. Zack. Her baby brother. He'd only been a year old, but from the day her dad and Angela brought him home from the hospital, he'd been hers. And she his. And she'd have done anything to keep from losing him.

Quinn had never pushed anyone like that again even though, as a teenager, she'd tried a couple of times. She'd never understood how she'd done it the first time.

The second time something happened was in high school. Her gut cramped. She'd nearly killed a kid.

Scrubbing her hands over her face, she pushed the memory away before it twisted her up again. She'd never done anything strange . . . *magical* . . . again.

Maybe it was time she tried.

Struggling out of the rope bed, she stood and looked around the tiny room for something to test her power on. Not the lamp. The chamber pot? She glanced inside, relieved to see it was empty and clean, then picked it up and set it a foot in front of the door.

Backing against the opposite wall, she stared at it. And felt like an idiot. Battling a chamber pot. A new experience, anyway.

So how did this power thing work? Slowly, she lifted hands that felt heavier than they should. As if, on some level, she resisted. It didn't take Freud to figure this one out. For most of her life, she'd denied her power. She'd pushed it down, locked it up, hidden it away. And *hated* it.

Dropping her hands, she shook them at her sides as she looked at the ceiling. It was time to unlock that door, to let the power out again. If it was still in there. Maybe she'd outgrown it. Maybe she'd never really had it and only thought she had. Angela might have tripped all those years ago. And maybe that kid really had had a heart condition as the adults had claimed.

But if she didn't have any power, why did the vampires insist she was a sorceress?

With a sigh, she pushed her hands out in front of her, stared at the chamber pot, and imagined it moving back, just a little.

Nothing.

So she imagined it flying back, shattering against the door.

Still nothing. Dammit. Maybe she needed some emotion to spur the power.

She glared at the chamber pot and threw up her hands. "I hate you!"

The door swung open, banging into the ceramic pot and sending it rolling. Arturo stuck his head in the room, peering around the door to see what he'd hit.

"Am I interrupting something?"

"Go away." Just looking at him hurt.

He entered the room and closed the door behind him, glancing at the pot. "I heard you yelling." He quirked a brow, wry humor crinkling his eyes. "Pretending it was me?"

She refused to gift him with an answer. "What do you want?"

He lifted his hands, then dropped them in a gesture that almost seemed . . . helpless. "I am sorry, *cara*, for deceiving you." His tone sounded genuine, but it hardly mattered. "My loyalty is to Cristoff first and always."

"I don't like being lied to."

"Understandable. In the future I will endeavor to—"

"Spare me the false promises, Vampire. *Snake*." She was playing with fire, but she no longer cared. If he wanted to retaliate, he could have at it. What difference did it make? What difference did anything make, now?

But if her words annoyed him, he hid it well.

"I sent word to my contact within Lazzarus's kovena. About your brother."

Her gaze snapped to his. She wanted to turn her back on him and his tantalizing words and pretend they didn't matter. But they did. Far too much.

"I should hear back within a day or two," he said softly.

"Days?"

"The kovenas are enemies, *cara*. And there are no telephones within Vamp City. Communication takes time, particularly when one must be very careful."

"What will your contact be able to tell you?"

"If your brother lives. And if he possesses sorcerer's blood. The vamp masters are very careful to screen all new slaves for sorcerer's blood. We have been looking for a savior for a long time. If your brother is a sorcerer, my contact will know. And, soon, so will I."

"If he is one, will you bring him here?"

"No. Lazzarus will not give him up." He tilted his head, studying her. "Do you believe your brother possesses power?"

Quinn looked away, debating what to tell him. Even if she lied, it wouldn't change anything. "No. My mother was the one they called a witch. Zack and I share the same father."

"That is too bad." He held out his hand to her. "Come. Cristoff wants you to attend him."

She shuddered at the prospect, remembering all too well the woman, bloodied and burned, in his throne room. "I don't suppose that's an offer I'm allowed to refuse?"

Arturo's eyelids dropped, his expression softening with pleasure. "It is not."

"Dammit, you're feeding on me again!"

He shrugged. "I am what I am."

"A fear-feeder? A *liar*?"

His lashes lifted, and he pinned her with that

dark gaze. "I cannot help the way I feed. But I do not wish to feed from you in that way. Not from you."

"Then don't."

"The feeding of emotions is not a choice. If there is fear, I will feed. I cannot turn it off."

"I don't know why you care one way or the other. You told me you don't want your slaves afraid, but I'm never going to be your slave. So what in the hell difference does it make?"

"I don't know." He caught her wrist and pulled her off balance, into his arms. As she struggled to right herself, he buried his nose against her temple. "Your fear offends me."

She forced some space between them and slammed her fists against his chest. "Well, your lies offend me. Let me go."

His arm tightened around her waist, holding her hips flush against him as his breath teased the rim of her ear. "It is your body I crave, *piccola*, your touch, your passion. When you are near, I can think of little but getting you beneath me and burying myself inside you."

His nearness, his warm breath, his *words*, sent damp heat pooling between her legs. The last thing she wanted was to be affected by him, to desire him. But her body had a will of its own. "*Vampire*," she said through clenched teeth. "Let me go."

Instead, he pressed his mouth to her neck, a kiss, not a bite. And a gentle one at that. Then he straightened and released her.

Quinn stepped back, out of his reach, struggling to get control of her unruly pulse. She hated that he still had this effect on her.

Arturo turned and opened the door. "Come."

She stared at him, her feet refusing to move, every bone in her body suddenly too heavy to push forward. Fear of the unknown, of what Cristoff might have in mind for her, had welded her to the floor.

Arturo turned back and met her gaze with surprisingly gentle eyes. "I do not believe he'll hurt you, *cara*. He will not wish for anything to happen to you before you renew the magic of Vamp City. And Cristoff, for all his vices, is a man of extreme control."

His words eased the simmering panic. A little. "And afterward? After I've renewed the magic?" Assuming she ever managed that feat, which was exceedingly doubtful.

"I am privy to neither Cristoff's plans nor his thoughts." He motioned to the open doorway with a nod of his head. "One day at a time."

And she really had no choice. If she refused to accompany him, Arturo would simply sling her over his shoulder and carry her out. Her pride was all she had left and he'd take that, too, if he had to.

Quinn took a deep breath and squared her shoulders before stepping toward the door. As they started down the long, narrow passage, side by side, she glanced at him sharply. "I don't believe you. You know exactly what's likely to happen to me; you're just not saying."

To his credit, he didn't reply, didn't compound his lies.

The passage was completely unadorned, lit only by a gas lamp every hundred feet or so, making the walk spooky. She should be glad to be leaving that miserable little room. And she was, or would be, if Cristoff wasn't waiting for her at the other end.

Arturo reached for her shoulder, squeezing it lightly before she shrugged him off. "Control your fear around Cristoff. He cannot taste it, as I can. As any fear-feeder can. But he'll see it in your face plainly enough if you let him. Cristoff may feed on pain, but he enjoys fear. The more he knows he distresses you, the more interest you will be to him. Ignore him, and he might do the same to you."

Eventually, their path led back to the grand foyer, which appeared all but deserted. She could hear voices and the clatter of billiard balls in the other room, but the grand party appeared to be over. "Where is everyone?"

"The banquet."

One of the guards she'd seen in Cristoff's throne room—the bald one who'd made her skin crawl, strode into the foyer from one of the side rooms yanking a whimpering girl along beside him by her hair. The girl's mouth had been bloodied, and there was blood smeared between her thighs, visible beneath the skimpy uniform all the castle slaves seemed to wear. But unlike the Slavas, her hair had no glow. Did that mean she was still new to Vamp City and not yet immortal?

Arturo halted their progress, turning to the guard, a fine vibration tensing his body. Anger? "She's not yet a Slava, Ivan. She'll not easily or quickly heal your abuse."

Ivan sneered. "She lives, doesn't she?" As if the girl was lucky he hadn't killed her.

And suddenly Arturo was no longer by Quinn's side, but standing squarely in front of the sadistic guard, his blade buried hilt deep in the guard's stomach. "Be happy you do, too. Now release her."

Quinn watched them, stunned. If Ivan were human, Arturo would have killed him, stabbing him as he had. Instead, as Arturo removed his knife, the guard merely straightened, hatred flashing in hard eyes. But he did as Arturo demanded, flinging the girl to the marble floor, eliciting a cry of pain from her.

Fury burned in Quinn's gut, and she started toward her. But before she could reach her, vampires began to flash around her as if she were standing still. Ivan disappeared. Arturo was suddenly at her side, taking her arm to hold her back, and a third appeared out of nowhere.

"Kassius." Arturo greeted the new arrival warmly.

"Ax." Kassius had to be close to six and a half feet tall, his shoulders as broad as a linebacker's. His dark hair was on the short side, but curly and untamed, several days' whiskers and a strong

Roman nose giving him a rough look. But the expression in his eyes belied that roughness as he went to the girl, lifting her into his arms with surprising care.

The girl began to cry with great wracking sobs, trembling harder than before. Both Kassius and Arturo tipped back their heads, clearly drinking her fear, before eyeing one another again.

"I wish you'd killed him," Kassius said. "I've ordered them not to touch the fresh ones. They can't take the abuse."

"Ivan's day will come," Arturo replied darkly. "But he's a favorite of Cristoff's."

Kassius scowled. "That's no surprise." He turned to Quinn, eyeing her with interest. "Is this her, then? The sorceress?"

Arturo led her forward with a nod. "Quinn Lennox."

Kassius watched her curiously. "She doesn't react to me."

"Nor can she be enthralled."

"She's strong, then." Relief softened the hard lines of his face.

"It would appear so although that is yet to be confirmed. But we have a banquet to attend."

Kassius nodded and left, cradling the weeping girl against his broad chest.

"A friend of yours?" Quinn asked, as he led her down another long hall. If she ever managed to escape her jail cell, she'd play heck finding her way out of this place without getting lost.

"Yes. Kassius is in charge of the Slavas. He's like

a mother hen with them. He does not take well to their abuse, particularly the fresh ones—those not yet immortal."

Another vampire with at least some compassion, some honor. How could such a man stand to live in a place where humans suffered abuse . . . and death . . . on a regular basis?

She glanced at the male at her side, intensely aware of all the contradictions he presented. He was a liar who'd betrayed her. But his own slaves seemed to adore him and he'd never physically hurt her. As much as she might hate him, she had to admit he wasn't all bad. There was compassion in him, too. And honor, buried in there somewhere. Maybe she hadn't been a complete idiot for trusting him the first time.

But that didn't mean she'd ever make that mistake again.

"Why do your friends call you Ax?"

He glanced at her, secrets in his eyes. "It is a long story, *cara*. One you will be happier not knowing."

Finally, they reached another set of open double doors. "The banquet hall," Arturo murmured, ushering her inside.

Quinn stared, her pulse thrumming. This room was twice the size of the throne room and lacked the gilt splendor, but it was still colorful and intriguing in a disturbing kind of way. Flat chaises covered in bright, solid-color cushions ringed the room on rising heights like four levels of stadium seating . . . or bedding. In the center of the room, at ground level, stood what appeared to be a shallow, waterless pool, marble and rectangular, with several spigots protruding from each side.

Dozens of people . . . vampires, she assumed . . . sat or lounged on the chaises, their excited murmurs rising and falling. They were dressed in flowing, sleeveless, brightly colored gowns, the men's loose-fitting, the women's clingy and sheer. Several nearby saw her, their expressions turning hungry. One male's fangs began to lengthen, his pupils slowly turning white. Yep, definitely vampires.

Quinn's heart began to pound, and she found herself sidling closer to Arturo, watching as a couple of the vampires threw their heads back in pleasure. Fear-feeders.

Arturo's hand shifted from her arm to the back of her neck in a clear display of possession. "Calm yourself, *cara*," he said softly, and ushered her forward, tight against his side.

"Arturo," the vampires murmured as they passed. Many greeted him with deference, some with genuine warmth. Most appeared intensely curious about her. Quinn met those who stared at her with her best *I'll-rip-your-eyeballs-out* look.

Arturo led her to one of four sets of steps. As they started up, she saw Cristoff at the top in a gown of gold, surrounded by half a dozen guards dressed all in black. Her pulse escalated, but she remembered what Arturo had said, that Cristoff couldn't taste her fear, only see it. Clenching her jaw, she pasted a hard expression on her face and prepared to meet the dragon.

When they reached him, Cristoff rose and took her from Arturo, squeezing her arm painfully as he pulled her beside him and turned her to face the room. All eyes rose to stare at her.

Cristoff grabbed her hair. Quinn stifled a cry, then lost the battle and cried out as he jerked her head back in a wash of scalp pain, exposing her neck. The damn vampire made a sound of pleasure deep in his throat, clearly enjoying her discomfort.

"I give you the last sorceress!" Gasps and exclamations erupted around the room, quickly followed by raucous cheers. Quinn trembled, tensing for his bite. "Vamp City and all who reside here are saved. Tonight, we celebrate. Bring in the feast!"

The cheers erupted all over again.

Cristoff released her as suddenly as he'd accosted her. Arturo gripped her arm far more gently than Cristoff had, steadying her, then seating her on the cool, peacock blue silk cushion between the two men. The two vampires. She blinked back the tears, knowing the worst thing she could do was show weakness. Of course, Cristoff knew he'd hurt her. Just as he'd intended to.

Double doors on either side of the room opened as if choreographed. Naked people started flooding the room. Slavas, by the looks of it, their hair faintly glowing in that weird way that meant immortal. She blinked. Cristoff had ordered the feast brought in. She'd expected servants carrying platters of food, but that was hardly a vampire feast, was it? No, the slaves themselves would be the feast. Some strode in with surprising confidence, others shuffling with misery. One light-haired female appeared to lose her nerve halfway into the room and turned to escape as a number of vampires threw their heads back, drinking her fear. The woman made it only as far as the door before a vampire grabbed her, gripping her chin as if to force her to stare into his eyes. To glamour her.

"Hold!" Cristoff commanded. "Put her in the basin as she is. Tonight she is mine."

The woman's color drained from her face, and she went absolutely hysterical, screaming, fighting to be free. The vampire picked her up and threw her into the marble pool with unnecessary force. The crack of bone preceded a horrifying scream. A different group of vampires gasped in pleasure. The pain-feeders.

Quinn began to shake. She had to get out of here.

Long, cool fingers curled around her arm. Arturo's. *Control your emotions,* cara, he murmured in her head. *If you cannot watch, look elsewhere. Appear bored.*

Bored? He was flipping crazy. But she forced herself to do as he instructed, ignoring the woman in the basin, pretending her screams weren't clawing at her nerves as she watched the other slaves instead.

Beside her, Cristoff rose. Her pulse stuttered, but he stepped past her and began to make his way down to the center of the room, leaving her behind. She thought again of the woman on the floor with the burn marks and wondered what agony the poor woman in the basin would endure. She did not want to be witness!

As Cristoff made his way down to his waiting victim, the other vampires, most of whom now wore rapturous expressions, grabbed a naked slave as they trooped past, deposited him or her on the nearest chaise, and sank their fangs into them. And, if they had them, their cocks.

Quinn turned to Arturo, her voice whisper-low. "They're going to kill them all."

"Most are virtually immortal by now. No matter how much blood is taken from them, they will survive without harm."

"That's why most of them don't seem to be afraid." Not only didn't they appear afraid, but most of the Slavas were now writhing in pleasure, active and eager participants in the sexual acts. "They're enjoying this."

"You've felt the pleasure of a vampire's bite, *piccola*," Arturo said quietly, a silken sensuality to his tone.

She swallowed and looked at him. "Aren't you going to join them?"

"My assignment is to guard you."

"Just . . . guard me?"

"Just guard you." A teasing light entered his eyes. A decidedly hot teasing light. "Do you wish more?"

"No." She was in no mood for teasing. Not here.

A movement caught her eye, a man moving toward them, dressed not in a gown but in the same jeans and shirt she'd seen him in before. Arturo's friend, Bram.

"Ax," he said, sliding onto the chaise beside Arturo. He nodded to her. "Sorceress." Unlike the other vampires, his expression was closed and rigid, revealing not a whiff of excitement or pleasure though he must be feeling it. "Cristoff is one sick fucker," he said quietly, pain, not pleasure in his words.

How terrible it must be for a moral man, a doctor no less, to be forced to watch people suffer for the pleasure of others.

"How are you holding up?" Arturo asked his friend.

"How do you think?" He leaned forward, pinning Quinn with hard eyes that reeked of desperation. "You've got to fix the magic."

"I'll try." Though wouldn't it be far better if this place failed? If all within Vamp City died? Perhaps not all. Bram seemed decent enough. Perhaps Kassius, too. She hadn't decided about Arturo. But what of the Slavas who'd been captured and forced to live out their lives here? Did they deserve to die? Did Susie? And Horace?

Then again, Horace had been alive far longer than any human should ever live. Death for many of the Slavas was long overdue.

Bram rose. "I've had enough. I'm getting out of here."

When he'd left, Quinn turned to Arturo. "When will I have to renew the magic?"

"I do not know. Magic is always strongest on the power days—the solstices, the equinoxes. There are others. A powerful sorcerer could call the magic even on a null day. I know not if Cristoff intends to wait for the equinox or test you on a null."

Would it matter either way? She had no clue how to do what they wanted. Regardless which day they tried, she'd almost certainly fail.

The poor woman's screams ratcheted, clawing at Quinn until she felt like she was going to crawl out of her flesh.

"You need to calm down, *cara*."

"*How?*" She didn't know what Cristoff was doing to his victim and had no desire to know. But the screams were cutting into her eardrums until she wanted to cover her ears and hide her face and try to make it all go away. And the smell. *God*. Sex and blood and raw, blinding fear. "I'm not sure how much of this I can stand. He's going to kill her. As we sit here."

"Doubtful."

She cut him a disbelieving look.

"Terese has been with us decades, long enough

to be immortal and to know that the worst thing a Slava can do is lose her nerve in front of Cristoff."

"So she'll . . . what? Heal anything he does to her?"

"Yes, unless he chooses for her to die, but that is unlikely to happen."

Quinn frowned. "What about the woman with the burns who was in the throne room when we first got here?"

"Healed."

"Physically."

"And mentally. The Slavas are glamoured the moment the abuse ends. The memory taken. She does not remember any of it. Neither will Terese."

Quinn thought about that. The fact that they wouldn't remember, and wouldn't suffer any consequences, didn't mean the torture hadn't happened. It didn't excuse it. And yet, the knowledge eased something tight and pained inside her.

"That's a gift . . . to be able to forget."

He nodded slowly. "One denied to you unless someone else has better luck controlling your mind than I did."

"I don't want to forget." What if they took her memories of her previous life? Of Zack? Of her very reason for living?

He gave her a look that said he expected her to be saying otherwise soon enough.

"Would you want to forget?" she asked.

He turned away, looking out over the gathering. "Yes. There are things I would prefer to forget.

Your life has been too short and too protected to feel the same."

She snorted. Her childhood had certainly been no trip to Disney World. Then again, it could have been worse. Much worse.

Without meaning to, she glanced at the horror unfolding in the center of the room, then desperately wished she hadn't. Her conversation with Arturo had helped her focus on something other than the screaming. But that quick glance was all it took to permanently imprint the horrific scene on the backs of her eyes—vampires lying around the basin, drinking blood from the spigots as the woman lay inside, spread-eagled on her back. Her wrists and ankles had been tied with barbed wire until the blood ran down her arms. More barbed wire wrapped around her head, the blood soaking her hair as it ran in rivulets from her scalp. Worst of all was the picture of Cristoff standing naked between the woman's spread legs, fastening a spiked band around his engorged penis.

The blood rushed from Quinn's head.

Arturo pushed her head between her knees. "Deep breaths," he said, his words low and urgent. "If he knows you're this sickened, he'll force you to watch every time."

The woman's screams turned bloodcurdling. Cold sweat broke out on every inch of Quinn's body. Bile rose in her throat. She wanted to vomit, to run away. She longed to tackle Cristoff and cut off his steel-clad dick. *The barbarity. . .*

Arturo's hand was at the back of her neck. "You must sit up, *piccola*. You cannot let him see you like this."

"I think he's a little busy to notice." But she took a deep breath and forced herself up, excruciatingly careful not to look toward the center of the room again.

"Watch the others, not Cristoff."

But the others . . . good grief. Sex and blood . . . everywhere. "How often does this happen?"

"Everyone together? At least once a month. But the torturing, the feeding, the sex, happens daily. It's how we feed, how we survive."

"That doesn't make it okay," she gasped. What if Zack and Lily . . .

She couldn't even go there. The thought of them suffering such torture had the blood draining from her head all over again, but she managed to stay upright this time.

"Quinn," the vampire at her side said warningly.

"I'm handling it." Breathing deeply through her mouth, trying to block out the thickening scent of blood and sex, she unfocused her eyes in the general direction of the nearest copulating couple. "I thought you only sensed my fear."

"I only feed on fear. But for some reason I keep getting blasts of your emotions, no matter what they are." He fished in his pocket for something and brought forth a half a roll of SweetTarts, offering her one.

Taking it gratefully, she popped the tart candy

into her mouth. "How can you be loyal to such a monster?"

"He is my master. He cannot help what he is any more than I can help what I am."

She watched Arturo, his darkly handsome face by far the easiest thing to look at in the room. "There has to be another way for him to feed."

Arturo shrugged. "This is the way he prefers."

"Because he's a psychopath. And a sadist."

"Because he is a vampire who long ago disposed of his conscience."

"And you gave me to him."

His mouth tightened. "I had no choice. We have been searching for a sorcerer to save this city since the magic began to fail. You are the first we've found. Sorcerers are all but extinct."

She turned away, then quickly back again as she remembered why she'd been studiously pinning him with her gaze. "Am I going to survive this? The saving of V.C.? Tell me the truth, Vampire. You owe me the truth."

This time he was the one who looked away, his lips turning in, working, before he slowly met her gaze. "Your death is not needed to renew the magic, no."

"But . . . ? You left a huge *but* dangling at the end of that sentence."

He opened his mouth, then shut it again, as if deciding against the denial that threatened to roll off his tongue.

"One day at a time, *cara*. One day at a time."

His words were no comfort at all.

CHAPTER NINE

The screams of the woman had finally faded away to be replaced by . . . music? Quinn turned in surprise to find a balcony high above her, where a dozen Slava musicians struck up a lively and incongruous rock beat with piano, guitars, drums, and various brass instruments.

One by one, the vampires around the room rose, leaving their depleted human meals lying limp and pale on the brightly colored cushions, and filed down the stairs to the wide swath of floor that surrounded the vat where the tortured woman remained, presumably healing.

As the music rose, the vampires began to dance in a wild revelry, some jumping, hands in the air, others clinging to one another, kissing, fondling, more sex than dance. A vampire rave.

Quinn shook her head, trying to take it all in. "They never get tired, do they?"

"After a full meal, a human often feels lethargic." Arturo shrugged. "Not so a vampire. The blood energizes. Never do we feel more alive."

He glanced at her, a hint of devilment in his eyes. "Would you care to dance?"

She looked at him askance. "You're kidding, right?"

"I tease you. Your dinner is being brought in. Once you've eaten, we can leave. Unless Cristoff demands you stay."

She shuddered. If she ever had to go near that monster again, it would be too soon. "Are you usually down there dancing with them? When you're not guarding prisoners."

"No. Not all enjoy the banquets. I avoid them whenever I can."

"So you're not as depraved as you like to let on."

"Have I shown you depravity, *cara*?"

"No. But you're always quick to defend it. 'We are what we are' and all that."

He shrugged. "It is best if you understand the nature of the beast. We are not human, *cara*. Our needs and our morality are very, very different from your own."

As he'd demonstrated with his betrayal. And yet . . . there *was* morality in this man though it might sometimes be buried deep.

"Here comes your dinner."

She followed his gaze to where a man climbed the stairs carrying a tray, dodging the gyrating vampires as he made his way up the rows toward them, striding as if he owned the place. He was dressed in what might have been considered nineteenth-century landowner casual—an ivory linen shirt, dark brown pants, boots—an anomaly in that room at the moment. His dark blond hair had the phosphorescent sheen of a Slava, but there was nothing cowed or subservient about the way he moved. With a close-cut beard skimming a strong jaw and bright blue eyes, he was strikingly good-looking.

He walked down the row in front of her, meeting her gaze with cool eyes as he handed her the tray. "Your dinner, sorceress."

"Thank you. But I'm . . . *really* not hungry at the moment." She'd been breathing through her mouth just to avoid the pungent smell of blood and sex for some time, now.

"You'll eat." Arturo's tone said she had no option. "You do not wish to offend Cristoff."

She wasn't sure Cristoff would even notice, but he was right. The last thing she wanted was Cristoff annoyed with her. For any reason.

She took the tray, then glanced down to find a plate of surprisingly-decent-looking food—chunks of ham, potatoes au gratin, a pair of large, fluffy rolls, and a metal tankard with beads of moisture clinging to the outside. Reaching for the tankard, she flipped open the top to find a frothy head of beer.

"Do you drink beer?" Arturo asked.

"I love it."

"We have our own microbrewery," the Slava told her.

She looked at him in surprise. Curious, she took a sip. Cold, crisp, tangy. "This is good."

At her praise, a smile pulled at the edges of his

bearded mouth, then disappeared just as quickly. "Everyone needs a hobby. Especially those of us stuck in this hellhole for eternity."

"Where were you, Grant?" Arturo asked, as the Slava climbed over the bench at her feet to sit on the other side of her, the spot Cristoff had occupied earlier. "You're late."

Quinn took another sip of the beer, liking the taste and the way it washed away the bitter fear and misery that coated the back of her throat.

The Slava grunted. "He insists I attend, but that doesn't mean I have to sit through his savagery." When Quinn glanced at him, he thrust out his hand to her. "I'm Grant Blackstone."

Blackstone. *Blackstone's ilk.* She cut her gaze at Arturo, then turned back to Grant, shaking his hand. "Quinn Lennox. You're a Slava?"

Annoyance flared in his blue eyes. "I'm a sorcerer. Like you."

She frowned. "Then, why . . . ?"

"Why don't I save VC and leave you out of it?"

"Yes."

"If I could, I would. I may be a sorcerer, but I've never had much power. A few parlor tricks, and that's about it. Nothing like my father."

"His father, Phineas Blackstone, created Vamp City," Arturo told her. "Vamp City was designed as a trap to kill every vampire within."

Her jaw dropped as she looked at Grant.

The other sorcerer nodded. "He failed and paid for it with his life. And two of my fingers." He held up one hand, wiggling his remaining fingers and the stubs of his pinky and ring finger.

Quinn's face turned cold. "Cristoff must have been furious."

Arturo nudged her shoulder with his own. "Eat."

Pulling her attention from the sorcerer, she pulled apart the soft roll, taking a bite that practically melted on her tongue.

"He was furious," Grant confirmed. "And more furious still when he realized neither of Phineas's sons had their father's power."

"There are two of you?"

"Grant and Sheridan, named by our mother after Civil War generals. Union, of course."

"Of course." *But, good grief.* "Were you born back then?"

"Right after. In 1865. Sheridan in 1866. He was turned when we were in our twenties."

"Turned? Into a *vampire?*"

"What else?" The man didn't have the most winning away about him, but she supposed he had a right to sound aggravated. She hated to think what she'd be like if she was still stuck here a hundred years from now. *Immortal.* It was hard even to comprehend what that meant. Forever youthful, yet . . . for what? To hang around in the dark, to try to avoid being tortured? To brew beer?

For the next few minutes, she ate in silence, surprised at how easily she devoured every bite of food on her plate. When she was through, she turned to Grant. "I don't know if I have the power to renew the magic. If I do, I don't know how to access it."

"Cristoff seems certain your power's strong enough. It'll come."

"Do you know what I have to do to save this place?"

Arturo's shoulder brushed hers. "Grant and Sheridan were there when their father renewed the magic that first time. They'll be able to help you."

The sorcerer frowned. "Sheridan will have to help you. Did I mention I lost two fingers that day?"

His words finally caught up with her. "You were . . . *five*?"

"No. Thirteen."

"But, I thought Vamp City was created in 1870."

"It was." Grant gripped his knees, hunching over slightly in a way that told her he didn't like reminiscing about that time. Understandably so. "It wasn't until 1878 that my father pulled the plug on the magic to bring it all tumbling down. Cristoff demanded he restore it. Dear Old Dad refused, of course. Cristoff's cutting off one of my fingers didn't make enough of an impression, so he took a second. Finally, my father saw the error of his ways. By then, I'd passed out." He rose and took her tray. "If you'll excuse me, I've made my appearance and now intend to get the hell out of here."

"It was nice to meet you, Grant."

He paused, met her gaze, a hint of warmth entering his blue eyes. "My pleasure." With a formal nod, he left.

Quinn turned to find Arturo watching the sorcerer's retreat with a small frown between his eyebrows.

"What?" she demanded.

He shook his head, his expression clearing as he met her gaze, then he rose and held out a hand to her. "We should go before Cristoff joins us again."

She placed her hand in his. "You'll get no argument here."

A smile lit Arturo's eyes as his fingers closed around hers. She followed him down the stairs to the nearest exit and took a deep breath when they'd escaped into the empty hallway, leaving the noise and horrors behind.

Her hand was still caught firmly in Arturo's, but she had no desire to tug it away. There was safety here, with him, or at least the closest she was going to get to it in this place.

She glanced at him. "Now what?"

"Now . . ." He gave her a rueful look. "I take you back to your room. I'm sorry to have to leave you there, but I have responsibilities elsewhere." Together, they started back down the hall.

"I thought you were the one guarding me."

"No one will bother you here. No one would dare cross Cristoff in his own castle." He glanced at her, and their gazes met, his expression unreadable. "I can bring you books or a deck of cards when I return," he offered after several quiet moments.

"Both, please. If there's anything that might teach me about sorcerers, I'd like to start there. I know nothing."

"I'll ask Grant."

"You don't get along with him very well." It wasn't a question.

"Grant Blackstone has never been particularly good at hiding his hatred of vampires."

"Then why doesn't he leave?" But she knew. "He'd revert to his true age, wouldn't he?"

"Yes."

"That wouldn't be pretty," she murmured.

Arturo laughed, surprising her. "No, it would not."

His smile burrowed inside of her, warming her. It was a mistake to like him. He was such a complex, contradictory man. Yet in a lot of ways she did like him. And she'd been attracted to him almost from the moment she'd first realized that he didn't intend to kill her.

As they descended the stairs to the prison level, the thought of returning to that tiny room sent a flutter of claustrophobic panic to flight in her mind. Locked up there, she'd never find a way to escape.

The vampire stopped, taking her arm and pulling her around to face him in the empty hallway. "What is it, *cara*? Something disturbs you." He acted like he cared.

Quinn shrugged. "Everything about this place disturbs me. I was just thinking about my home sweet jail cell."

"You do not wish to return just yet?"

"You're kidding, right?" She raked the hair off her face with both hands. "I'm going to go stark raving mad if I have to spend much more time in there. I need to run. I need some fresh air to clear my lungs, then a hot shower to wash off the depravity that feels like it's coating my skin half an inch thick."

"A run is impossible, of course."

Quinn rolled her eyes and dropped her hands. "Of course." Unless she found a way out of here, then she would never stop running.

A gleam entered his dark eyes. "The shower, however, might be arranged."

She looked at him with surprise. "Are you playing with me or telling me the truth?"

His mouth kicked up on one corner. "I would very much like to *play* with you, *tessoro*."

"Don't, Vampire. Don't even tease about sex right now. Not after what I just saw."

His expression lost all hint of playfulness. "I wish you had not looked."

"Trust me, so do I. I'll never get that vision out of my head."

He turned back, waiting for her to follow, and she fell into step beside him, a decided bounce to her stride. He led her down another, far shorter hallway to a door, then ushered her outside, onto a brick patio. Outside! Quinn had begun to wonder if she'd ever see the steel gray of day again. The air was warm and humid, gusts of sun-heated breeze brushing against her skin interspersed with cooler air, as if night and day had tried, unsuccessfully, to mate.

"Where are we going?" she asked warily. While she was thrilled to be outside the castle, even if only for a little while, she was still firmly within the castle's walls. Cristoff's prisoner.

"The showers are outside."

She gave him a hard look. "*Open* showers?"

"Trust me a little, *cara*. They are not open. You will have your privacy."

The tension leached out of her shoulders. "Okay. Sorry."

"Forgiven."

Her mood lightened as they started across the patio. "Do you get weather here?"

"Whatever weather you get in your world, we get here." Arturo took her hand and she let him, liking the feel of his long, cool fingers wrapped around hers. "Rain, wind, snow. Even the summer heat, though not nearly as hot. It is always cooler in the dark. Sometimes, we even smell the diesel from your trucks."

"The smells carry, then. But not the sounds?"

"Not the sounds." He ushered her down one of several brick pathways that branched off the patio. This one led to a group of buildings at the back of the mansion's walled compound, where something seemed to be going on. If the mansion had been silent, the yard was anything but—resonating with the sound of voices and the loud clank of hammer to metal as if a blacksmith had a workshop back there.

"Is this where the slaves work?" she asked Arturo.

"And live. We call it the food compound." His mouth twisted ruefully. "Perhaps not the best name."

Definitely not.

She caught sight of a couple of women hanging wet clothes on a long clothesline. The sun certainly wouldn't dry them, but perhaps the warm air would.

"Do the Slavas do normal slave work along with the . . . banquets?"

"Yes—laundry, sewing, mending, blacksmithing, construction, cooking, cleaning. Everything necessary to run the castle."

"The vampires aren't big into work, are they?"

Arturo snorted. "We are not the most industrious lot, no. Most cannot be bothered even to run their own households."

"Where do the humans sleep, then? Out here, or in the slave wing where you put me?"

"Out here. The servants' wing—where your room is—was intended for some of the key Slavas—better living conditions than the food compound. But the Slavas were unhappy there. They were far too accessible to the vampires. While they fear Kassius, they know he protects them well."

She frowned. "He seemed pretty decent to me."

"He is. He would never hurt them, but he possesses the gift of fear."

"Which means?"

"Humans feel afraid of him the moment they are near him. Without justification. Without reason.

"That must be awful for him."

Arturo looked at her thoughtfully. "Vampires always say, 'How wonderful'. But you're right. He hates it. Fortunately, those humans who've been around him long enough eventually lose their fear of him. Unfortunately, it often takes decades. He's the one who clears their minds of the abuse and guides them toward the work for which they are best suited. Susie is with me because of Kassius."

"Why? What happened?"

"She was a pretty little thing and timid as a mouse when she was first captured. Though Kassius tried to steer her toward the kitchen work, the moment she was out of his sight, she was set upon, raped, terrorized until Kassius feared her mind would break. Removing the memories isn't always enough. Sometimes the damage goes too deep when the slaves are fresh."

"Cristoff let her go?"

"I bought her from the kovena. Kassius made the sale, as was his right."

"No wonder Susie adores you."

"I am no saint, *cara*. She has been one of my blood-and-sex slaves ever since, but I seduce and cajole. I never harm one of my own. And I never take."

"And you never make her fear you."

He glanced at her, a look of gratitude passing through his eyes. "No. Never. I prefer a calm household."

"You're no saint, but you're not a monster."

Arturo shrugged. "My conscience, while not my guiding force by any means, is still intact. I can still feel empathy when I choose. Most of the time, I do not choose. There is no changing us, Quinn. It is important that you understand that. We are what we are. We feed or we die."

He tugged on her hand, pulling her along toward the women hanging the laundry.

"Good day, ladies."

"Hi, Arturo!" one of them called. All three laughed as if this were *Little House on the Prairie* and he a dashing and unmarried male. Which she supposed he was, in a warped kind of way.

"They like you," she said quietly, not quite hiding her surprise.

The look he gave her was a little affronted. "Should they not?" He turned back to the women. "My new slave is in need of a towel for the shower."

The women's gazes all shifted to her, curious, maybe even a little jealous. They really did like this vampire.

One of the women stepped forward, a winning smile on her face. "I'll fetch it, Master."

"Bring it to the shower." As the woman hurried off, Arturo ushered Quinn the other way, stopping in front of a wooden shed at the far end of the compound. He grabbed the lantern hanging on the hook beside the door and lit it, then opened the door, waiting for her to precede him in.

The lamplight flickered eerily over the shadowed interior—a simple stall with wooden benches on either side. Deeper in hung a partial door that reached from her chin to her knees. Over the door, she saw an old, rusted showerhead.

"How do you have plumbing in this place?"

Arturo hung the lamp from a hook on the ceiling. "We may not have much in the way of infrastructure here, but we understand the concepts. The plumbing is very rudimentary, but it works. The water is warm."

"How? Magic?"

He grinned. "The water in the tank is heated by a wood fire."

"Not constantly."

"No. Only on banquet days."

The thought of all those naked Slavas . . . "I'm wasting their water."

"It will have reheated by the time they've recovered and returned."

He reached over the door and turned on the spray, then turned her to face him and grabbed the hem of her shirt.

Startled, she pushed his hands away. "Whoa, what are you doing?"

"Undressing you."

"Obviously," she replied with exasperation. "I can undress myself, thank you."

"No, *tessoro*, you will not." His eyes turned hot, making her shiver, though whether with desire or dread, she wasn't sure. He reached into the stall and turned off the water again. "If you want the shower, you will pay the price."

She stared at him. "You didn't hear anything I said. I'm in no frame of mind for sex play right now. If that's the price, then I don't want the shower."

"Yes you do," he said gently. Lifting a hand, he cupped her cheek. "I wish only to help you into the shower. Then, perhaps, to watch you."

Despite herself, she shivered again and this time she knew the source as damp heat pooled between her thighs. She remembered the words he'd used when he was talking about Susie. Cajole. Seduce. Cristoff's snake was a master manipulator.

His thumb stroked her lips ever so lightly. "I will not take you against your will, *cara*. That I will never do."

"Why not? You said yourself you don't usually let your conscience bother you."

His gaze turned thoughtful. "You are special, Quinn Lennox. Necessary to our survival if your power proves true. And you cannot be enthralled or made to forget. But . . ."

"But what?"

He turned her, pulling her back against him, sliding his arms around her waist. "I like you." His warm breath brushed her temple. "And I want you. I want the passion I've glimpsed within you, but I will never get it by force."

"Cajole and seduce," she murmured, her breath

unsteady at the feel of his arms around her and of the thick ridge at the small of her back.

"Yes. Perhaps. But never force." He tilted her head and pressed his mouth against her neck, nuzzling her. Kissing her. But she felt no fangs. "As you've said, today is not the day for such intimacies, not after what you've seen. But I will watch." His hand slid down over her abdomen and lower, his touch tense with desire, his fingers just brushing her pubic bone. "And I will want."

"Watching that orgy . . . aroused you."

"I may no longer be human, but I am still male. Decide quickly, *cara*. I do not have all day."

Everything inside her rebelled at the coercion. But he was giving her a choice, and he didn't have to. It was rather remarkable that he was. And, heaven help her, she was nearly shaking from the desire to step beneath the spray of that shower. So what if he watched?

"All right."

Wasting no time, he lifted her shirt over her head, then reached for her pants. She tried to brush his hands away, but he ignored her.

"I can do it, Vampire."

"As can I." He pushed her pants down over her hips.

"My boots."

"Sit."

She did, finding the bench rough beneath her bare thighs.

The vampire knelt on the wooden floor of the shed and pulled off her boots and socks, then her pants, tossing them into the corner with her shirt. Then his hands went around her, and he unfastened her bra, tossing it onto the pile, too.

When he reached for her hips, and her panties, she grabbed his wrists. "Enough. I can do the rest."

The look he gave her was rich with heat and a gleam she didn't entirely understand . . . or trust. But he capitulated, turned to sit beside her, and pulled off his own boots.

Quinn remained where she was, uncertain how she wanted to proceed. "Are you going to watch me from over the door?"

"I am going to join you." He stood and pulled off his shirt, revealing far too fine a six pack. "I am going to wash you."

Quinn lunged to her feet, crossing her arms over her bare breasts. "You said watch. *Watch.* Not wash."

"Easy, *cara.* I will not remove my pants. I said I will not take you today, and I will not."

She eyed him dourly. "You are pretty free and easy with the lies, Vampire. Your word doesn't mean a lot, does it?"

His eyes flashed and she wondered if she'd gone too far this time. But he only shrugged. "My tongue is glib, I'm afraid." He reached for her, cupping her face in both hands, sliding cool fingers into her hair. "Have I ever hurt you?" His gaze grew infinitely serious, surprisingly soft. "Have I?"

"No."

"Trust my actions, then, if not my words. Trust your instincts. I tell you I want more than to watch you. I want to touch you, to pleasure you. Only that. Do your instincts believe me?"

"You're hard as a rock. I know you want sex."

"I am ready for sex. Of course I am. I'm staring at a very beautiful, very naked woman. But I do not want that from you today."

"You won't take anything for yourself?" she said dubiously.

"And why do you think that touching you is not for me, also?" At her frown, he leaned in, brushing his lips against her temple, her cheek. "I love the way you respond to my touch. I feel your pleasure rise every time I touch you, even in the simplest way. You are sensual, magnificent. I am not usually this sensitive to another's pleasure, but your pleasure feeds my own." He pulled back, lifted her chin. "Will you trust me? In this?"

It wasn't like she had much of a choice, but the truth was she really didn't believe he'd hurt her or take her against her will. That didn't mean he wouldn't still try to seduce her, but she honestly didn't think he'd push her if she said no. And the thought of his hands on her . . . just that . . . set up a deep, sensual longing. "Yes. I will trust you in this."

His smile was swift and delighted. Without warning, he kissed her, his lips cool against her own yet infinitely warm. His lips moved softly, a first exploration, a first kiss despite the fact she stood naked before him, having just given him permission to touch her wherever he pleased. His mouth moved over hers, his tongue sliding lightly along the crease of her mouth until she opened for him, giving him access. And then he was inside, his tongue sliding against hers, stealing her breath, her thoughts, the last of her inhibitions.

He tasted of dark liqueur and darker nights, lush and crystal clear. Without thought, she wrapped her arms around his neck, pressing her breasts to his chest, the feel eliciting a moan deep in her throat.

Firm hands slid up her rib cage and down over her hips, back and forth, making her moan with the pleasure. She loved being touched. Especially by a man with a sure, if gentle, hand. A man who knew what he was doing.

His fingers slid into her butt cheeks, gripping them hard, kneading them as he pulled her against him and the hard ridge that lay between them within his pants. Her own hips began to rock of their own volition, seeking . . . needing . . .

Oh yes, her vampire knew what he was doing.

Her moan turned to one of dismay as he released her mouth, pulled her arms from around his neck, and set her away from him. Once more, he cupped her face, forcing her to look at him through the haze of passion.

"Your body screams for mine, *cara*, but I fear it is your passionate nature speaking and not truly your will. Do you wish me to remove my pants?"

She closed her eyes, trembling with desire, and tipped her forehead against his shoulder. "No."

He gathered her against him with a sigh, holding her against his warm length. "I feared as much."

"Do you want to stop? And let me take my own shower?"

"Never. My control is exquisite. And there is nothing I want more at this moment than to touch you. Not sex, not blood, not fear. Just to touch you." His hands traced wide, warm circles over her back.

She blinked. "Why aren't your hands cold anymore?"

He pulled back with surprise, meeting her gaze. "You can feel the warmth?"

"Yes. You feel hotter than I am."

A funny look crossed his face. "When I touch you, when I kiss you, I feel as if I've stepped into the sun for the first time in centuries. You smell like sunshine to me. And I feel a warming of the flesh I've not known in far too long. I thought I was being fanciful."

"You're actually warm to the touch." She looked at him curiously. "Is this my magic?"

"I do not know." He frowned, his fingers running through her hair. "I wish you had no magic."

"Why?"

"Because then I could keep you for my own."

CHAPTER TEN

Turning away, Arturo opened the inner door of the shower stall and started the water, then stepped back out and began to remove his belt.

Quinn stared at him with disbelief. "You said you were keeping your pants on."

"Pants, yes. Belt, no. I would not ruin the leather."

"Oh. Fair enough."

But the moment he tossed the belt aside, he reached for her, long fingers catching in the waistband of her panties. "Hold on to me."

She did, gripping his shoulders—hard, muscular, lovely shoulders—to steady herself as he pulled her panties down and off. Arturo straightened slowly, caressing her body with his gaze in a wash of sensual heat. With a quick shake of his head, as if to clear it, he opened the door behind him, took her hand, and led her inside under the deliciously warm spray of water.

"Oh, this is heaven," she murmured, stepping into the stream, tilting her head back to soak her face and hair.

"You, *cara mia*, are magnificent." He dipped and nuzzled her neck even as the water sluiced down the back of her head, neck, and shoulders. Slowly, he straightened, then reached for the bar of soap sitting in the soap dish on the wall. A bar that looked a lot like what she used at home.

"Dove?"

"So it says." He thoroughly lathered his hands, then dropped the bar back into the dish. "Step out of the water. Let me wash you."

She did, missing the warmth until his soapy hands slid over her shoulders, cupping her neck and throat, then down to cover both breasts. Tipping her head back, she sighed with pleasure at his firm, slick touch. "This place is such a strange blend of the old and modern. Fire-heated water, hand laundry, and Dove soap."

"And Herbal Essences shampoo."

Quinn laughed softly, happily lost in a haze of pleasure as her vampire companion thoroughly washed one of her arms, then the other.

He turned her away from him, lifting her hands, placing her palms against the wall as he placed a kiss on her shoulder. "Keep your hands there and move back, bend over."

"I don't think . . ."

His hand slid softly up her spine. "Trust me."

"I have no idea why I should do that," she muttered, but did as he asked, the water hitting her lower back, her body beginning to tremble in anticipation of his touch. And she didn't have long to wait. A moment later, soapy hands were sliding over her back and shoulders, down over her hips. But his touch was firm, no-nonsense, as he thoroughly cleaned one leg and foot, then the other. Disappointed, she was beginning to think he truly meant to take no advantage at all. Until his foot tapped her inner ankle.

"Spread your legs." She did, and, a moment later, one soap-slick finger started at the base of her spine and slid down, over her anus, and further, straight into her hot, wet core. She cried out, arching her back at the pleasure.

His other hand, equally slick, corralled her from the other side, sliding across her stomach, delving into her nether curls, finding and plucking at the center of her pleasure. His mouth caressed her shoulder, her back, her neck as both of his hands played her until she was rocking, crying out, screaming with release. And then she was in his arms, her back against his chest, one of his hands covering her breast, the other deep between her legs, finger-fucking her, milking the orgasm for all it was worth.

She reached behind her head, running her fingers through his hair as she arched back into him, rocking, moaning, loving his touch. Gradually, she calmed. Slowly, he released her, turning her around to face him, pulling her back into his arms and kissing her with a passion that threatened to drive her up all over again. Until the water at her back began to turn cold.

Quinn gave a squeak and dove out of the water, looking at Arturo with dismay. "I haven't washed my hair."

His eyes were soft as he watched her. Infinitely warm. "Tip your head forward under the water, then shift toward me, and I'll wash it for you."

She did as he directed, enjoying the feel of his long fingers massaging her scalp before she shoved her head back under the now-chilly water for a quick rinse and repeat. When her hair was clean and clear of the fragrant shampoo, Arturo turned off the water, reached through the door for the towel, and wrapped her up snugly. How strange to feel taken care of by a vampire.

He towel-dried her hair, then helped her back into her clothes. As she pulled on her boots, he donned his shirt, not appearing to care that his pants were soaking wet.

A shriek split the air from one of the buildings nearby, a loud wail that had Quinn turning rigid as stone. "Not again."

"No one is being tortured."

"Sounds like it to me." She tied her second boot and rose.

"That is a cry of anguish, not pain."

"You know your screams."

His expression turned wry, but he took her hand and led her out of the shower shack, to a low, wooden structure that looked like it belonged in a campground packed full of day campers. He ushered her inside. The interior was open, furnished only with a couple of long trestle tables. Built into one wall was a huge stone hearth, unlit.

Firelight flickered on the walls from half a dozen lamps, and on the faces of half a dozen stricken women, one of whom was in full-blown hysterics.

Quinn watched as Kassius strode up to the group, grabbed the hysterical girl by the jaw in a grip that appeared surprisingly gentle, and forced her to look into his eyes. Instantly, she calmed, her tears ending, her expression falling into one of sleepy indifference. As a woman put her arm around the girl and led her away, the others followed, eyeing Kassius with an odd mix of fear and gratitude.

She glanced at Arturo and caught the look of pleasure on his face. "You're feeding."

"I am," he said unapologetically.

One woman remained behind, a woman with a thin, pinched face and the shimmering hair of a Slava, who eyed Kassius with a haughty belligerence. Kassius turned on her with a look that Quinn thought warranted a little fear.

"You enjoy the hysterics," Kassius accused her. "You should be one of us."

"They are weak."

He stared at her until she began squirming beneath his gaze. "Perhaps I'll recommend to the council that the next game's theme be dark-haired bitches."

She closed her mouth with a snap and whirled away.

Kassius growled low in his throat, then came to join them. "The Games," he spat. "They should be for warriors, not women."

Arturo shrugged. "They are what they are."

"You are too damned complacent, Ax!"

"And you care too much, Kas. You grow fond of them, and they die."

Kassius glanced at her. "And you don't?"

"Caring has never changed anything."

"I can't stop. Not anymore, though, gods, I wish I could." He turned toward the door and strode out, anger vibrating in every step.

"What just happened?" Quinn asked softly.

Arturo's expression told her she wouldn't want to hear it. And he was probably right. But Zack was caught in this place somewhere, and the more she understood, the better her chance of getting him back.

"I want to know. The truth, Vampire."

He frowned. "She's been chosen for the Games."

"Which means?"

He gave a snort of frustration. "One of Vamp City's prime selling points, over and above the fact that the sun never shines, is that it is a place where vampires can engage freely in our favorite sports."

"Which are?"

He met her gaze, warning her not to press. She stared at him, insisting he finish.

"The hunting, terrorizing, and torturing of humans."

Quinn shivered. "The Games." He was right. She didn't wanted to know this. "Tell me the rest."

Arturo swung away from her, staring at the cold hearth. "You are familiar with the gladiator games of ancient Rome?"

"Of course. At least superficially."

"Soon after V.C. was built, the coven masters joined together to build a coliseum, though on a far smaller scale. Once a month we hold the Games, often with different themes, though one thing remains the same. Humans fight. Humans bleed. Humans die. Each kovena sends a pair of their freshest slaves, humans who have not yet turned to Slavas, have not yet turned immortal. The girl who was crying had just been told she will be going, I suspect. Though it's possible someone close to her is to be sent."

Quinn stared at him. "So she'll be forced to fight. With no training? Will she even be given a weapon?"

"Sometimes yes, sometimes no. It depends on the whim of the organizers. The males chosen are often sent to a gladiator camp in the city for training. The second and third rounds are generally between at least minimally trained combatants and tend to be good fights. But the first round . . ." He shook his head.

A slaughter. "Zack could be involved."

"Yes."

The thought of it, of her sweet, smart, nonathletic brother thrown into a gladiator ring filled her with a cold and silent terror. He wouldn't survive for five minutes. Yes, he could battle with the best of them when it came to computer games, but in real life? He wouldn't even know how to hold a real weapon.

"I have to free him."

"I've told you . . ."

"I know! I know you won't help him."

"Not won't. *Can't.* The politics of this world makes the machinations of your own political parties look like kindergarten squabbles. I'm Cristoff's chief negotiator, but I do nothing without his will because if I fail, war ensues. And I will not risk that kind of disgrace over a human. Any human."

"Can you at least ask your contact if Zack's been chosen for the Games?"

The vampire gripped her by the shoulders, hauling her around to face him, all softness gone from his expression. "If he is not a sorcerer, he is dead, Quinn. Or will be soon." His grip tightened, and he gave her a small shake. "Fewer than one in five slaves brought into Vamp City lives long enough to turn Slava. He may die at these Games, or the next, or in a fit of anger or hunger at the hands of one of his masters. *He is lost to you.* I do not know how to say that any clearer. You must mourn him and move on."

Her eyes burned as a shaking started deep inside her. She would never move on. *Never.* "Do you go to the Games?"

He growled in frustration. "All Cristoff's most trusted accompany him. Anytime the kovenas gather, there's the risk of war."

"When are these Games?"

"You are the most stubborn female . . ."

"It's a simple question."

"Three days hence," he snapped. "Come." He started toward the door, once more the master with his slave. Discussion over.

Three days. And if Zack was involved? She might never know. *He is lost to you.*

No. As long as she drew breath, she would fight to find him. Or, at the very least, to learn his fate. Then, perhaps, she would find the strength to move on.

But not a minute before.

"In the yard, bloodsacks. Now!"

Zack gave a silent groan, pushing off the narrow rug that served as his bed on the damp floor in the Dungeon. It looked like a dungeon, with its stone walls and damp stone floor, but it was really just the basement of the Smithsonian Castle . . . Castle Smithson, the vampires called it, now. This place was so fucked up.

Around him, the other new slaves stumbled to their feet looking . . . and smelling . . . like hell. Not a one of them had seen a shower, comb, toothbrush, or razor since they'd gotten here. He didn't care. At least, he wouldn't have cared if Lily weren't here somewhere. He hadn't seen her since the kitchen yesterday. Thank God none of the vamps appeared to have overheard his lapse as he'd yelled for her. She hadn't looked bad, not like he suspected he did. She'd looked . . . tired. And kind of shell-shocked. But still so fucking pretty.

The vampire's whip snapped through the air. The slaves rushed for the open door, pushing and jostling one another, none wanting to be last. None wanting to feel the lick of that lash. Zack clamped down on a groan of pain and stumbled after them. One sorry bastard remained asleep on the floor. Or, maybe dead. Zack hoped he was just sleeping, mostly because if he was dead, that meant Zack was last in line.

He was becoming as cold-blooded as the vampires.

Exhausted and starving, every one of his muscles ached as if it had been wrenched and twisted a hundred ways, then left to harden that way. But the worst part, by far, was the constant, gnawing hunger. All they ever fed them was oatmeal, canned stew, or canned chili. Cheap stuff. And never, ever enough.

Behind him, he heard the whistle of the lash, then the cry of pain of the guy who'd been sleeping. Not dead.

As he pushed through the door into the torchlit yard, he saw that two more sadistic vampire guards were already pushing them around. "Line up! Two lines, facing one another." One of them grabbed Zack and shoved him to one side. "You in this line." Still more asleep than awake, Zack stumbled as he found his place in one of the lines, righting himself at the last minute.

Why two lines? Since he'd gotten here, he'd done more physical labor than he'd done in his entire life. He'd hauled bricks, hammered shingles onto a roof, carted boxes and crates, and dug a trench for a new water line. Lining up like this was new. Were they going to be carrying something long and heavy?

Facing the castle, he glanced up as a movement caught his eye. Lily. She stood in the open second-story window, watching him, a scrub brush in one hand and pail in the other. As the torchlight flickered over her face, she looked so sad, he wanted to hit something. When was the last time she'd smiled or laughed? She had the best laugh. Had the vampires stolen that, too?

If only he were some kind of superhero and could whisk them both out of there. They'd find Quinn and escape this sorry world once and for all.

But he was no fucking superhero. Not even close.

One of the vampires started down the line of slaves, handing something to each of them in turn.

Zack gaped. *Swords? You've got to be fucking kidding me.* What did they think this was? Ancient Rome?

As one was shoved into his hand, he realized it was made of wood, the point rounded off. Okay. His heart started beating again. Just pretend. Sort of.

The head vampire stopped at the end of the line, addressing them. "You will fight your opponent, the man you face."

Zack's gaze flew to the guy across from him, Reggie, one of the ones who'd been here a few months, who always seemed to know what to do. Reggie's expression changed before Zack's eyes, transforming from one of tired resignation to hard-eyed warrior. Fuck. He was supposed to fight him . . . with a wooden sword?

"You may draw blood," the vampire continued. "But you will not kill."

Jesus. Zack gripped the wooden hilt, a frisson of excitement fizzing inside of him. A real battle. If only he had a serious weapon, like a laser gun or a light saber, he'd take them all down, vampires included, chopping off their heads left and right. All the slaves would clap him on the back, and he'd lead them in an uprising like Vamp City had never seen. Then he'd grab Lily and Quinn and get the hell out of there.

The vampire lifted his arm high above his head, then brought it down like he was waving a flag at a NASCAR race. "Go!"

Before Zack knew what was happening, Reggie lunged, swinging the sword, slamming it hard into the side of Zack's head. The next thing Zack knew, he was on the ground, struggling to get up, something wet running down his cheek. He brushed at the wetness with the back of his hand. Blood. *He'd lost.* As he pushed to his feet, swaying, three Reggies danced in his vision, their swords hanging at their sides.

Where was his sword? His hands were empty. *He'd failed.*

"Enough!" the vampire cried.

Zack swayed, stumbled back, and caught himself before he fell. Slowly, the three Reggies merged into two, then back to one.

"You've made your decision already?" one of the vamps asked the one in charge.

The first vampire snorted and looked at Zack. "That one, with the red hair."

"He won't last five minutes in the arena."

"Let the Games have him. He's useless here."

Zack's face flamed. *Useless?* He wasn't useless! He could program circles around every last one of them. But they didn't care about that here. His shoulders sank. It didn't matter here. Nothing mattered but muscle. And he didn't have nearly as much of *that* as he'd thought he had.

With a sinking gut, he looked up at the window and found Lily standing there still, tears streaming down her cheeks. She'd seen it all.

His humiliation was complete.

CHAPTER ELEVEN

Forty-seven, forty-eight, forty-nine . . . Quinn pressed through the push-ups, her hands damp on the unpolished wood floor of her miserable little room. There wasn't much else she could do in here, but she had to do something. Never in her life had she been sedentary. Even at work, she spent more time standing than sitting, moving every chance she got. If she was stuck within these four tiny walls for much longer, she was going to become claustrophobic.

She'd tried, over and over, to access that small burst of power she'd had as a kid, but it was gone, and she had no idea how to get it back.

At the sound of a key in the lock, she jumped to her feet, brushed her hands off on her pants, then pushed back a sweat-dampened lock of blond hair with her knuckle. Arturo pushed open the door and stepped inside. Under one arm, he carried a bottle of wine and an old book. In his hand, two wineglasses and a tray of bread and cheese.

He eyed her flushed and damp state and her uneven breathing with amusement. "Training to take me down?"

She shook out her arms, eyeing him coolly.

They'd parted on a sour note after the trip to the food village and the shower. As nice as he was sometimes, nothing she said made a difference in his attitude toward helping her find Zack. And her refusal to give up thoroughly annoyed him. It was a huge sticking point between them. But, dammit, Zack was her brother.

"There's not much else to do in here."

He glanced at the bed. "I can think of something."

A bolt of heat lightning arced through the air between them as she remembered the feel of his hands on her body . . . *in* her body. The thought had her legs weakening all over again. But it did nothing to ease her anger with him. He wanted her, but he didn't give a damn about her. Not when he knew Zack's loss was killing her, yet he refused to do *anything* to help. He claimed he couldn't. And maybe that was true. But he could damn well quit telling her to forget about the only person she'd ever loved.

Who was this vampire, deep down? He was definitely attracted to her. She'd felt the way his hands shook every time he touched her. She'd felt the evidence of that attraction pressed against her hip. Still, he had yet to actively seduce her. The moment he touched her, she turned to putty in his hands, and they both knew it.

So, what did he really want from her? Was he carefully working to win her trust, or did he honestly possess a conscience? Maybe even a heart.

A man with a heart could be swayed to do the

right thing. Perhaps. If he cared. And if she didn't continually annoy him with her begging him to help.

Arturo set everything on the washstand, then handed her the book. "Grant sent this for you."

Quinn handled the dusty volume with care as she turned it over. *A History of Witchcraft in America.* "Is this a joke?"

"He said it's important that you understand your heritage in order to call forth your true gift."

"He thinks I'm a *witch?*"

Arturo's brow lifted in amusement. "And what do you think a sorceress is?"

Something I'm not. She turned the book over in her hands. Could anything look more boring? "It's a history text. Clearly, everyone in this place enjoys torture." She hated history. Absolutely hated it. "I wouldn't mind a novel, though. Maybe a Mary Higgins Clark or Nora Roberts?" Of course, Grant wouldn't have sent her this one if there wasn't something in it she needed to know. Maybe the Blackstones were discussed at some point.

"I might be able to scare you up a Stephen King."

She snorted. "Why doesn't that surprise me?"

A crack of thunder rattled the mansion, followed by the pounding of raindrops against the outer walls.

Arturo poured two glasses of white wine, handed her one, then carried the plate and his own glass to the bed. She was still angry enough to be tempted to tell him to leave. Except she didn't want him to go. Not yet. As much as she hated being trapped in this room, being trapped in it alone was a hundred times worse.

Quinn eyed the sagging mattress dubiously. "We might want to sit on the floor. The bed is a bit . . . soft."

His smile turned devilish. "You just have to know how to sit on it."

"And you do?"

"I've slept on worse, *cara*. Many a time."

"I suppose you have."

He handed her the plate. "Hold this." She took it and watched as he lowered his long frame to the middle of the narrow bed like one might a hammock, then leaned his back against the wall, looking annoyingly comfortable. He reached for the plate, set it in his lap, then held out his hand again. "Give me your wine."

Quinn hesitated, then, with a huff, did as he asked and managed to join him with a minimum of grace. Arturo handed her the wineglass. Leaning back against the hard wall, she wasn't exactly comfortable, but she wasn't too uncomfortable, either. Especially not with the bed pitching her shoulder to shoulder with Arturo.

The vampire looked at her with approval. "There now. Was that so hard?" He handed her his wineglass, then set about cutting slices of cheese and tearing off chunks of bread. When he was through, he reclaimed his glass and set the plate in her lap, snatching a piece of cheese before he pulled away.

She glanced at him before placing a slice of cheese onto one of the bite-sized chunks of soft bread. "It surprises me every time I see you eat. Vampires should only drink blood."

"Many things you see in the movies are not true. You must know that."

"Like vampires being pasty white? You're not. Your skin tone is . . ." She almost said *gorgeous* and caught herself in time. "Normal-looking."

He made a sound of amusement as if he knew exactly what she'd been thinking. "Vampires are whatever color they were originally."

"Without suntans."

His mouth twitched. "Without suntans."

"You're Italian. Clearly. All the *caras* and *piccolas*."

"I am."

"I didn't know there were vampires in Italy."

"And you knew there were vampires in Washington, D.C.?"

"Good point." She took a sip of the wine, making a sound of approval at the smooth, fruity taste. "This is delicious."

"But of course. When one has lived a long time, one learns to appreciate the finer things in life. And has had the time to discover them."

"And to save the money to buy them?"

His eyes danced, a small smile hovering at his mouth that did all kinds of crazy things to her pulse. "That, too."

She took another bite of cheese and bread. The bread was soft and still warm, the cheese delicious. Never would she recommend this place for its hospitality, but the food was another matter. "You're entirely too charming for a vampire, do you know that?"

"Am I, now? I'm not sure I should take that as a compliment. Your vampire legends are rife with charming scoundrels."

"And Cristoff calls you his snake."

He shrugged turning away to take a sip of wine. "I am what I am."

"A fear-feeding, bloodsucking vampire." She glanced at him. "I understand the blood thing. Blood is life. But not the emotions. Even if you drank blood as often as you wanted to, you'd still die if no one feared you?"

"Die? No. But my control would weaken, and my conscience would be overridden by the drive to feed. The more I try to limit my need to terrify, the more harm I'll do, perhaps attacking innocents or children, killing instead of merely feeding."

"Do you ever terrorize children?"

"Never." The word snapped from his lips. "Before Vamp City began to crumble, my friend Micah hunted swine—the humans who preyed on the innocents. Pedophiles, rapists, wife- and kid-beaters. He'd bring them to me before delivering them to Cristoff, and I would delight in terrorizing them. I have an entire dungeon outfitted in the basement of my house for the purpose. I've never actually used the instruments. The sight of them is all that is needed to send such vermin into paroxysms of fear. For decades, I've fed almost exclusively on Micah's offerings, but they've ceased now that we are trapped."

She studied him, considering his words, stated so matter-of-factly. "You're surprisingly comfortable with yourself and what you are, aren't you? No anguish over being a soulless monster."

He grunted. "And why would I be soulless?"

She looked at him curiously. "Do you consider yourself dead? Or undead, maybe?"

"Neither." He took her free hand and drew it to curve around the side of his neck, pressing her finger against the pulse point beneath his ear. His skin was cool, but very much alive. "Do you feel it?"

"Your pulse? No."

"Wait for it."

A moment later, she felt the unmistakable throb of his heart blood, strong and clear. "Yes," she breathed, and waited to feel it again. Seconds passed, perhaps more than seven, before she felt another kick. Withdrawing her hand, she looked at him in surprise. "It beats incredibly slowly."

"Yes. It will beat faster right after I've fed and far more slowly when I'm hungry and depleted of blood. But my heart beats, Quinn. I live."

"And yet when you became a vampire, you died."

"I was transformed. Near death, yes. And without the blood of my maker and the transformation, I would have died. He'd drained far too much of my blood for me to have ever recovered. But, no, I never truly died."

Quinn took another sip of her wine, mulling his answers, overlaying the legends in her mind with the truth as she now understood it. "Why did he turn you?"

Arturo stilled, then slowly lifted his glass and drained the wine. "He did what he did." Without warning, he stood, levering himself up and off the rope bed far too easily, then set his glass on the washstand.

She looked up, starting the awkward scoot off the bed with wineglass in one hand, plate in the other. "Are you leaving?"

He grabbed her glass, then took her hand and helped her up. "I have responsibilities other than you, *cara*."

"I wish I could say the same. Seriously, Vampire, what's the plan? To keep me locked up here for the rest of my life?" Which, in this place, might not be very long.

He handed her back her glass. "Get some sleep. Night has fallen. In the morning, we shall accompany Cristoff to the Crux to test your power."

That sounded . . . ominous. "What's the Crux?"

"The Crux is the term for the inner lands of V.C., farthest from the Boundary Circle, lands not claimed by the kovenas. Within their very heart lies the Focus, the spot upon which Phineas Blackstone stood and cast his magic to create this world. It is there that the magic must be renewed."

"You do know that I have no clue what to do, right?"

"Grant and Sheridan Blackstone will accompany us, along with a dozen of Cristoff's guards."

"You're afraid other vampires may attack us? Don't they want Vamp City saved?"

"Vampires are not always the most logical of creatures. But there are other things within the Crux that would enjoy seeing us dead." He touched her hair. "Nothing for you to worry about."

"Right. Go to sleep and don't worry about the monsters, even though *these* monsters are real." Arturo turned to go, and she stopped him. "Vampire, what if I fail? What if I can't save this world?"

"We'll try again at the equinox."

At least failure wasn't an automatic death sentence. "And if I succeed?"

He gave her a small smile. "We will be grateful."

"That's it? Will I be freed?"

Frustration glimmered in his eyes. "You will never be free. If you are of no worth to Cristoff, I will offer to buy you from him." His eyes darkened, his hand lifting to touch her hair. "I wish you for my own."

"For your slave."

"For my bed." Vampire-fast, he took the glass and plate from her hands, deposited them on the washstand, then pulled her against him, dipping his cool face to nuzzle her neck, making her shiver with pleasure. His dark, decadent scent filled her nostrils, his soft hair sliding along her jaw. A moment later, he shifted, rising, claiming her mouth in a kiss that was soft and sensual, a tasting, a sharing.

When he pulled away, she stared at him, breathless, trying to make sense of the inconsistencies in him. He could be so hard. Yet when he touched her, so gentle.

His hand cupped her jaw, his thumb tracing her bottom lip. "Such a frown. Did my kiss displease you?"

"No. I just . . . I don't know what to make of you sometimes."

"And why is that?"

She watched him for long moments, debating whether to be honest and deciding she might as well be. "My instincts tell me to trust you, but you've told me yourself that I should never do that. And you've proved it. You lied to me about taking me to find Zack, then turned me over to Cristoff. And you refuse to help me save my brother. I hate you for that. I *want* to hate you. And I can't."

He mirrored her frown, then cupped her face in his hands, looking at her in earnest. "This is the truth, Quinn. You must understand it. My loyalty is to Cristoff. His needs and desires come first above those of anyone else, including myself." His smile was small, his eyes deep and fathomless. "But I do not hate you either, *tessoro*. I quite like you. And I would not see you come to harm."

"You'll protect me. But never from Cristoff."

He slid his fingers into her hair, running the

blond locks between his fingers. "Correct. And no, never from Cristoff."

He'd protect her from all but the worst of the monsters—the master who ruled them all. Which was little protection. And yet, she believed him.

"Will you continue to lie to me?"

The charmer smile blossomed. "I am what I am."

She laughed despite herself. "A hopelessly unapologetic reprobate."

He grinned, his eyes going tender. "A pretty sound, your laughter. I would hear it more often." He kissed her forehead. "I fear I am a reprobate who cannot stop thinking about you." His lips brushed her cheek. "About the beauty of your breasts or the feel of your satin flesh beneath my hands." His mouth teased the corner of her own. "Or the cry of your passion when pleasure breaks over you." His lips grazed her jaw, then slid to her neck. "The sweet smell of your skin invades my thoughts at the most inopportune times, and your taste." Once more, he rose and claimed her lips, sliding his tongue deeply into her mouth.

Quinn moaned, wrapping her arms around his neck and giving herself up to his kiss.

As he pulled back, she pressed her hand to his cheek, marveling at the feel of him. No longer cool. "Kissing makes you warm."

"Only when I kiss you." He smiled, running his fingers lightly down the sides of her neck. "You may smell like sunlight, but you taste of peaches, utterly delectable." Their gazes caught and held until she thought she might happily drown in those dark pools. "Someday soon, you will open your arms and your thighs and welcome me, *cara*. But not today." He gave her nose a tiny kiss, then released her. "Sleep, Quinn." A moment later, he was gone, the lock clicking into place.

Quinn leaned back against the door, running her own fingers through her hair, hair he'd been playing with just moments before. He made her feel soft and excited, warm and unsatisfied. At once marvelously content and thoroughly frustrated on so many levels. He was stubborn and unbending and yet . . . sweet. Loving. And what strange, strange words to attribute to a vampire.

With a sigh, she pushed away from the door and poured herself another glass of wine. He'd told her to get some sleep, which meant she wouldn't see him again for hours. And she didn't even have a clock or a window to give her any clue of the time.

She picked up the book Grant sent and sat on the floor beside the washstand. Starting at the beginning, she quickly began to skim, searching for any reference to a Blackstone. Soon, the words began to run together, and she knew she was about to nod off, which wasn't a bad thing. Sleep was the best way to make the time pass. But as she flipped the page to see how many more she had until the end of the chapter, her eyes started playing tricks on her. The type beneath her fingers began to dance and fade.

As she stared at the page, the type slowly disappeared, handwriting appearing in its place—a tight male scrawl she could nevertheless read clearly.

Her pulse began to race.

My dearest Quinn,

I am writing to you in sorcerer's text, which you will be able to reply to by writing over the same page with your finger. Only another sorcerer can see it, so our communication is perfectly safe. It is being said that you escaped V.C. in a sunbeam. Is this true?

Your humble servant,
Grant Blackstone

For long minutes, Quinn stared at the writing, reading it over and over as chills ran down her spine. This was true magic.

Finally, she set her finger to the page beneath Grant's note.

Yes. The sun burst through outside Arturo's house, and I could see my world in it. I ran into the sunbeam and out of V.C.

Now what? She supposed she'd have to ask Arturo to send the book back to Grant and hope— New writing appeared, overlaying the old.

It is rare for one to see either world from the other, even in a sunbeam. Is that how you found your way into V.C. in the first place?

She pressed her finger to the page and replied.

If this is one of the parlor tricks you were talking about, Grant, I can't imagine what kind of power. . .

She stopped. She'd been about to write, *a real sorcerer might have,* but that would probably offend him. Especially since she was supposedly one herself. Good grief, his father had created V.C. Created this entire world. *That* was real power.

She started a new line.

Yes. I'd been getting short glimpses of V.C. for several weeks. Then a friend went missing, and as my brother and I searched for her, I saw your world clearly in front of me. My brother and I got sucked inside. After I escaped, I returned to look for my brother and ended up in a slave auction. So much for brilliant plans.

Your brother?

My half brother, Zack. I have to find him and Lily, who is the friend who went missing. I suspect she might be here, too, somewhere.

She stopped writing, then pressed her finger once more to the paper.

Can you help me find them?

She waited for a response. And waited.

Was that it, then? Was the exchange over?

And suddenly the original text reappeared, the finger-written conversation bare shadows on the page. Shadows she suspected only a sorcerer would see.

And now yet another person refused to help her find Zack. Well screw them both. She'd find Zack herself.

The righteous determination left her on a defeated sigh. Who was she kidding? She was trapped as completely as any rat in a cage. Escaping Cristoff would take a miracle.

Or a hell of a lot of magic.

CHAPTER TWELVE

The next morning, Arturo led Quinn out the back of the mansion to where several horses stood, their reins held by vampire guards. The dirt had turned to mud in the overnight downpour. The morning had dawned dark—as they all did around here—and stiflingly humid, a light fog obscuring what little she'd normally be able to see. There was a reason this part of D.C. had been named Foggy Bottom at some point in the distant past.

Arturo stepped off the bottom step onto the muddy ground, but when she would have followed, he held her back with his hand, reached for the reins of one of the horses, and pulled it toward her.

Quinn backed up a step as the massive head swung her way. She looked to Arturo with disbelief. "You want me to get on it?"

His mouth kicked up on one side. "I wish you to mount, yes."

Great. Okay, she'd seen Westerns on television. She could do this. When Arturo had the horse parked parallel to the step, she reached up and grabbed the pommel, lifted her knee nearly to her shoulder, and managed to get her foot in the stirrup. With a lot less grace than she'd have liked, she swung aboard the big animal.

Arturo handed her the reins. "Don't move," he warned, then mounted another horse, a big black one, with an ease that made her envious.

A chill went through her as she caught sight of Cristoff, a short distance away, already mounted and waiting. Today he was dressed in what appeared in the low light to be a purple silk shirt. Were those really purple pants? Mounted on another horse near him was a young man, perhaps a few years older than Zack, dressed in the style of the nineteenth century, his shirt white, his sleeves wide, his pants black. His dark blond hair brushed his shoulders, framing a good-looking, if ill-tempered, face.

Arturo brought his horse beside hers and took the reins from her hands. "Since you've never ridden, I'll lead."

"You don't think I can drive this thing?"

His eyes laughed at her. "I'll teach you to ride when the ground is no longer mud."

She supposed that was fair, especially since she didn't need anything else to worry about today. Not with Cristoff so close, the threat of magic breathing down her neck, and the threat of failure and what that might bring.

When Arturo didn't kick his horse into gear,

she looked at him with confusion. "What are we waiting for?"

"Grant."

"Oh. Who's the guy with Cristoff?"

"That is Sheridan Blackstone."

"Grant's brother?" Holy shit, that *young man* was over 150 years old. She could see the family resemblance between the two brothers, each with that dark blond hair and the strong, attractive features. But Sheridan still possessed the leanness of youth while Grant had filled out into a man.

"They look so much more than a year apart. Is that because Sheridan was turned?"

Arturo nodded. "Slavas sometimes continue to age for a time, even after they've turned immortal. Not always, and those who do, generally quit aging by thirty or thirty-five. Grant was one of the latter. Vampires remain whatever age they were when they were turned."

"How old was Sheridan?"

"Twenty-four."

"That's kind of young."

"He was not given the choice."

Perhaps that's why he looked so sullen. Although after 130 years, she'd have thought a guy would get over something like that. Maybe not.

Several minutes later, the back door opened, and Grant descended the stairs unhurriedly, as if he were the first one there instead of the last.

"Nice of you to join us, sorcerer," Cristoff drawled from across the courtyard.

"This is a waste of time. She'll never pull the magic on a null day."

"We'll find out, will we not?"

Grant mounted the remaining horse with an ease that rivaled Arturo's. Immediately, Cristoff and the Blackstone brothers started toward the gate.

Arturo followed after them, leading Quinn on her horse. She felt like a five-year-old. It was true that she'd never tried to drive something that had a mind of its own. Well, other than the ancient Oldsmobile she'd had in high school that refused to start whenever the temperature dropped below freezing and had a nasty habit of stalling at stoplights whenever she was late. But she was pretty sure she could figure it out. Really, how hard could it be to snap the reins, and say, *giddyap*?

Then again, Arturo rode as if he and the horse were one, with a beautifully flowing motion and strength, while she bounced along, her butt slapping the saddle with every stride of the beast. She was definitely going to need lessons if she got stuck here too long.

As they left the gates, a full dozen of Cristoff's vampire guards joined them, half leading the way, the other half bringing up the rear. Clearly, Cristoff was taking no chances, though whether he feared his rivals or one of the other creatures that made its home in the Crux, she didn't know. They headed north, and it only took a few blocks before the remnants of old buildings gave way to open mud fields interspersed with dead forests. The City of Washington in 1870 hadn't extended much past modern-day downtown, apparently. The rest of D.C., she was beginning to realize, had been distinctly rural.

Quinn glanced at Grant. A dozen times last night, she'd opened the book he'd sent her, hoping to find another message, but none had appeared. There wasn't much chance they'd be able to talk today, certainly not privately. Not surrounded by fifteen vampires.

The ride was slow though it became more manageable as the ground became less and less muddy. Apparently, last night's downpour had been fairly isolated. But as the horse moved faster, Quinn only bounced more in the saddle, until she began to wish the mud would return.

How did they know where they were going? Even after the fog lifted, the landscape rolled on in every direction, with few if any landmarks, though she did see an occasional stream or pond. And an occasional house. Houses that actually appeared to be lived in. The question was, by what?

"Who lives out here?" Quinn asked quietly.

Arturo heard her and brought her horse up closer to his so they could talk more easily. "We're traveling the wolf lands at present, though Rippers are known to haunt the Crux as well."

"Rippers?"

"Another race of vampire. They feed only on blood, not emotion. But unlike the Emoras, they lose all conscience when they are turned, all trace of humanity. They live to feed, and they do so without mercy."

Vampires that were even more dangerous than the ones she'd met. This place just kept getting better and better.

"How big is Vamp City, anyway?"

"Approximately six miles in diameter. The vampires wanted a large dark city, far larger than Washington City, so Phineas Blackstone rode to nearly the center of the ten-mile square that was originally D.C. to perform his magic. The city he created extends out approximately three miles in every direction from that spot. The Boundary Circle is where the vamps enter and exit the dark city . . . or did when the magic was intact. Most of the kovenas have strongholds near the Boundary. The unclaimed land around the kovenas we call the Nod. The large, unclaimed center, the Crux. It's a dangerous place, home to the wolves and Rippers and anyone else who longs to stay away from the kovenas and has the fortitude to survive."

"How are there wolves in V.C.? There haven't been wolves in the D.C. area in centuries."

"Werewolves, *cara*."

"Oh." *Shit.* "Don't the wolves and Rippers kill one another?"

"All the time."

"And are we in danger of being attacked?"

"Yes, of course." He eyed her expectantly.

Quinn glared at him. "You're waiting for my fear."

He smiled that devilish smile of his. "A small morsel, perhaps."

"I thought you didn't like my fear."

"I do not. Particularly when that fear is of me."

But he'd happily make her afraid of something else. Or he was just being contrary. She rolled her eyes. "So we're not really in much danger?"

The vampire shrugged. "It is unlikely they'll attack so many of us. Especially since we follow a straight path to the Focus, the very heart of the circle, where the magic still throbs with power. All know that Cristoff alone possesses Blackstone's sons. And most wish for V.C.'s magic to be renewed. Most wolves, at least. The Rippers rarely give much thought to consequences. They seek only the kill." He nodded front. "Look ahead. You can see the Focus."

She saw only the backs of the Blackstone brothers, riding directly ahead, at first. As they crested a small hill with dead trees on either side, she glimpsed a flash of colored light ahead. And suddenly she had a clear view of what appeared to be a small aurora borealis grounded and writhing in one fixed and open spot, its colors a brilliant blend of fuchsia, orange, and blue.

"It's beautiful," she breathed.

"None but a sorcerer can walk through it."

She looked at him in surprise. "What happens?"

"If I try to breach the Focus, it will throw me back like any good science-fiction force field."

"Except this one's real."

He nodded. "This one is real."

As they neared, Quinn watched, fascinated by the pulsing, gyrating colors that appeared to form a small dome over the ground, perhaps the size of a one-car garage. Finally, they were upon it, and Cristoff's guard rode to encircle the Focus, facing out to fight off any enemy.

Arturo dismounted, then grasped her waist and pulled her down before she could even attempt it on her own. Quinn gripped his shoulders as he set her on the ground, which was, thankfully, solid.

"You're nervous," he murmured.

Always the fear-feeder. "I'm fine." But he knew the truth. He knew exactly her level of anxiety, and she *was* nervous. Despite having tried to push the chamber pot, she wasn't at all sure she was ready to come face-to-face with her magic again. But it was Cristoff who scared her most.

Together, she and Arturo walked to where the vamp master waited with the two Blackstone brothers, her heart rate escalating with every step. Quinn avoided Cristoff's gaze as they joined the threesome, nodding instead to Grant.

Grant returned her nod in kind, then turned and headed toward the shimmering lights. "Come."

Quinn started after him without hesitation, anxious for any excuse to escape Cristoff's company. As Sheridan fell into step beside her, she turned to him. "I'm Quinn."

"I know who you are."

"And you're clearly not happy to meet me." How could a hundred-fifty-year-old man act so much like an ill-tempered teen?

He looked at her sharply, then away. "Were you expecting a brotherly hug?"

Her eyes narrowed. "And why would I expect that? Are we related?"

"How should I know?"

Fine, wonderful. Apparently all vampires were a pain in the ass, one way or another. They followed Grant the rest of the short distance in silence. Without pausing, Grant stepped right into the swirling mass of color. Quinn's eyes widened, and she followed, with a quick, mental, *here goes nothing.*

It was far from *nothing.* Like the sunbeams where the worlds bled through, she felt that strange tingling on her arms, the hair rising. But the magic here was far more dense. It was thick, like a heavy fog that clung to her skin, soaking in. No, *digging* in. It felt . . . strange. Uncomfortable, like fingers poking beneath her flesh.

"What's going to happen?" she asked, as they reached the center and turned toward one another.

Grant answered. "Sheridan knows the ritual but has little sorcerer's power. I have more, but not enough. We're hoping that by joining ours with yours, we'll have enough to renew the magic."

"So I don't have to do anything?"

Sheridan glared at her. "You could shut up."

Grant gave his brother a look of disgust. "Ignore him, Quinn. Everyone else does."

Suddenly, Grant was hanging two feet off the ground, his brother's hand around his throat as the younger Blackstone flashed a pair of wicked fangs.

"Sheridan!" Cristoff shouted from outside the aurora.

Sheridan ignored his vamp master for half a dozen seconds before dropping his brother to the dirt. The pair glared at one another, the animosity thick between them. Then, in that way men had of shaking off discord, they appeared to forget their animosity a moment later. As one, they turned to her, each reaching for one of her hands. Their palms pressed against hers, one human-warm, the other vampire-cool.

The second they gripped one another's hands, completing the circle, a stinging heat clawed at her palms, and she jerked away from them, running her hands down her hips, easing the ache.

"What happened?" Grant asked. They were both staring at her.

She looked at them in surprise. "Didn't you feel that?"

Grant watched her as if not entirely pleased. "What did you feel?"

"It hurt."

"It shouldn't have. Not if you're a sorceress." He glanced at his brother, but Sheridan just shook his head, his expression mirroring Grant's. "The magic let you in. You're one of us, or it wouldn't have."

Sheridan held his hand out to her. "Shall we continue?" The hard edge of his tone challenged her to man up. *Asshole.*

She glanced behind her at Arturo and Cristoff standing side by side, watching her, Arturo with concern, Cristoff with a sharp look that had her pulse ratcheting as she turned back. She did not like that man . . . vampire . . . whatever.

Taking a deep breath, she once more placed her hands in those of the brothers Blackstone. Like before, the magic stung, but she clamped her teeth together and rode it out, praying that the ritual didn't take long.

Beside her, Sheridan began to whisper words, a running chant so low and quick, she barely caught half of it. As he chanted, the stinging spread from her hands into her arms, and up, like a slow, acidic burn. The pain moved into one of her shoulders a second before the other, sliding into her chest, making her gasp as it traveled down her body, through painfully sensitive parts, and into her legs and feet even as it rose up her neck into her head until she was rigid with misery. Still, the chanting continued, over and over, until her forehead was damp, her body shaking.

"I can't take much more of this," she managed between gritted teeth, realizing belatedly that she was squeezing the bejeezus out of their hands.

Abruptly, Sheridan's chanting ended. Both men

released their grips and pulled their hands from hers. Slowly, the pain began to ease and die.

Grant looked at her with concern. "What happened?"

"I was going to ask you that."

"Cristoff will not be pleased," Sheridan warned.

Grant took Quinn's arm. "Does it hurt when I touch you like this?"

"No."

Grant led her back out of the aurora, and suddenly Cristoff was in her face, grabbing her jaw with a cruel hand. "The magic attacked you. What did you do to make it attack you?"

"I don't know. Believe me, I didn't enjoy it."

He smiled. "I did." He released her suddenly and swung away. "Perhaps you need a bit more persuasion to accept the magic and save our world. I believe you have a brother?" He grabbed Grant's left hand and lifted the three-fingered appendage. "It's extraordinary what a bit of familial persuasion can do."

His meaning slammed into her, draining the blood from her face. Zack. He'd hurt him, maim him just to force her to cooperate. And she didn't know how! Out of the corner of her eye, she saw Arturo staring off into the distance, his expression closed. He'd told her he'd never come between her and Cristoff.

Grant was the one who came to her aid, jerking his hand free of Cristoff's hold. "Her magic is untapped. Trying to call it forth on a null day was precisely as successful as I predicted it would be."

Cristoff glared at the Slava with ill-disguised dislike, but he turned and started back for the horses without another word.

Quinn turned to Grant, gratitude in her eyes, but he walked past her without a glance. Sheridan met her gaze, his own cool, before turning to follow his brother. She felt like a first-class failure. If only she had some idea of how to do what they asked. It was one thing to refuse, another entirely to be inept. Heaven help her if Cristoff got his hands on Zack.

With a shuddering breath, she started after them. Arturo fell into step behind her, but cold fury had her turning away. She longed to tell him to go to hell and leave her alone, but she needed his help to get out of this place in one piece, and she knew it. *Damn him.* If Cristoff ordered Arturo to find Zack and cut off his fingers in front of her, he'd do it. He'd do it!

Arturo said nothing, not even bothering to attempt an apology. In silence, he helped her mount, then led her horse back the way they'd come, following the others, as before. Several of the vampire guard in front turned toward the west, and she followed their gazes. Her breath caught at the sight of six large wolves sitting on the rise beneath the trees, watching them depart. Holy shit. From this distance, they looked just like wolves, if big ones. *Werewolves.*

Quinn shivered, but the wolves made no move to attack, and the vampire procession passed them without incident. She ought to feel relieved, she supposed. Instead, she felt beaten and bruised from the magic's attack, and cold in the pit of her soul at the thought that her love for her brother might end up destroying them both.

The one vampire who could possibly help her would never do so. He'd turn his back on her, betraying the strange connection between them all over again.

CHAPTER THIRTEEN

Arturo's temper simmered the entire ride back from the Crux, frustration like an itch beneath his skin he couldn't scratch. When they reached Gonzaga Castle's courtyard, he swung the sorceress off her mount, gripped her arm, and hauled her inside and downstairs, back to her room before Cristoff demanded her attendance . . . and subjugation. Before he himself lost control and began railing at her for all to see and hear.

She quaked beneath his hand, her fear not a sweet bright burst in his mouth but a cold, tasteless misery he wanted nothing to do with because the fear wasn't for herself. Not an ounce of it. It was all for that damnable brother of hers.

He unlocked her door and shoved her inside, keeping hold of her so she wouldn't fall. Honey hair swung, sending sunshine warmth into the air even as frosty green eyes turned to glare at him, accusatory. Hurt.

He rued the day he'd found her. No, he didn't. If he hadn't shown up when he did, Quinn Lennox would be dead, and he didn't wish that. But he could heartily regret that he'd been the one to save her, to become entangled in her fate. To become enchanted by her beauty and strength, and heartily exasperated by her obstinate, unbending, single-minded insistence on finding her brother.

Slamming the door behind him, he grabbed her by the shoulders, resisting . . . barely . . . the urge to shake her. "You are strong, *cara*. Strong as steel, yet you allow your feelings for another to make you *weak*."

"He's my brother!"

"He has no future!" The words were harsh, but she had to understand. "He is dead, Quinn. Perhaps already. Perhaps in the Games this week. Both would be a blessing, for if Cristoff brings him here to use against you, he will suffer more than you can possibly imagine. And it will destroy you."

Her face paled. Her trembling grew worse, and he hated it.

His fingers tightened, then gentled on her shoulders. "You must let him go, *cara*. Say goodbye to him in your heart."

"Never!"

Arturo released her. Just as he urged her to cease to care about her brother's fate, so, too, he must cease to care about hers. She was nothing to him but his charge and the potential savior of Vamp City. A thorn in his side, for all that she intrigued him. But that was the way of a sorceress, was it not? To enchant and enthrall, even if she did so unintentionally with her spirit, with her smile, which appeared all too rarely, and with the unaccountable sunshine that lived in her hair, her touch, her kiss. Were she just a human, he would keep her for his slave, but this sorceress was becoming far too much trouble. Cristoff had made him responsible for the woman's safety, but once the magic was renewed, he was done with her. What became of her then was not his concern.

His mind told him to turn away, to leave her to her obsessive thoughts of freeing her brother, but his own obsession reared its head, and he was helpless to deny himself one more taste. He took her face in his hands, her skin like silk beneath his palms, warm, fragrant, seductive. Green eyes snapped, but within the temper rose tendrils of a need that matched his own. Lush lips parted in an invitation he'd no intention of denying.

The moment his lips touched hers, he warmed, feeling the sun on his shoulders and back, and he sighed with pleasure at the way she met his kiss, at the way her arms slipped around his neck. He hauled her into his arms until their bodies molded together, a perfect fit—hard and soft, cool and warm, male and female—as his tongue swept inside her mouth, deepening the kiss, tasting sun-warmed peaches.

He longed to take her. His body throbbed with the need to part her thighs and make them one. His fangs ached to drop, to lengthen, to prepare for penetration of a different kind. His hand cupped her derrière, pulling her against his erection, arching against her as he fought the hunger tugging at his fangs. They still frightened her, as adept as she was at hiding it. And he hated that fear. He would not take her so long as she feared him. But his hunger for her was becoming more and more fierce, more and more difficult to control.

Wrenching away from her, from the temptation he was nearly helpless to resist, he released her and stepped back, his fangs and cock throbbing in equal measure. Her lips were damp and swollen from his kiss, her eyes dark with desire, and he had to fist his hands to keep from reaching for her and finishing what they'd begun. Would she welcome him without fear this time? Was she ready to take him into her body?

With Herculean effort, he turned away. The last thing he needed was to fall even further under the sorceress's spell. And he had a very bad feeling that once they'd become one, he'd find it impossible ever to turn away from her again.

Quinn stared at the door Arturo had just closed, feeling hot and chilled, such a tangle of conflicting emotions. His kiss melted and soothed even as it made her tense and trembling with wanting, a desire that was far from gone. But she was so angry with him, so disappointed that he refused to help her against Cristoff.

Dear God, what have I done? She should never have told them about her brother, never told any of them. Her only remaining hope was that Arturo had been telling her the truth when he'd claimed that snatching Zack from a rival vamp master could lead to war. That alone might give Cristoff pause. Then again, she got the strong feeling that Cristoff wouldn't let anything hold him back if he wanted something. And if he thought snatching Zack would force her to give him what he wanted, he wouldn't hesitate.

She pulled off her boots and sank down onto the soft bed, lying back, her fists to her eyes as she struggled to block out the image of Zack's being hauled before her, his fingers cut off one by one as she was forced to watch. Bile rose in the back of her throat, her stomach clenching, her eyes stinging. Hatred burned inside her for the monster who could threaten such an atrocity with such ease, one who'd done it before and so much worse. So much worse.

In that moment, she hated Arturo, *hated* him for his loyalty to such a man, such a creature. He would stand there and watch his master torture her brother and refuse to say one word to stop him. She knew it, and she couldn't forgive him for that. Why did she keep letting him kiss her?

Swiping at the tears that were slipping down into her hair, she blinked, staring up at the ceiling. She let him because she liked it. She liked *him*, dammit. The lesser of a hundred evils, and all that, she supposed. Compared to Cristoff, he was a certified saint. But he was also a manipulator. A liar, when it suited him. And he was utterly loyal to a monster.

Rolling onto her side, she curled into the fetal position and let misery and, finally, sleep, carry her away.

Quinn stood in the frozen food aisle of the grocery store, staring at the door of the ice-cream section, which had begun to bulge strangely. Light suddenly burst out around the edges. Quinn gasped and lunged, pressing against it. No! The light pushed to escape, screaming in her ears, fighting against her until the door pulsed and groaned, threatening to shatter. But she held on tight, turning to push her back against the freezing glass. No! If the light escaped, something terrible would happen. Terrible!

Across the aisle, twelve-year-old Zack sat, leaning back against the frozen-orange-juice door, his legs crossed, head bent low over his GameBoy.

Don't look, Zack.

She struggled against the troublesome, stubborn light until she was panting from exertion, her arms weak with strain. But she couldn't stop fighting. If she pushed hard enough and long enough, the light would die and go away. No one would ever know.

Zack would never know.

Quinn woke with a start, sitting up, groggy and confused.

A sound. At the door.

She tensed as the door opened, then frowned as a woman she'd never seen before slipped inside. A woman with the faintly glowing hair of a Slava.

Quinn struggled out of the pit of the bed and

onto her feet, brushing her tangled hair out of her face.

The woman, as tall as Quinn and dressed in black pants and a black T-shirt that had been turned inside out, clasped her hands nervously in front of her. "I'm here to help you escape."

Quinn's flesh tingled. "Why?" She shook her head, trying to clear it. Was she still dreaming?

Impatience crossed plain, sharp features, lightning-fast. "Grant sent me. Do you want to leave Vamp City or not?" With that, she opened the door, looked both ways, and slipped outside.

Crap. Give a girl a minute to wake up before you spring something like that. But . . . hell, yes, I want to escape.

Quinn grabbed her boots and slipped out the door, closing it behind her, then, on silent feet, ran after the woman. She caught up to her just as the woman stopped in front of a door four down from Quinn's own and clicked her fingernails against it, one after the other, in a careful rhythm. A moment later, the door opened.

The woman slipped inside, and Quinn followed, nodding to the man holding the door, a tall, dark-skinned male dressed in the same all-black clothing as the woman, an impressive dragon tattoo curling around his forearm. But his close-cropped curls were lacking that Slava shine. Holy hell.

As he closed the door behind him, she whirled on him. "You're a vampire."

"No way." He turned and lifted his shirt, show-

ing her a back sporting fresh, ugly welts that probably looked a lot like the ones decorating her own
back now. "New slave, just like you. Hopefully, a
soon-to-be ex-slave. Move," he said stiffly.

Quinn turned back to the room—one identical
to her own except for the manhole in the center of
the floor. And the ladder leading down.

Escape. If this was a dream, she was going to be
thoroughly pissed.

The woman grabbed a flashlight off the washstand as the man started down the ladder. Quinn
shoved her feet in her boots and tied the laces
with fast, excited fingers.

"Quickly." At the woman's silent urging to precede her down, Quinn hurried to the hole, grabbed
the top rail, and swung herself onto the ladder. As
she started down, she heard the woman follow,
accompanied by the soft squeak of hinges and the
click of the hatch. The room's light disappeared,
to be replaced by the flashlight beam. How was
such an obvious manhole hidden from the vampires' eyes?

Down and down she climbed, damp rock on
every side. She knew nothing about these people,
whether they were really sent by Grant, whether
Grant was even friend or foe. But any risk was
worth the chance of escape and the possibility of
finding Zack before Cristoff went after him.

She heard booted feet hit the stone floor below
her and knew that the man must have landed. A
second flashlight erupted behind her, allowing
her to see the last few rungs. The man said noth-

ing as she joined him, but his eyes gleamed with excitement. Why? Had these two been sent by another of Cristoff's rivals to kidnap her? Was this guy looking for some kind of reward for bringing her in?

It didn't matter. One way or another, she'd make this work to her advantage.

The woman completed her descent, then led the way down a long tunnel deep beneath the castle as Quinn followed, the man bringing up the rear.

Finally, the woman stopped, rapping softly on what appeared to be solid rock. How were there tunnels in the rock this far below D.C. . . . and no water? She thought this part of D.C. had been built on a swamp. Then again, this wasn't D.C., was it?

To her surprise, a narrow, short strip of rock swung open. A door. For midgets.

The woman bent low and swept under. Quinn hesitated only a moment before doing the same. *In for a penny, in for a pound.*

On the other side, she straightened, taking in a cave easily three times the size of her apartment back home, the walls unadorned except for the three lanterns sitting on various natural shelves, their light flickering over the damp walls. Around the cave, close to a dozen people stood watching her, as many men as women, all dressed similarly to the first two in varying shades of black and navy, some with shoes or boots, others barefoot. None of them had hair with that phosphorescent glow except the woman who'd come for her.

And Grant Blackstone.

He stepped forward, the only one still dressed in nineteenth-century landowner garb, his expression no more friendly than it had been any other time she'd met him. "I have a proposition for you, sorceress."

Nice to see you, too, Grant. "What's the proposition?" And really, was she likely to say no? Even if she wanted to, she probably couldn't find her way back to her jail cell. And she certainly didn't want to.

"I want you to free these slaves." His hand waved to encompass the entire lot.

"And how am I supposed to do that?"

"Send them through a sunbeam."

Quinn frowned. "They can't walk through on their own?"

One of the slaves stepped forward, a petite young woman with a bit of a weight problem. "I heard how you escaped. So a couple of days ago, I was in the right place when a sunbeam broke through, and I ran right into it and out the other side, still in V.C. Three times. It didn't work."

"Could you see the real world in the light?"

She looked surprised. "No."

Quinn turned to Grant. "Why can I do it, and she can't?"

"Because you're a sorcerer."

"What about you? Are you able to see the other side through the sunbeams?"

Grant lightly scratched his beard, his nails clicking at his whiskers. "I don't know. I rarely leave the castle and haven't seen the sunbeams." A wistful look crossed his face. "I should like to. It's been far too long since I've seen the sun."

Quinn frowned, turning to look at the girl thoughtfully. "Even if she couldn't see the outside world, she should have been able to run into it. The sunbeams are the real world breaking through."

"True," Grant replied. "But perhaps it takes a sorcerer to lead a human."

She was a human, dammit. He made it sound like she was one of the weirdo creatures that inhabited this place.

"Was your brother touching you when you came through together?"

"Yes." She'd been holding his arm. She glanced at the hopeful faces, then back at Grant. "You want me to help them escape."

A chorus of whispered *yeses* and sighs echoed off the cave walls.

Grant nodded. "The ten in this room."

She took a quick count. There were eleven in all—nine with normal hair plus the woman and Grant. With understanding, she met the sorcerer's gaze. "Not you."

"No. I can never leave."

"What about her?" Quinn glanced pointedly at the woman who'd sprung her from her room, the other one with the glowing Slava hair.

"Celeste only turned Slava a year ago. She should be able to escape."

Celeste stepped forward, her features pinched. "I don't care about the risk. My children were left orphans when I was captured. I have to get back to them."

Quinn's heart went out to her and the children whose mother had been missing for . . . what? Three years, now? She turned to Grant. "If I can hand them through without going myself, I will. But I'm not leaving Vamp City." She resisted adding *without my brother*. It was time she started keeping that to herself.

"Good enough. But if you're going after your brother, you should know he's no longer at Smithson Castle."

So much for the secrecy. "Smithson Castle?"

"Lazzarus's stronghold."

So, had Arturo lied about that, too? Or was Grant lying, now? Was there anyone she could trust to tell her the truth? "Where is he now? And how do you know?"

"He was moved yesterday to the Gladiator camp."

Her eyes widened, her blood turning cold. "The Games?"

"Yes. He was the one chosen for this week's."

She swayed. Her head began to pound. "*How do you know?*"

"I may not leave this castle often, but I have a valuable network of spies."

"You don't even know what he looks like."

"No, but Arturo does. It was his spy my own learned this from."

Arturo had probably seen him that day when she and Zack first came through.

"So Arturo knows that he was moved."

"He does."

Hell. Would the traitor grab him and take him to Cristoff or leave him there to die? She squeezed her eyes shut, pressing her fingers to her eyelids. She wasn't sure which she preferred.

Zack.

Not the Games. Was there ever a kid less suited to violence than her brother? He had height, but little muscle, and had never been into sports or skateboarding or anything physical. He'd always been a mind kid—video games, computer games, school. He was a great student with a quick, agile brain. And now they were going to put him in an arena and order him to fight to the death.

The cold seeped from her blood into her flesh and down into her organs, a debilitating frost that threatened to strip her of her ability to think, to act.

She turned to Grant. "Tell me how to find the gladiator camp."

"Not until you've fulfilled your part of the bargain."

She blinked. "Not until I've freed all these people?"

"Yes."

Her temper flared. "Do you have any idea how long it can take for the sunbeams to appear? It took me six days . . . *six days* . . . to get back in after I escaped." From the moment she'd first arrived in this place, she'd been chained, enslaved, ordered about, and punished . . . by vampires. She'd be damned if she was taking it from a slave, too. She closed the distance between them, eyes shooting fire as she got in his face. "We're doing it *my* way this time. You tell me where the gladiator camp is, and we'll start in that direction, hunting sunbeams as we go. But the Games are in two days. Zack will be dead *in two days.* Two days that aren't likely to matter one bit to your buddies here."

But Grant wasn't one to be cowed, especially by a sorceress who couldn't find, let alone control, her power. Blue eyes flashed with a temper equal to her own. "You do realize you're not getting out of here without a guide."

Quinn straightened, folding her arms across her chest. "Then it looks like we have a stalemate." She frowned as the implication of his demands hit her for the first time. "Or a trap."

It was his turn to frown. "A trap?"

"If Vamp City's magic fails, you die. Are you convinced I don't have the power to renew it? Is that it?"

"I have no idea what kind of power you possess." But he looked away as he said it, making her think he knew precisely. Making her think, too, that he was a lousy liar.

"If I escape Vamp City with my brother, I'll never be back. You know it, and I know it. So either you think I'm going to be of no use in helping you renew the magic, or you don't think I'll ever escape. Which is it, Grant? Am I powerless, or are you planning for me to be captured once I help your friends?"

He scratched his jaw absently, studying her with those blue, blue eyes. "I have no plan for you to be captured. Escape Vamp City with my blessing." So he did think she was powerless. Or he was just one more liar.

"Where's the gladiator camp?" she persisted.

A muscle leaped in his jaw, but he told her. "Approximately H Street and North Capitol."

That was only a few blocks from Union Station in the real D.C., which wouldn't help her much in this world since she was pretty sure Union Station hadn't been built until long after 1870. Still, she knew the general location. She'd find it.

Quinn met Grant's gaze. "I promise you, I will do everything in my power to see these people free of this place. But my brother is not going to die for it. He comes first. If we run across a sunbeam as we head for the gladiator camp, I'll get them through if I can." She lifted her hands and dropped them again. "You have to understand, I don't know how the sunbeams work. I don't know if I can send them through without going with them. And I can't risk leaving Vamp City and not being able to return for a week, again. But, I'll do everything I can to get them out of here."

The woman, Celeste, moved beside Grant, eyeing Quinn with eyes bright with hope. "I can live with that."

"Me, too," the dark-skinned man said. "If I can help free your brother, I'm down with that, too."

She nodded, then swallowed as she remembered Lily. She didn't even know if the girl was in Vamp City, though her pen's lying on the sidewalk precisely where the worlds collided made it more than likely. Still, how was she supposed to find her, let alone free her? How, for that matter, was she supposed to free Zack from the gladiator camp? Her odds of accomplishing any of it were practically nonexistent.

For one dark moment, the weight of those impossible odds threatened to crush her, stealing her breath, her hope. Leaving either Zack or Lily behind was not an option. Yet how would she ever save them both when twice she'd found her freedom within this world devastatingly short-lived?

Celeste walked over and took Quinn's hand. "Thank you. Bless you. You're the only hope we have."

The dark-skinned man joined her. "Yes, thank you, sorceress. We'll be forever in your debt."

Quinn felt that terrible weight lift slightly, enough for her to take a deep, unsteady breath. "Okay. Who's leading us out of here?"

A guy with a stylishly shaggy haircut and silver reflective glasses unfolded himself from the back wall of the cave. "I'm your guide. Grab your packs and your stakes, boys and girls." He turned and slammed his palm against the wall beside him, and yet another door opened in the stone. "We're going home."

She would never get used to this place.

Grant kissed Celeste's cheek. "Be happy." As she hurried to join the others filing through that back door, Grant turned to Quinn, his gaze probing, his expression enigmatic.

"Thank you," Quinn said quietly.

He nodded once. "Stay out of the Crux." She started to turn away, but he stopped her, his three-fingered hand on her arm. "Good luck."

She might escape, but he never would. And his hatred of this place was palpable. She wasn't sure what got into her, but she found herself leaning forward and placing a quick kiss on Grant Blackstone's cheek. "Thanks, Grant. May you find happiness in some form."

A small smile lifted his mouth, warming his eyes a few degrees. "Go."

And she did.

CHAPTER FOURTEEN

Quinn left Grant and strode quickly across the cave, to where the dark-skinned slave waited for her by the hidden door in the stone.

The man handed her a twelve-inch-long wooden stake. "Don't lose this. Vamps die if you stake them through the heart with wood."

"So that legend really is true?" She ducked through the doorway into another dimly lit passage through the rock. The other slaves were already a distance ahead.

"It's true," he said, following her in.

"Who built all these tunnels?" The tunnels were barely tall enough for her, let alone anyone taller than her own five-foot-nine. "I would think we should be up to our eyeballs in water down here."

"Slaves built them about fifty years ago. With Grant's help."

"With magic?"

"Your guess is as good as mine."

"Are they hidden from the vampires?"

"Concealed. If the vamps find the tunnels, they

can get into them. Grant's magic is good, but it's not that good."

Parlor tricks, he'd said. *Yeah, right.* The man was a wizard. Literally. And yet he couldn't renew the magic of Vamp City. But they expected her to? They were crazy.

"I'm Quinn, by the way," she said quietly.

"Marcus. They say you walked into V.C. on purpose."

She glanced at him. "The second time."

Understanding entered his eyes. "Your brother."

She nodded. "I lost him."

Marcus squeezed her shoulder lightly from behind, a warm gesture that strengthened and settled her more than any number of words could do. She'd thank him for it. Later. By finding a way to get him home.

As they rounded the next curve, Quinn saw the rest of the group ahead, the guy with the silver reflective glasses holding up a lantern, waiting for the stragglers. Was he really wearing sunglasses in the dark?

When Quinn and Marcus caught up, the leader began to speak, his voice low-pitched and quiet. "We'll come out of the tunnel in an abandoned row house about a block from the castle. Getting out of the Gonzaga kovena lands may be the most dangerous part of the journey. I'll go first to ensure that the coast is clear. Stay here until I give the signal. Once you're topside, don't go near the windows and don't make any noise. Not a sound."

"Jeff?" Celeste asked. "If the coast isn't clear?"

"If there's trouble, follow Celeste deeper into the tunnels. She knows them almost as well as I do." Jeff turned and started climbing a wooden ladder that rose straight up.

Quinn glanced at Marcus. "Is it day or night, now?"

"Day."

"Why not wait until full dark?"

"The vamps can see perfectly fine in the dark, and we can't. The little bit of daylight provides an even playing field." He shrugged. "Though not fucking much." He lifted his finger to his lips, his gaze following Jeff as their leader slowly pushed open the trapdoor above.

Quinn and the others turned silent as stone, barely breathing as they listened, tense and ready to run. If the vampires found them, they'd almost certainly catch them. Vampires were way too fast.

A soft click sounded, a tap similar to the one Celeste had made on the two doors. At the sound, Celeste grabbed the ladder and started climbing. One after the other, the remaining slaves followed until only Quinn and Marcus remained. As before, he waited for her to go, then brought up the rear.

Moments later, she emerged into a small, dark room, deep with shadows, that might have once been the living room of a small town house. The remains of rotted furniture littered the wood floor while the smell of mildew and decay thickened the air, along with swirls of dust.

Jeff, his back pressed against the wall, peered out a window so dirty it let in only the faintest of light.

Quinn followed the woman in front of her into the shadows at the back of the room while Marcus closed the trapdoor. Did they really think there was a chance that a group this large could pass through the city unnoticed by the vampires? They must.

Jeff slowly opened the front door, but only far enough to slip through. Halfway out, he nodded, then disappeared. One followed, a second, a third. Seven of them were out the door, Quinn only two back, when the house began to shake just as it had right before the sunbeam burst through the last time.

Upstairs, something crashed. Timbers creaked, one snapping. The whole damn house was going to fall on top of them!

Marcus grabbed her arm with one hand and yanked open the hatch with the other. "Down," he hissed.

Quinn hesitated. The others didn't, diving for the hatch like rats escaping a fire. "But this is it," she hissed back.

"No. Not here." He pulled her to the floor, until she was on her hands and knees. "There are too many vamps around. We'd never make it."

The others were rushing back in the door, bending low as they, too, dove for the hatch. Marcus shoved her into line between two of the men. Just as she started down, Jeff slipped into the house, shutting the door a split second before sunlight erupted into the room from the street outside in a blinding, fiery burst.

Quinn scrambled down the ladder, speeding up simply to keep her fingers from being stepped on by the bare feet of the man above. She felt hands at her waist and allowed herself to be pulled aside as the man above her jumped. Someone turned on a flashlight, but she was still sunblind and would probably remain so for several more minutes. Vaguely, she was able to make out Marcus's solid form coming down the ladder.

A shout sounded from above, then a woman's scream.

Quinn's eyes widened, her heart beginning to pound.

Jeff closed the hatch and quickly joined them. "We lost Crystal and Rick."

"How?" one of the women demanded. "You *left* them up there?"

"Crystal fell over a fallen beam," Jeff said, as if discussing the weather. "Rick stayed to help her. Apparently, they were caught."

Marcus grunted. "Because you closed the door."

Jeff scowled. "And if I hadn't before the light erupted, we might all have been found. We might still be. All it takes is one vamp to ask the right questions, and we're all dead. Let's move."

"Back to the castle?" Quinn asked no one in particular.

Marcus answered. "No. There is a maze of tunnels down here. Jeff and Celeste and I are the only ones who've been down here though none of us are experts. Far from it."

"This way," Jeff said. And now only eight followed.

Quinn.

Quinn started at the sound of Arturo's voice, her heart catching, then racing as she looked around.

"What's the matter?" Marcus grabbed her shoulder.

I do not know who took you, but I'll find you.

Holy shit. Could he really speak to her from this distance, or was he a lot closer than he should be? If he could sense where she was, they were in deep trouble. She wondered if he could read her mind. *Vampire, can you hear me?*

I will find you. The words sounded as much promise as threat. And they hadn't answered her question.

Marcus squeezed her shoulder. "Quinn?"

"Nothing. I just . . . nothing." Her heart racing as much from Arturo's contact as the near miss, she followed the others. Dammit, it was as if she hadn't escaped him at all.

She had no idea how long they'd walked, or how far, when Jeff finally started up another ladder.

"Do you know where this one goes?" Celeste asked.

"No clue. There's one way to find out." He put his finger to his lips, then slowly lifted the lid as those below doused their lights. As before, the rest of them waited silently, listening.

Quinn felt the change in the air as the hatch lifted and smelled the faint scent of manure. A moment later, the soft telltale click of fingernails gave the all clear, and the others started up the ladder. Quinn scrambled after them, climbing into the dark, her hands landing on a hay-covered wooden floor. A barn? It was hard to tell in the low light though the place did appear big enough. It certainly smelled like a barn—one with animals. Downtown like this, it was probably a stable.

As Marcus closed the trapdoor behind them, Jeff crept toward the large, open doors that were letting in the only light. The other slaves waited behind, ready to make a hasty escape, if needed.

Several minutes later, Jeff returned. "There's a house that way, and it looks lived in. We'll go out the other way. There has to be a back door." He turned on a flashlight, revealing the stable she'd imagined. Jeff motioned them to follow, and he led them around several large piles of wood that appeared to be old building timbers. Finally, they stopped before the back wall. Quinn could just make out the outline of a door in the dark wood. Jeff grabbed the latch and lifted it slowly, but as he pushed the door open, rusty hinges squeaked loudly enough to wake the dead.

Or the undead.

"Look what we have here."

Quinn whirled, along with the others. Not ten feet behind them stood a male vamp dressed in jeans, a red Washington Nationals T-shirt, and muddy boots, his fangs long and deadly, his eyes dotted white.

"My favorite snack." He laughed. "Blood rats."

He moved too fast to track, but a moment later, two of their number were gone. Jeff began pushing people out the door. "Go!"

Quinn grabbed her stake and whirled to Marcus. "We need to kill him."

"He's too fast."

"We can't just leave them!"

Marcus pushed her toward the back door. "Know when to cut your losses."

But they never made it to the door. One moment she was standing by the back door arguing with Jeff, the next she felt herself flying through the air, a hard band around her middle. Then she was being slammed back against something hard.

Her vision swam, her senses tumbled. Slowly, she realized she was standing within one of the stalls, shoulder to shoulder with Marcus as he struggled to free himself. The vamp must have carried them back here with his superhuman strength and speed. He now had them both pinned between his bulk and the wall.

Turning to Marcus first, the vamp gripped her companion's face, forcing him to look into his eyes. Marcus's struggles quickly fell silent. Slowly, the vampire turned those white-centered eyes on her.

Tell him you're a sorceress, tessoro. He will not kill you.

Jeez, could Arturo see what was happening to her? Could he feel the push of glamour?

She forced herself to relax, forced her eyes to unfocus even as her pulse raced. Finally, the vamp released her, then darted away so quickly that Quinn barely saw the stall gate swing open and shut. Marcus wandered a short distance away, moving as if in a trance to join the first two women to disappear. All were now enthralled.

Clearly, the vamp wanted to collect the whole set of humans. Which meant she might actually stand a chance of taking him down.

But the minutes passed, and he didn't return. Marcus and the two women walked slowly, aimlessly, around the stall, and Quinn forced herself to do the same in case the vamp returned with more victims. If only she could unenthrall the three. She refused to leave them at the mercy of the vamp like this.

Where was he?

Had the other slaves killed him and taken off? No, she was the one they would never leave behind. She was their ticket home. Maybe the vamp had killed the others. But, then, why hadn't he come back right away? Maybe he was fetching Traders to pick up the lot of them for auction.

That final thought chilled her to the bone.

But as she tried to come up with an explanation she liked better, the vamp pushed open the stall door, holding it. "Come," he said. Marcus and the two women moved toward him as commanded. Quinn quickly followed. Outside the stall, she found Celeste and one of the male slaves already enthralled. So he *had* gone back for more. And he seemed to have decided six were enough.

Quinn slid the stake out of her pocket, gripping it tightly. As the vampire led the way out of the stables, Celeste and the male tried to merge into the line, jostling the others. Quinn took advantage and cut to the front, right behind the vampire.

Gripping her stake, she took a deep, nervous breath, knowing she'd only get one shot at this. Okay . . . *go!* She leaped, circling the vamp's neck from behind with her left arm as she drove the stake into his back, up beneath his ribs, with all her might.

A second later, she was flying through the air, crashing back first into the soft ground with a whump that left her struggling for air. Terrified, she was about to be leaped upon and her throat ripped out, she rolled, pushing to her feet. And saw the vamp on the ground, facedown.

Hot damn. I did it.

"Quinn?" Marcus blinked, confused.

She smiled, unable to help herself, and nodded to the downed vamp. "I got him."

Marcus's mouth dropped open. To her surprise, he dove for the vamp, rolling him onto his back. The vampire, who'd looked no older than his late twenties moments ago now looked sixty. No . . . seventy. Eighty? He was aging a decade every three seconds.

Marcus dug through his pockets, pulling out coins, keys, tossing them in the dirt a good distance away. Then he scooted down to the man's feet and yanked off his boots, one after the other, tossing them, too. Behind him, the others stirred, and they all watched as the skin began to fall off the vampire's bones.

Quinn grimaced. That was just . . . gross.

Marcus jumped back. "Quinn, back up!" Quinn did what she was told and was glad a moment later when the skeleton, clothes and all, erupted in a puff of flesh and ash that rained onto the dirt a good five feet in every direction.

No wonder Marcus had taken what he could. Everything he'd left had disintegrated along with the vampire. Very, very strange. As the three women swooped in to pick up the things Marcus had claimed from the body, Marcus strode over to her. "You staked him?"

Quinn nodded. God, she'd just killed a man. A vampire, but still.

Marcus gripped her shoulder. "Are you okay?"

"Yes. Fine."

"He would probably have killed us, you know that."

She looked up, met his gaze with a frown. "I know." She'd been so proud of herself at first. Now she felt . . . numb.

Releasing her, Marcus motioned for the others to join them. "Let's get going. We'll find Jeff if we can. If not, we'll head toward the gladiator camp."

As they left the stables, she realized they were still downtown. There were buildings all around them though more suburban in density than modern D.C. And most appeared long abandoned.

As they started down the sidewalk, keeping close to the buildings, none of them seemed as tense . . . or were watching for vampires as carefully . . . as they probably should be. Quinn suspected they all felt the same—that if there were any vamps close by, they'd have heard the commotion and already come running.

Quinn kept feeling Marcus's gaze, his brows drawn as if he were trying to decipher a puzzle.

"What?" she finally demanded.

"He didn't enthrall you. Why not?"

"I suppose because I'm a sorceress. None of them seem to be able to."

"A handy trick."

"Especially since they never expect it."

Marcus grinned. "Thanks for the save."

And just like that, the pall lifted, and she found herself smiling back. "You're welcome."

Marcus made a funky little move that was almost a jig. "I might actually get home."

"How long have you been gone?"

The smile left his face. "Over a year. It was spring when I was captured. My wife was five months pregnant. I'm a dad." But the words held no joy, no pride, only a devastating heartache. "I wasn't there for her, to help her give birth, to take care of her afterward." Fury leaped into his eyes. "I've missed my son or daughter's entire first year. And my wife probably thinks I'm dead. For all I know, she's found someone else."

"At least she wasn't caught with you."

The sound he made was heartfelt. "Thank God for that. I was walking home from the gym after work. A drunk bumped into me, then turned and stared at me. The next thing I knew, I was in the slave auction." He glanced at her, his heart in his eyes. "I need to get back to my family."

Quinn touched his arm. "I'll do what I can, Marcus. If I can get you home, I will."

"I believe you. And if we get out of here, I want my wife to meet you. My full name is Marcus Aurelius Washington." He shrugged. "My mom was a history professor. I live on California Street in Kalorama. Look me up?"

"Yes, of course."

They lapsed into silence, taking the back roads and alleyways as much as possible. When a form detached itself from the shadows, they all pulled their stakes, but it was only Jeff. And he was alone.

"The vamp?" he asked, joining them. They told him what happened.

"Where are Tim and Janika?"

Jeff shrugged. "Tim's dead. Janika was captured by a Trader." So matter-of-fact.

Marcus eyed Jeff sharply. "And you, of course, got away."

"What's that supposed to mean?"

"Not a fucking thing, man."

But Quinn knew exactly what he meant. Jeff was a survivor. He might be their guide, but the only one Jeff was looking out for was Jeff.

"Come on." Jeff took off in a different direction,

heading south. Not in the direction of the gladiator camp, damn him.

"Where are we going?" Marcus demanded, as if reading her mind.

"A safe house, where we can get some food and regroup."

As badly as she wanted to get to Zack, she had to admit that food sounded like a good idea. There was still time to go after Zack. And she didn't really expect to manage it with a cast of thousands. Or of seven, for that matter. Hell, she had no idea how she was going to manage it at all. The only thing she knew was that she had to find a way. First, she'd get Marcus home to his wife and baby. As her boss liked to say, you had to count your wins, not just your losses. She'd be glad for any win at this point.

They'd traveled half a dozen blocks when Jeff led them down a narrow alley and motioned them behind a small wooden storage shed. "Wait here. There's a hot spot nearby. I want to make sure it's not being watched."

When he'd gone, Quinn leaned close to Marcus. "What's a hot spot?"

"One of the places where the sunbeams are breaking through. They're multiplying." He grunted. "I'm surprised Jeff didn't take one of us to act as bait."

She'd had the same thought. "Can the vamps smell us?"

Marcus smiled, laughter in his dark eyes. "Fee fi

fo fum? I've never heard of one who could, and it's a good thing, or we'd stand *no* chance against them. They may be as fast as Superman, and damned near as strong, but their senses aren't that much better than human." He frowned. "Other than the night vision. And the fear and pain feeding."

Jeff returned a short time later and motioned them to follow. At the end of the alley, he led them through the back door of a small row house that appeared to have been lived in fairly recently. Maybe in the past four or five years. The windows were still intact, the furniture appeared more 1960s than 1860s, but there was inch-thick dust everywhere and no sign of habitation.

When they were all inside, Jeff closed the door, then motioned to Quinn to follow. He led her to the front window and pointed next door, where there appeared to be yellow crime-scene tape roping off a good section of sidewalk and part of the street.

Quinn looked at Jeff. "What is it?"

"The hot spot. The vamps mark them if they can so they don't accidentally get caught next time it opens. Vamps fry in the sun, in case you were wondering."

She'd gathered as much.

Jeff turned to the group, moving until he stood in the middle of them and could talk quietly. "We're going to be watching out the windows, carefully. Three upstairs and three down while I rotate between you. If the ground shakes, we meet right here. If no one's seen any sign of vamps, we go. Understood?"

All nodded. All but Quinn. "I thought you said we were going to a safe house to get food."

"We are. Later. If the sunbeams don't break through."

She stared at him, her temper firing. "You lying scum."

But Jeff turned away. "Take a window and keep your eyes open."

Her fury should have blazed a hole in his back. Marcus touched her arm, regret in his eyes, along with a healthy dose of excitement and hope. The hope that the sun would blaze through. That he'd finally get home to his wife and baby. And dammit, she couldn't deny him this.

But she was getting so tired of people lying to her!

She and Marcus wound up watching the downstairs front window, one on either side, peering in opposite directions. But Jeff didn't like them to talk—any of them, and she couldn't say she blamed him. The whole game was lost if a vamp wandered by and heard voices within a supposedly deserted house. Of course, if he was a fear-feeder, he'd know humans hid nearby. A pain-feeder probably wouldn't.

There were so many ways they could get caught, but the more careful they were, the more likely they'd remain free. So she stood there, out of sight of anyone who passed by, watching, listening to the sporadic sounds of this dark, dangerous city—a bloodcurdling scream, a horse and carriage.

A Jeep.

Was Arturo looking for her? If Grant was right, he knew Zack had been moved to the gladiator camp. Would he try to catch her there?

You think of me, cara, *but your emotions do not cry out for help. You are safe. Or you believe yourself so. For now.*

The sound of Arturo's voice in her head was becoming almost familiar. And not altogether unwelcome. As long as he stayed in her head and didn't show up in the flesh.

She glanced at Marcus, breaking the no-talking rule. "Have you ever heard of a vampire speaking in someone's head?"

"You mean telepathically?"

"I guess. But it only seems to go one way."

"You've got one talking to you, now?"

Quinn nodded.

"He's drunk your blood."

"A couple of times."

"I've heard of weird connections forming when that happens, but it's not common."

She sighed. "The story of my life."

As long as you remain in Vamp City, I will search for you, tessoro, *you must know that. I will find you. There is no escape, Quinn. Come back before you fall into hands that will harm you.*

As if she ever would, knowing he'd only deliver

her back to Cristoff. No, she was getting Zack out of V.C., that was all there was to it. Or die trying.

Zack tried to parry the blow with his wooden training sword, but his arm was like rubber, his opponent too fast, too strong. Paul slammed his sword against Zack's ribs, then against his calf, knocking Zack's leg out from under him. Zack hit the ground hard, the collision rattling everything inside him that hadn't already come loose, shooting pain up his spine and into every cut and bruise he'd suffered since his arrival in the gladiator camp yesterday.

Was it only yesterday? This has to be the longest fucking day in my sorry, fucking life. And it isn't over yet.

Paul thrust the point of his training sword against Zack's throat, forcing him onto his back. "Dead. Again." With calm satisfaction, the shorter man turned away, heading toward the water station. In the movies, this was the point when the downed hero would jump up and take the asshole from behind. Right. He was certainly no hero. And if he had that much energy left, he wouldn't have been knocked down in the first place.

Instead, he lay back in the dirt with a grimace, his ribs aching, his muscles on fire, his lip split in three different places, one eye swollen nearly shut from a blow he'd taken last night during his very first sparring match.

He'd fought as hard as he could every fucking time, but he just didn't have it. He closed his eyes against the burn of humiliating tears, pressing the heels of his hands against the lids until he got control. *Fuck.* He didn't stand a chance.

The Games, they called them. A fun time for the vampires, maybe, as they threw humans into the ring like slaves in the Roman arenas, ordering them to fight to the death.

The thought of it had his stomach churning, and had ever since he first learned what the Games were, since he first realized they were sending him in there like some joke. *Useless,* the vampire had called him. *I'm not fucking useless!*

Though, yeah. He was. He couldn't even save himself, let alone his sister and his best friend. Useless didn't begin to describe the worthless piece of shit he'd turned out to be.

If there was any good news, it was that his death would almost certainly be quick. In the arena, they used real swords. Every blow he'd taken today would slice right through him. When the time came for the real fight, he'd die fast.

And there was no doubt in his mind. In two days, he was going to die.

CHAPTER FIFTEEN

Quinn tipped her head against the dusty window frame, peering out at the empty street and that strip of crime-scene tape that marked one of the hot spots, as Jeff called it. One of the places where the sunbeams occasionally broke through, blending the two worlds in such a way that apparently she alone could travel between them. She and whoever was holding on to her as she walked through.

At least that's how they thought it worked.

And the six slaves in this deserted house with her were all counting on that being true. They were counting on her to free them of this place once and for all.

She was hungry—they'd eaten the last of the little bit of food they'd brought in the packs a couple of hours ago—and crazed with the need to head for the gladiator camp. If a sunbeam didn't break through soon, they might just lose their ticket home. It was all she could do to stay here *waiting* when she knew where Zack was. But she'd promised to help the six slaves with their escape back into the real world, and this deserted place was the perfect spot to send them through. If the earth would only rumble.

Jeff appeared on the stairs, followed by the three slaves who'd been watching through the upstairs windows.

"Looks like we're calling it quits," Marcus said quietly.

Finally. She pushed away from the window and went to meet Jeff as he reached the foyer. "It's time to free Zack, then we'll all go through together."

Jeff shook his head. "It's going to be dark in an hour."

Quinn scoffed. "How can you possibly know that?"

Marcus came up beside her. "He's right. You learn to read the light, and it's nearly sunset in the real world."

Dammit. To. Hell. "So now what?"

"We're not far from that safe house. We'll get dinner there and spend the night, then set out again in the morning."

"To the gladiator camp." It wasn't a question. Tomorrow, she was taking charge, and if they didn't like it, they could find their own way home.

Jeff didn't reply. Instead, he turned to the others, motioning them to gather 'round. "The safe house is a Slava hideout. Say nothing about Quinn's being a sorceress. If they find out, they may send for the vamps in order to keep her here to save V.C. and their own skins." He turned and motioned them to follow.

After hours of frustrated boredom, fear once more ate at Quinn's nerves as the now smaller group darted across streets and down alleys, dodging a passing carriage and hiding from a pair of strolling Traders. Finally, down another block, they turned into an alley and came to what appeared to be just one more broken-down doorway. But when Jeff pushed aside the door that hung partly off its hinges, another, far sturdier door appeared behind it.

Jeff rapped lightly on the wood in four places with an even more distinctive series of taps and knocks than the ones she'd heard before. A small section slid back in the middle of the door, just enough to reveal a pair of eyes. Feminine eyes that turned angry. "What do you think you're doing bringing so many here?"

"They're runaways, Barbara. They need shelter."

"No." The eyes moved away. Quinn expected the little slider to slam closed any moment, but Jeff was quicker.

"I bring news."

The eyes reappeared, sharp with interest. "What news?"

"Of the sorcerer."

The little slider slammed shut.

Quinn turned sharply to Jeff. Hadn't he told everyone to not say anything about her?

He lifted his hand with a small wave, a silent *don't worry*.

The door opened, and a woman with long phosphorescent hair, dressed in one of the *Little House on the Prairie* dresses, stood back to let them in. "You'd better have something useful, whelp, or you're all out on your ear. It'll take half of our supplies just to feed all of you."

"Bitch, bitch, bitch," Jeff said under his breath, then led the way inside a fairly large space that looked like it could have at one time been a storeroom. The walls were made of stone, the ceiling, low-hanging wooden beams. The floor was hard-packed dirt overlaid in places by wood-slat flooring. A long, rough-hewn trestle table sat in the middle of the room, chairs all around. Along the edge of the room, small curtains had been hung from the rafters, sectioning off privacy corners for many of the inhabitants. This place, too, smelled of mold and mildew, the air humid and damp. Not exactly the Ritz. But there were no windows, not a one, and a good six oil lamps cast a comforting amount of light.

"Do you see another way out?" Marcus asked close to her ear.

"No. Maybe behind one of the curtains." A single escape route was never a good thing. If the vamps found them, they were trapped. And yet what choice did they have but to stay here? They were out of food, out of water, and she didn't have a clue how or where to scavenge for more.

She hated being dependent on others, hated feeling so helpless. All her life, she'd been a take-charge person, but it was difficult as hell to take charge when she felt like a babe in the woods. And, for all practical purposes, was one. And these woods had big, scary, bloodsucking monsters inhabiting them.

You sense danger, cara. *Be wary of everyone. Each has his own agenda. Be very, very careful, Quinn.*

Arturo's voice was but a low whisper, though a frighteningly clear one, as if he stood at her shoulder, whispering in her ear. As if she needed his reminder to trust no one. All she could do was take the opportunities that came her way and pray she could find a way to make the most of them. Trapped inside a jail cell, she'd been all but helpless. At least out here, she stood a fighting chance.

Barbara started leading them across the room, where more than two dozen people, all with that glowing phosphorescent hair, sat or stood watching the newcomers with as much wariness as Quinn felt. Jeff took another route, leading them instead to a corner, where he plopped down on the dirt. Barbara scowled but turned away in a huff. One by one, the small group slowly sat in the dirt around Jeff, Quinn joining them.

"The first thing I'm going to do when I get out of here is take a shower," one woman muttered.

"I just want to stand in the sun."

Jeff grunted. "I want a huge platter of barbecue ribs and a gallon of ice-cold beer."

"Hug my babies," Celeste replied.

Marcus glanced at Quinn. "You?"

What *was* the first thing she wanted to do when she got out of this place? Honestly, it didn't matter as long as Zack and Lily were with her. But the others were waiting for her answer, so she gave them one. "Get a change of clothes."

Marcus smiled, but his eyes told her he'd read her hesitation right. Her situation was a lot more complicated than the rest of theirs.

"I know your answer," she told him.

His smile died, a fierce flame of love lighting his eyes. "I'm going to hug my wife and hold my child."

The strength of his emotion both bothered her and yet resonated deeply. But hers was a devotion to brother, not spouse. Not child. Could she possibly feel more strongly, or be more weakened by love than she already was? She never wanted to find out. But she would find a way to get Marcus home.

Quinn rose and moved to where Jeff sat, pushing her way between the others to sit beside him. "Are there escape routes out of this place if we need them?"

He stared into the room, neither acknowledging her question nor answering it.

She leaned forward, turning until she was in his face, her voice low. "Are you afraid that if you tell me how to escape, I will, leaving you behind? I wasn't the one who ditched in that stable, was

I? I'm not you, Jeff. I'm not only looking out for myself. If you want my help, you're going to have to start working with me. You're going to have to trust me and start giving me a reason to trust you."

She sat back and waited for him to reply. Because she had little doubt he knew another way out. And if the vamps attacked, he'd escape, leaving the rest of them to fend for themselves.

Finally, he leaned close, his mouth nearly against her ear. "There's an escape hatch at my back, which is why we're sitting here instead of where Barbara tried to seat us."

"Where does it go?"

"To a hallway that leads to the back alley. The spring latch is at the base, where it connects with the floor. You can't see it, but you'll feel it with your fingers. If the vamps raid the place, run for it. It's one of three such escape routes, but the Slavas in this group know them all. The vamps will see us disappearing quickly enough. Most won't escape. Be one of the first to reach the door, and you will. Probably."

When Jeff pulled back, Quinn met his gaze with a brief nod. Then she rose and returned to Marcus's side.

"Did you learn what you wanted to?" he asked quietly.

"I think so. If I tell you to stay close, don't argue."

He smiled at her. "I wouldn't dream of it."

Several minutes later, a man strode across the room toward them, and Jeff rose to meet him. "Richard."

The man was perhaps the oldest she'd seen in Vamp City, over fifty, his phosphorescent hair graying at his temples. "What's this about news of a sorcerer?"

Several of those in her group tensed, but Quinn kept her face impassive as she watched Jeff. He wouldn't give her away, not unless there was something in it for him. And best she could tell, he still wanted to escape.

"There's news that Cristoff has found the sorcerer to save Vamp City."

"Tell me."

"They say he's old, older than you."

Richard's expression tightened at the dig, but he remained silent, encouraging Jeff to continue. Quinn relaxed back against the stone, settling in for the tall tale.

"They say he's a descendant of Blackstone and far more powerful than either of Blackstone's sons, but that he's making demands and refusing to cooperate until they're met."

"What kind of demands?"

"I'm not sure. As soon as I know more, I'll send word."

"Cristoff will kill him the moment he renews the magic."

Jeff nodded. "No doubt about it."

Richard's gaze narrowed as he looked over the

group. "What do you mean to do with this lot?"

"There's a rumor that several new slaves managed to escape V.C. through sunbeams. We're going to try."

The older Slava rolled his eyes. "I've heard this rumor. It's false. And you're fools." He shrugged. "But be my guests and try. You don't have much to lose, do you?" With that, he left them.

Jeff met her gaze with what might have been a smile but was probably a smirk. A short while later, two women brought a couple of large baskets over to them, baskets filled with dried apples and drier rolls, along with a large jug of water. They ate in silence.

With the edge off her hunger, Quinn tipped her head back against the wall to attempt to get some sleep.

"Use my shoulder for a pillow, if you want, Quinn," Marcus said quietly. "Or my thigh. I did two tours of duty in Iraq a few years ago. I can sleep standing up, sitting down, even standing on my head, if I need to."

Quinn smiled. "Thank you. I'm going to take you up on that." She tried getting comfortable against his shoulder and finally gave up, curled up on the floor beside him, and laid her head on his thigh. His warm hand curled around her shoulder, and the last of her tension dissipated. She was safe. For now.

"No! Richard, don't let them hurt him. He's one of the good ones!"

Quinn woke, sitting up as commotion erupted in the hideout. Half a dozen Slava males dragged a seventh, struggling, male into the room.

"He's a monster, Delilah," Richard said coldly. "They're all monsters."

"That's not true!" The woman, an attractive redhead, was growing frantic, and Quinn could see in her face that she had feelings for the captured male.

She glanced at Marcus, watching tensely beside her. "Is he a vampire?"

"I think so."

"I would have thought a vampire could throw them all off. Or dart away."

"They've cuffed him."

Quinn stared in consternation at the vampire, whose hands were clearly unbound. "What do you mean?"

"See the silver chain around his throat?"

She did. Its large links made it look like a choke chain.

"Silver doesn't burn them, but it acts as a powerful damper for their powers if it encircles their heads or necks. You'll never see a vampire wearing a silver necklace. As long as we humans can get our hands on silver, we have a weapon, though a minor one. It's damn hard to collar something that can move faster than the eye can see."

"You have to use something . . . or someone . . . as bait," Quinn murmured. Is that what had happened here? She watched as the vampire was thrown to the floor and chained on his back, spread-eagled.

The woman, Delilah, ran to him, falling at his side. "You idiot! Why did you come after me?"

"I thought . . . you were in trouble."

She slammed her fist against his chest. "I hate you!"

"No," he said quietly. "You don't."

Delilah made a sound like a sob. "Damn you." When she looked up, tears gleamed on her cheeks. "Richard, please. Don't hurt him."

"Don't be a fool, Delilah." Richard turned to one of the other males. "Get her out of here."

"No!" the woman cried.

As one man grabbed her arm and pulled her away, another pulled out a knife and stabbed the vampire in the side, sinking the blade all the way to the hilt.

The vampire threw his head back in pain. The metallic scent of blood, an oddly-spicy-smelling blood, began to fill the room.

A second human stabbed the vampire through the throat as the first human pulled out his knife and stabbed the vamp in the stomach.

Quinn looked away, breathing through her mouth. She neither wanted nor needed to see this. "I thought he had to be stabbed through the heart."

"He does. And only a wooden stake will kill him."

"So they're just torturing him."

"Yes. Taking out their hatred on him."

If it were Cristoff they were stabbing, she'd have watched. She might have even enjoyed it. Arturo? *God, no.*

Delilah sobbed, begging them to stop. "He's done nothing! Hurt no one."

By the time the blood-coated men and women backed away from the prone vamp, Quinn was sick to her stomach. And angry as hell.

"Enough." Richard turned to one of the attackers. "Jose, you get the killing blow. You've lost the most at their hands."

Quinn rose. Marcus grabbed her arm, but she shook him off and stepped into the circle of bloody attackers. "What is this vampire accused of?"

Richard threw her a sharp look of warning. "Proceed, Jose."

A broad-faced, broad-shouldered Mexican stepped forward and positioned himself over the vamp's chest.

"No, Jose!" Delilah cried. "He's not evil!"

"Have we become the monsters, now?" Quinn asked. "Do we kill the innocent because we don't like their eating habits?"

She didn't see the fist coming until it was too late. The male beside her punched her in the mouth, splitting her lip and knocking her back in a minor explosion of pain.

Cara! Arturo's voice.

Careful hands gripped her, pulling her back.

Through tearing eyes, she saw Jose lift a wooden stake. "For my wife and my children," he snarled. And drove the stake down into the vampire's heart.

Delilah screamed, the sound cut off suddenly as Richard clipped her beneath the chin with a swift uppercut, knocking her out. Quinn allowed Marcus to turn her away, to lead her back to the wall. Jesus.

Tell them you're the sorceress, Quinn. Tell them you're their only chance of survival. Don't let them hurt you!

He thought she was the one being tortured.

Jeff moved beside her, his face a mask of fury. "Are you *trying* to get us thrown out?"

"Oh, go fuck yourself." She sank to the ground, angry, frustrated, hurting.

Vampire, if you can hear me, don't follow me here. Please. They've just killed a vampire who I don't think deserved to die. I don't want that to happen to you.

He didn't deserve that kind of death. She wasn't sure anyone did.

These people had suffered too long at the hands of the vampires. They'd had too much taken from them—lives, freedom, loved ones. They'd been tortured repeatedly, whether they remembered each instance or not. And had been made to suffer in God only knew how many ways. They couldn't strike out at the ones they hated, so they struck out at the ones they could. It was wrong. Horribly unfair. And sadly inevitable.

The vampires, through their own cruelty, had created another breed of monster.

Richard stalked over to them, turning a vivid glare on her. "*Out*. You're not welcome here."

She rose, meeting his gaze. "A little truth presents that much of a threat to you?"

Jeff leaped up beside her and grabbed her arm. "Shut it, Blondie." He turned to Richard, his demeanor changing in an instant. "Richard, I'm sorry. If I'd known what a bitch she was, I would never have agreed to bring her along, but I made a promise, and I'm stuck with her. Let her stay until morning, please? Then we'll all go."

Richard snorted. "To find a sunbeam. You're an idiot." His rancor spewed over the lot of them. "You're all idiots! And I want you all out of here at first light." He turned and walked away.

Marcus pulled her back down beside him and put his arm around her shoulders. "You've got a soft heart, Quinn, but soft hearts have a way of getting torn to pieces in this place. I've crossed paths with that vampire before, the one who just died. He had a streak of compassion a lot of vamps lack, but he was far from the paragon Delilah seemed to think he was. More than once, I saw him torture Slavas in front of new slaves just to scare the new ones. Yes, he cleared the minds of the Slavas when he was through, but torture is torture. Even the 'good' ones are monsters, Quinn. The sooner you understand that, the better off you'll be. There's no such thing as a good vampire."

He patted his thigh, and she curled up and laid her head down as she had before, his words living in her head beside thoughts of Arturo. She knew that the vampire couldn't be trusted to tell her the truth, but she had seen goodness in him. At least she thought she had. Was that just one more lie, or was he truly the exception to the rule?

Did it even matter? If she succeeded in escaping Vamp City this time, she would never see Arturo again.

She was lying on the beach, the towel beneath her soft and sun-warmed, the sun a blazing ball in the clear blue sky. A breeze blew across her heated skin, cooling, soothing. Heaven.

A shadow fell across her closed eyelids, and she looked up, blinking at the man standing over her. He was dressed all in black, his skin hinting of the Mediterranean, his dark eyes gleaming with a heat that had nothing to do with the sun.

In the blink of an eye, his shirt was gone, his broad, muscular chest on full display. For her. Only for her. There was no one else on the beach, no one in the world but the two of them.

He wanted her, she could see it in his eyes. And she wanted him.

She only had to think the words and he was kneeling beside her in the sand, lifting her hips as he pulled off her bikini bottoms. Then his hand was between her thighs, his other pulling aside her bikini top as his mouth dipped to claim her now-bare breast. His fin-

gers stroked her sensitive flesh, back and forth, sliding through her wetness, delving into the dark heat of her body.

You were made for me, cara. Though she heard no words, his thoughts flowed freely into her head. *You are mine.*

And then he was over her, his pants mysteriously gone, his cock pressing against her, sliding inside her. And it was good. So good.

Quinn!

Arturo's sharp voice startled her awake and she sat up, blinking in the dim light in confusion. Someone had turned out all but one of the oil lamps.

"You okay?" Marcus asked quietly beside her. Around them, the others slept, some snoring softly.

"Yes. Just . . . dreaming."

Ah, were you asleep, cara? *Were you dreaming of me? I felt your passion rise, and I admit to a strike of jealousy.*

The dream had fled, thanks to him, but she couldn't deny the feeling of restless heat that still throbbed between her legs or the tingling sensitivity of every inch of her skin. That had been one hell of a dream. She supposed she should be grateful for the interruption, or she might have truly embarrassed herself.

I think of you, cara, *constantly. The way your skin smells when you're aroused, the way it flushes a beautiful shade of rose when I stroke my hand over you.*

Quinn groaned. *Go away, Vampire.* If only he could hear her.

If only she could deny she felt any attraction for him. But she tried hard never to lie, especially to herself. She might have seen the last of him, but it would be a long, long time before she forgot Arturo Mazza, her onetime vampire master.

CHAPTER SIXTEEN

The flicker of lanterns beat against her eyelids, waking her. Quinn sat up, feeling more rested than she should, considering her midnight visit. Around her, the others rose as the Slavas once more lit all six oil lamps. With no windows, and no real light either way, morning had to be manufactured.

Jeff came over to them, handed out chunks of hard-as-rock bread. "Eat, then we'll leave." He cut her an annoyed look but didn't say anything more. It wasn't like they'd intended to spend more than the one night here. She certainly hadn't. This morning, she was heading for the gladiator camp and nowhere else. The others could come with her or stay behind. Their choice.

The bread was truly awful, not much better than cardboard, but she managed to get it down. As they rose to go, Delilah came over to them, her eyes swollen and red from a night of crying, her jaw resolute.

"I'd like to travel with you if that's all right."

Jeff looked at her stonily. "It's not."

"Jeff . . ." Marcus said quietly.

"I don't trust a vamp-lover."

Quinn had had enough. "You're welcome to come with me, Delilah."

Jeff rounded on her. "You selfish little bitch."

Quinn whirled until they were face-to-face. "You, who considers no one but yourself, is calling *me* selfish? That's rich."

Temper, cara, Arturo chided.

Oh, shut up, Vampire, she snapped, wishing that for once he could hear her.

"If you want me to lead you—"

She cut Jeff off. "I don't need you half as much as you need me, and you know it."

Marcus's hand landed firmly on her shoulder. "This isn't the place for this discussion."

He was right, dammit. Not unless she wanted Richard and every Slava in here to know she was a sorceress. Maybe a weak one, but a sorceress all the same. Quinn pulled back, folding her arms across her chest. "Delilah comes. Nonnegotiable."

Jeff shook his head in disgust. "You're a fool." He swung one of the packs onto his shoulder and stalked toward the front door.

The others hesitated only a moment before following.

Quinn looked at Delilah, motioning her with her head to join them.

With a look of relief, the Slava fell into step beside her. "Thank you. I'm sorry I've caused you so much trouble."

"Is there ever anything *but* trouble in this place?"

The Slava smiled weakly. "I suppose not."

Jeff led the way outside, where the streets were dim and colorless, faintly lit by the steel gray of day. But Quinn no longer trusted him to lead her to the gladiator camp.

"Do you have your bearings?" she asked Marcus, who'd waited for her.

Delilah touched her arm. "I know exactly where we are. Where do you want to go?"

"The gladiator camp."

Delilah lifted a brow, but asked no questions. "I can take you there."

"Lead the way."

Jeff scowled, but Quinn ignored him.

They walked through the empty streets as they had before, disappearing into the shadows and the old buildings whenever the sound of a carriage or automobile sounded nearby. Quinn thought she heard Arturo's Jeep, but only in the distance. He couldn't find her. She wouldn't allow that to happen.

"How long have you been a Slava?" Quinn asked the woman, as they walked past a block that consisted now of little more than rubble.

"Oh, I don't know. Close to seventy years, I imagine. I was captured only a few months after the stock market crash of '29."

"A little over eighty, then."

"Is it? It makes so little difference here. Nothing ever changes."

"Do you have someplace to go, Delilah?" Marcus asked. "Where we're going . . ."

The woman waved a hand absently. "You're trying to get home, I know. And, yes, I have someplace. My sister is married and free. If I can find her, she'll take me in."

Quinn frowned. "Is she in a hidden enclave, too?"

"Yes. In a way."

Clearly, she didn't intend to say more, and Quinn couldn't blame her. She'd already run afoul of one enclave. The less anyone knew where she was going, probably the better.

They continued on in silence down a couple of blocks of run-down buildings before once more crossing the street. A movement ahead caught Quinn's attention. All their attentions, it seemed, for they stopped as one.

A vampire?

"Wolves," one of the women whispered, the word radiating fear.

Quinn glanced at Marcus. "I thought the wolves lived in the Crux."

"They do," Delilah replied, "but they often hunt in the Nod—the unclaimed boundary lands."

"What do they eat?" The moment the question was out of her mouth, Quinn wanted to take it back. "Do I want to know?"

"Meat," Delilah said simply. "Human or vampire."

Lovely. Vamp City was definitely not a people-friendly place.

In front of her, two of the slaves pulled switchblades out of their pockets. Out of the corner of her eye, she saw Marcus pull one, too.

"One wolf isn't going to take on this many of us," he murmured. "Not when it's obvious we're prepared to fight."

From the building across the street ran another, and another, and still another, until there were ten in all.

"Too bad it's not just one," Quinn muttered.

As the wolves began to circle them, their lips pulled back in hungry snarls, Delilah stepped away from Quinn, into the street, her arms up as if in surrender. None of them called her back. Quinn had a feeling that none of them knew what she was doing.

"I am Delilah," the woman called. "Sister to Nirina, the wife of the alpha of the Herewood pack. I ask that you deliver me to my sister. And I request safe passage for my friends."

One of the wolves, a large gray one, broke from the others and walked to Delilah, sniffing her thoroughly, before backing up several steps. As Quinn watched in amazement, the wolf shifted into a man in a process that was neither fast nor slow, and appeared to cause him little pain. He stood naked, a large man with a hard-boned face and a dark braid that hung halfway down his back.

"You are who you say." He looked at the humans with dispassion. "We'll not take them all, but the price of your passing is two. You may choose which two, if you like."

Delilah shook her head. "They are new to V.C., with wives and husbands and children mourning them in the outside world."

"There is no escape for them."

"There may be. Several of the new ones have managed to escape through the sunbeams." Which was false as far as Quinn knew, but she wasn't about to correct her. "Let these people go, I beg of you. Let them escape this place as we cannot."

The werewolf frowned, eyeing the group of them, then turned back to Delilah. "You will owe me a boon, sister of Nirina." His gaze skimmed the woman's body before slowly, hungrily, returning to her face. "And I will collect."

To Quinn's surprise, Delilah smiled. "Thank you." She turned and ran back to Quinn, throwing her arms around her neck before releasing her. "Godspeed."

"You're going to be okay?" The werewolf was huge. In every way.

A hint of mischief lit Delilah's eyes through the sadness that would remain for some time, Quinn suspected. "I need to forget. And to kick up my heels a bit. He's just what the doctor ordered."

Quinn snorted, then laughed. "Good luck, Delilah."

By the time Delilah turned away, the werewolf had returned to wolf form. He waited for Delilah to join him, brushing against her leg as she ran her hand through his fur. The other wolves followed, and the pack disappeared behind the buildings across the street.

Quinn had been watching for street markings and had seen enough to know they were on

G Street, only about five blocks from her rough understanding of the gladiator camp's location. Finally.

She turned to Marcus as she started walking in that direction. "How am I going to free my brother from the camp?"

He gave her a small grimace. "I've been thinking about that. A lot. I know I said I'd help you . . ."

"But you can't be captured, or you'll be enthralled and enslaved again. If I'm captured and can make them think I'm enthralled . . ."

"You might be able to surprise them as you did the vampire in the stables. That's the only chance I see." He gripped her arm. "I know you don't want to hear this, but it's not much of a chance, Quinn. Maybe no chance at all."

"I know. But it doesn't matter. Do you have any siblings?"

"Two sisters."

"If it were one of them in there?"

He smiled grimly. "No one and nothing would stop me from trying to reach her."

Quinn nodded. But she knew he spoke the truth. Mission impossible, Vamp City style. She was going to need a miracle.

As they reached the corner of the next block, the earth began to shake.

As one, they froze, turning, waiting for the sunbeam. Marcus gripped her shoulder, and she could feel the tense excitement in his touch. This was it.

But when the sun broke through, the closest beam appeared to be at least a block or two away. There was a long line of buildings separating them from it. If it closed quickly, they'd be too late.

"That way!" Quinn said.

Jeff and Marcus both leaped forward. As one, the group took off running to the end of the block, made a quick right turn, and ran down the next block. Quinn had always been a runner, and though she was a little out of shape, she kept up with Marcus and one of the other guys, the others following close behind. She saw no need to wait for anyone. She probably couldn't get them all through at once anyway. And there was no telling how long the light would last. Even if she only got Marcus through, she'd call it a victory.

Quinn rounded the block and finally got a good look at the sunbeam. She groaned. This one didn't conveniently illuminate a spot on the street as the other two had, but spilled its light directly on top of a pile of rubble from a building that had finally lost its fight with time, weather, and gravity. Nothing was ever easy. She darted across the street and onto the dirt, then began picking her way over broken timbers, Marcus at her side.

"This whole pile could collapse, Quinn," Marcus warned. But he wasn't slowing down, not at all, not when his wife and baby lay on the other side of the climb.

Taking her eyes off the timbers for just a moment, she looked into the sunbeam to see what lay on the other side. It appeared to be an office space with cubicles. Huh. Even though it wasn't technically in the sun, it was the part of the real world that occupied this particular space. The office appeared to be empty. If there was anyone there, she couldn't see them, which was a good thing. People dropping in from thin air might raise a few eyebrows.

The boards beneath her feet tilted, nearly dumping her, but she managed to keep her balance and continue climbing. The closer she got, the more the energy crawled along her skin. Finally, balancing upon a mountain of rubble, she was close enough to touch the light. With Zack, the magic had pulled her through, and she couldn't afford for that to happen again, not unless she had time to leap back out again. But perhaps the pull wasn't the same on this side as it had been on the other. She could hope.

She grabbed Marcus's hand. "Give that baby a kiss for me."

The big man pulled her hand to his lips, tears gleaming in his eyes, then swung the pack off his shoulder and onto hers before grabbing her hand again. "Look me up. I want to know that you got out okay."

"I will." When the time was right. When this was over. She grabbed the hand of the man on her other side and told them both, "Walk into the sunbeam."

Carefully, they picked their way forward and

stepped directly into the light, gripping Quinn's hands. For a brief moment, she felt the cool rush of air-conditioned air as the two men stumbled into that office, but no pull of magic. The expressions on the men's faces brought tears to her eyes. Euphoria. Boundless joy. Marcus turned in her general direction, unable to see her, and called, "I owe you," before backing away for the next pair to come through.

A moment later, Jeff was at her side, one of the women at her other, and she pushed the two of them through as she had the first pair, smiling as they jumped together in a triumphant hug.

Quinn turned to watch the plump girl and Celeste making their way up the pile of rubble. From this height, she had a good view of the ruined landscape of Vamp City.

Her pulse started to race, her stomach twisting with the knowledge that escape was within her grasp. And she wanted that—to leave this place and never return—with a desperation that nearly made her ill.

She turned back to the sunbeam, staring at the world she belonged in, a world with fluorescent lights and office furniture and air-conditioning. It would be so easy to step through with the others and leave all this behind. God knew, her chances of saving Zack were about as good as winning the lottery. And it wasn't like she hadn't tried. She'd come back for him, hadn't she? And then gotten herself captured again.

Maybe it was time to save herself. She began to shake with the need to do just that. To escape while escape was at hand.

The two women, helping one another, reached her at the same time. Celeste grabbed for Quinn, then lost her balance, nearly tumbling them all. But Quinn righted her, and, a moment later, the pair were close enough to reach the sunbeam.

"Walk into the light," she told them, and handed them through. As desperately as she wanted to follow, her feet refused to move.

Stepping into the air-conditioned office, the girl squealed in delight. But Celeste's eyes went wide as she clutched her chest and slowly crumpled to the ground. Susie had warned her that once a human turned immortal, there was no going home. Grant had seemed to believe Celeste would make it. And perhaps she would, if they got her medical attention in time.

But as the others rushed toward her, the sunbeam disappeared, leaving Quinn in the dark atop the rubble heap, light-blind, shaking, and very, very alone. For a moment, she'd actually considered leaving Zack behind. But though her mind had considered it, her heart remained steadfastly resolute. She refused to leave Vamp City again without her brother. Which probably meant she'd never leave Vamp City at all.

As her sight returned, she slowly picked her way down the rubble pile, each step feeling heavy and stiff. Two of the others had left their packs on the sidewalk, and she went through them, adding their meager contents to the pack Marcus had given her. In all, she scrounged two stale rolls, half a bottle of water, a flashlight, and extra batteries. Not enough to live on for more than a day but more than enough to last her until she reached the gladiator camp.

With a noisy sigh, Quinn reclaimed her bearings, searching for sign of wolves or vampires, then started out again, alone. A chill crawled down her spine as she crossed the street, a feeling that she was being watched. Perhaps it was just one of the wolves making sure she moved on. Just in case, she pulled out her switchblade and a stake and gripped one in each hand as she walked.

Her chest ached. It was foolish to feel abandoned, but she couldn't help it. And the thought of what came next scared her shitless. Was she really going to walk up to the gates of the gladiator camp and ask to be let in? What kind of a fool-ass move was that? She'd wind up raped, tortured, probably dead. She'd never be able to save Zack. Never. She'd just force him to watch her die.

God, she was such a fool for ever thinking she could do this. She should have escaped with the others.

Quinn.

At the gentle sound of Arturo's voice, she closed her eyes, feeling the sting of tears.

You're not alone, cara. I'm here.

Such simple words, and not entirely true, but

they calmed her all the same. She swallowed the unshed tears, took a deep breath, and let it out slowly, feeling warmed, even comforted, by his presence. Even if that presence wasn't real. Even if that comfort was a lie.

Quinn hadn't traveled more than two blocks alone when a distant shout carried to her on the wind, followed by a chorus of yells. She slowed, looking around. Was that coming from the gladiator camp?

Her steps quickened, her desperation to reach the camp a thrumming need, though she still had no plan for getting inside short of walking up to the nearest vamp and demanding to be enslaved.

The remaining blocks passed quickly, the clack of wood on wood and the occasional shout of pain growing louder. Sweat began to dampen her scalp as she half walked, half ran, driven as much by anticipation as fear. *Zack, buddy, I'm coming.* She wondered how big the camp was, how spread out. Surely, there would be buildings. Maybe even fences, though fences could be climbed. But if the slaves were enthralled, maybe there was no need to fence them. There would be little chance of their escaping.

She hadn't considered what she might do if Zack were enthralled. Would she be able to break through vampire mind control enough to lead him away? So many questions. So many ways for her to fail.

As she turned the next corner, she could see

light rising from behind the line of row houses on the next block. She was nearly there. Quinn darted across the street and back into the shadows closest to the houses, then slowed as she made her cautious way to the corner, where she could peer at the encampment without being seen. As she reached the corner, she pressed her fist to her chest, attempting to quiet her stuttering nerves, praying she might, at last, catch a glimpse of her beloved brother.

But as she pressed back against the building and slowly peered around the corner, her heart fell to her stomach. They'd called it a camp. She'd envisioned something open, accessible. Instead, she stared at a freaking fortress. The brick wall, a good twelve feet high, extended all the way down the block and back at least as far, encompassing an entire city block. Maybe two. Halfway down the block, light gleamed from what appeared, from this distance, to be thick iron-barred gates.

Holy hell. She'd imagined grabbing Zack and slipping away unnoticed. There would be no escaping this place. Her lashes swept down, her jaw tensing, as she absorbed the blow of disappointment.

From behind the wall rang the clack of wood and the shouts of anger and pain. She'd almost certainly found the gladiator camp. But the question remained, was Zack within those walls? Grant had claimed he was. At least, that he had been. But what if she got herself captured and taken inside only to discover that Zack wasn't there?

Maybe there was a way to see inside before she committed herself. Gripping her switchblade and stake tightly, she turned back the way she'd come, deciding to go around the block and try to come at those gates from a different angle—one that might afford her a little cover.

An alley provided the path she'd been looking for and led to a building directly across the street from the gates. Perfect. As always, she approached quietly, carefully, in case this happened to be one of the houses that was actually occupied. As she drew closer, she saw that the door hung askew. Clearly abandoned, like most in V.C.

Cautiously, she slipped inside, the old wood creaking beneath her feet. What little light the day provided barely penetrated the house, but she didn't dare turn on her flashlight with the vampires right across the street. And she could see well enough without it, well enough to make out the stairs to her right. From an upstairs window, she might have the best view. The treads appeared to be intact. Hopefully, they'd hold her weight.

She tried the first step, slowly. While it creaked, it held, and she moved up the stairs, keeping to the better-braced ends rather than the middle. The fourth step cracked, and she quickly moved on to the next, but the rest held. At the top of the stairs, she moved just as cautiously down the hall to the front bedroom, where the smell of mildew was rampant, the furniture crumbling and ghostly-looking in the dim light of day.

One of the windows was still intact but too

thick with dirt to see through easily, so she moved to the broken one, where she discovered a clear view across the street. And into the surprisingly wide gates.

The interior of the camp was well lit, firelight and shadows dancing on the far walls. She could just glimpse one of the torches hanging in an iron holder.

Movement caught her eye through the bars, a line of bare-chested young men, marching as if in formation. A shout, and they dropped to do push-ups, sweat and blood gleaming on their backs. And that's when she saw him. *Zack.* She'd know that mop of curly red hair and that long, skinny back anywhere. That back, now crisscrossed with welts and straining with exertion.

Oh, Zack.

As she watched, a thick-armed brute strode up the line, cracking a whip seemingly at random, knocking one recruit onto his chest, then another. Several more withstood the flick of the whip, continuing with the push-ups as if nothing had happened. The whip scored Zack's flesh, and Quinn gasped. But though Zack's form wavered, he didn't crumble. Her own skin crawled with misery at what he suffered even as she cheered on his determination.

There were no women in the group even though a woman had been chosen to represent Cristoff's kovena. Then again, why bother training the ones who were only there to be slaughtered?

Another shout, and the line of men jumped

to their feet. Zack rose a beat late, for which he earned another lash. Then they were marching off again, out of her sight.

She had to get him out of there. Getting in herself should be easy. It was getting back out again that was going to be the problem. But that was a worry for later. Right now, right this moment, all she cared about was reaching Zack.

Taking a deep, bracing breath, she retraced her path down the stairs, careful to avoid that missing step. But as she reached the back door, a shadow appeared in the doorway.

Her pulse leaped as a second joined it. And a third. All three male. All three with the faintly glowing orange eyes of Traders.

Her heart plummeted. She refused to return to that slave auction. No way in hell. Not when she was so close to reaching Zack.

Quinn flicked open her switchblade and took a step back. If she could make it out the front door and across the street, would the vampires snatch her from these vermin? Or would they let them take her? She didn't know and couldn't risk their choosing the latter. She was going to have to fight off this lot herself.

The Traders weren't particularly big men—no taller than she was, but they moved into the house with a wiry grace that boded ill for her ability to fight off any of them, let alone all three. She'd expected to have to deal with men today, probably even rape. But at the hands of vampires within the gladiator encampment. Not here!

"What do you want?" She tried to keep them in her sights, but the way they were circling her, it was impossible.

"You." The first one eased closer. "An escaped human fetches a higher price than a fresh one. Though you look plenty fresh." He lunged for her.

Quinn struck with her knife, slashing a bloody line across his arm. "Oh, I'm fresh all right."

"Bitch!"

The second two attacked at the same time, and she whirled, kicking back at one as she swung at the other, but this time they were prepared, and she missed on both counts. They circled her, laughing, as she crouched, waiting for their next attack, desperately trying to keep them all in sight.

The first one lunged again, and she struck out, but the moment her arm was extended, the other two pounced on her from behind, knocking the knife out of her hand. Quinn slammed her elbow back, connecting with a nose, and heard a satisfying crack. That attacker fell back with a yell as a second lunged. She lashed out with another back kick, but a hand gripped her ankle, a foot swiped her other foot out from under her, and she slammed onto the floor, back first, her head splintering wood behind her. Pain exploded, her sight shorting out for one terrifying moment before returning in sunburst flashes of pain.

Rough hands groped her breasts as another pair pulled off her boots and reached for the waist of her pants. Terror burst inside her, and she struggled to fight them off, but a third set of hands grabbed her wrists and pinned them high over her head.

Heat began to crawl beneath her skin, rushing from her hands down through her body, an unnatural heat that neither warmed nor burned, reminding her of what she'd felt in the Crux when Grant and Sheridan took her hands. Except there was no pain this time, just a hot itchy feel. Of power? Could she do something this time?

She flattened her palms and pointed them toward the Trader who gripped her arms, imagining him flying backward, away from her, willing it with all her might.

But nothing happened.

Instead, a blinding storm of fear and fury roared through her as her pants and panties were wrenched off, as the man who'd taken them pulled a thick, distended cock from his own pants.

He was going to rape her. They all were. Terror hit her in a blinding rush, and she struggled, kicking out, missing.

And suddenly her would-be attacker flew backward, slamming against the wall. Was that her doing? But she'd barely formed the thought when the man who'd been groping her breasts disappeared just as suddenly in a yell of outrage and pain, and the crunch of bone.

She hadn't done *that*.

The last of her assailants released her hands and leaped up, ready to take on whatever had attacked his comrades.

Only one thing moved that fast. A vampire.

Free at last, Quinn rolled over, away from him, the room spinning sickly as she struggled to crawl away. Slowly, she pulled herself to her feet, wanting her clothes, but choosing escape instead. She stumbled toward the back door, her head pounding, her heart threatening to beat out of her chest.

Behind her, the sound of battle continued, the crack of bone, the cry of pain. Of death. Silence.

And suddenly cold hands gripped her shoulders, shoving her back against the nearest wall. She lashed out, struggling against a grip five times stronger than the Traders' had been.

"Quinn."

A familiar scent filled her senses—that intoxicating scent of almond liqueur. Arturo.

The relief hit her hard, weakening her knees. Tears burned her eyes. But when she would have reached for him, his hold on her shoulders tightened, a punishing grip. She blinked back the tears, her vision clearing, only to be assaulted by his face inches from her own, by the fury in his eyes. Clearly, he hadn't forgiven her for escaping.

She wanted to yell at him that she didn't need this right now. She was shaking, the adrenaline of the attack ricocheting inside her, trying to find a way out.

He gripped her chin, his cold fingers biting into her cheeks as he forced her to look into those furious eyes. "What game are you playing?" His voice radiated with barely leashed violence.

What *game*? How was she supposed to answer that? It was too much. She was shaken, hurting, naked. The tears started to slide down her cheeks. "I found . . . Zack." Her voice caught on the last.

But Arturo wasn't sparing her an ounce of sympathy. His grip on her only tightened, painfully so. "You have power. Loads of it. When I found you just now, your eyes were glowing with it."

She just stared at him and began to sob.

"Answer me!"

"If . . . if . . . I had power, don't you think I would have stopped them?"

For long moments, he didn't say anything, but she felt his grip on her jaw ease. Then he was pulling her into his arms, holding her tightly against him where she so badly needed to be. She clung to him, burying her face against his neck, as the storm of tears swept through, leaving her beaten and exhausted.

Finally, when the storm had passed, she pulled back, swiping the moisture from her cheeks, horribly embarrassed. Naked, crying, helpless—was there anything she was missing to make her humiliation complete?

The vampire's hand slid down her hair. "We need to talk."

A sigh trembled out of her. "I'll tell you everything I can, but it's not much. If I have power, I don't know how to access it." She met his gaze, willing him to understand. "I *tried*, Vampire. When they had me pinned, when he was unfastening his pants, I tried to push him away. *I tried*."

He gripped her face with gentle hands this time. "Shh. You're safe now."

"Did you kill them?"

"Yes."

She nodded, bowing her head again, needing her clothes.

As if she'd spoken the thought aloud, he released her and went to fetch them, then helped her dress with quick, clinical movements.

As she sat on the floor and pulled on her boots, she looked up to find him watching her, frowning. "I saw Zack. He's in the gladiator camp."

A look of disgust crossed his face. "And I suppose you were planning to ask them to let you in?"

She returned her concentration to her boots, choosing not to answer that derisive question.

"Do you know how many would have raped you? And drank your blood? They'd have killed you!"

Boots on, she rose and met his gaze, knowing there was desperation in her own. "Help me get him out of there. Please?"

But all she got was a scowl in return. "You ask the impossible." He clasped her arm in a steel grip and steered her through the front door, where his yellow Jeep sat.

The last hope that he might still help died as he shoved her into the front passenger seat, then drove off, gripping her wrist to keep her from escaping again.

Quinn turned away, her elbow on the window opening, the wind raking her hair back from her face as the tears once more began to roll. He refused to bend. And she'd lost this fight one too many times.

Deep within, her soul withered, crumbling, as the last hope of saving her brother slowly died.

CHAPTER SEVENTEEN

Quinn's head pounded, her heart cold and aching, as Arturo led her up the steps of Gonzaga Castle and into the grand foyer. She should be terrified to be back here, but she felt nothing. Empty.

She'd failed. Cristoff would never allow her to escape a second time. And Zack would soon be dead.

The castle once again streamed with music and laughter, the foul joyousness of a savage and dangerous race.

"Where is Cristoff?" Arturo asked one of the guards strolling through the foyer.

"In the throne room, Arturo."

Arturo gave a nod, took her upper arm, and led her up the wide staircase and down the hall to the room where she'd seen the burned and naked woman being fed on by four vamps. That might end up being her fate if she failed to call the magic a second time.

She couldn't summon the will to care.

Outside the doorway, Arturo stopped, pulling her around to face him. She glanced at him, noticing the regret in his expression before she looked away.

"I am sorry, *cara*. It is a hard world we live in."

She said nothing. What was there to say?

Arturo sighed, touching her hair, then turned her back toward the large double doors, opening one to lead her inside. The room was empty this time but for Cristoff and a pair of guards, one standing on each side of the dais. Dressed in a bloodred silk caftan with intricate gold embroidery on the stand-up collar and cuffs, Cristoff sat upon the great throne with a naked woman draped across his lap as he sucked at her neck. He glanced up, his gaze landing on Quinn, his eyes hardening. He pushed the unconscious woman onto the floor as if she were so much trash, wiped his bloody mouth on his sleeve, and rose.

Quinn's apathy fled. Her heart began to beat a frantic rhythm as the vamp master strode toward her, human-slow, drawing out the moment to a fine-honed edge. Arturo made a sound of pleasure deep in his throat, and she growled and glared at him, jerking her arm free of his hold. To her surprise, he let her go, stepping aside as Cristoff reached her. Anger crackled in the vampire's eyes, and he grabbed her hair. Pain tore across her scalp as he wound it around his fist and lifted her onto her toes. Tears bloomed until she could barely see the cruel face inches from her own.

"How *dare* you escape me. Who released you?" He jerked her up higher, and she cried out at the pain. "*Who?*"

"Celeste. And Marcus." Which was true enough. And they were safely out of his reach.

He turned to Arturo. "Call Kassius."

"Yes, Master." Out of the corner of her eye, she saw him turn and go, leaving her alone with this monster.

Her fear spiked even as she knew Arturo's staying wouldn't help her, not at all. Because *he* wouldn't help her. Not against his master.

Cristoff backhanded her hard, splitting her lip. Tears scorched her eyes, blurring his angry countenance, hiding his hand as he hit her again, and again. The coppery taste of her blood ran over her tongue, her cheeks running wet with tears. Finally, he released her, tossing her by her hair. She landed hip first on the marble floor, crying out from the shattering pain. The taste of blood coated her mouth until she thought she would vomit.

She tried to roll off her injured hip, but fell back, biting down to keep from crying out. *Damn Arturo. Damn him to hell.*

Finally, the traitor returned, Kassius at his side. As she stared at Arturo, hating him, his jaw turned hard, but nothing in his expression gave any indication of regret. Or apology. How she wished she'd gone through that sunbeam with the other slaves.

No, she didn't. She'd have never been able to live with herself if she'd abandoned Zack without one last try to save him. Now, she probably wouldn't live at all.

"Bite her," Cristoff commanded. "Tell me who freed her and how."

Kassius loomed over her moments later, kneeling beside her, compassion in *his* gaze, at least. "My bite won't hurt, and it will help you heal," he said quietly. Then more loudly, "Think of your escape, sorceress, and it will go more easily for you."

As he lifted her into his arms, Quinn cried out as pain exploded in her hip at the movement. When he bit her seconds later, she felt no pain. And within moments, the fire in her hip began to ease.

Cool lips clamped onto her flesh as Kassius pulled at her blood. The sensation was pleasant enough though without the passion she'd felt the couple of times Arturo had bitten her.

Something began to happen.

Her vision spun and she reached out, gripping Kassius's arm. When her vision cleared, she was seeing through another's eyes in a land . . . and time . . . far, far away. Not only seeing. She felt the sun beating down on her sweating back, tasted dust and her own blood in her mouth. Felt the pounding of her heart and heard the roar of the crowd as she stood in a sunbaked arena, her body moving with strength and speed, her blade swinging, stabbing, drawing blood from her opponent—a man dressed in the short, leg-baring armor of a Roman gladiator. She was strong. Invincible. Her blade swung again, slicing open her opponent's neck. The man went down. Sweat dripped into her eyes as a cheer went up from the crowd, chanting, "Kassius! Kassius! Kassius!"

These were his memories.

Her sight twisted, the scene changing, and she was carrying a heavy load into a cage, hunger rumbling in her belly. The door clanked shut behind her, but she didn't care. She tossed her burden onto the dirt floor at her feet. The gladiator she'd just killed. She tore off his armor and clothes, tossing them aside, then stripped off her own. The moment she was naked, she fisted her hands, threw back her head, and called on the power within her, feeling it answer in a primal howl and a rush of glorious pain.

Suddenly, she was on the floor, on four feet, her snout long, her mouth watering from the smell of blood and flesh.

She ripped into the dead man's abdomen, the meat fresh and delicious, the juices running into her mouth.

Her stomach heaved. The room spun again, and she was back in Cristoff's house of horrors, in Kassius's arms, sweating, shaking. Stunned.

Kassius jerked back, his mouth bloody, his dark eyes wide as he stared at her in shock. Then he blinked, hiding his thoughts behind a mask of calm. She'd thought he was a vampire. He *was* a vampire. But was he a wolf, too? Had anything she'd seen been real? He licked his lips of the blood and set her on her feet beside him, angling that big body between her and Cristoff. Her hip felt bruised but no longer broken. Amazing. She had to get these vampires to bite her more often.

Her gaze found Arturo, who stood stiffly across the room, his face hard as stone.

"Well?" Cristoff demanded.

"Two slaves freed her," Kassius replied. "Marcus and Celeste."

"Who ordered them to do it?"

"The sorceress believes the slaves were acting on their own. There was a group of them looking for escape from Vamp City. They banded together to free her, hoping she could help them leave through a sunbeam."

"How did they get her out of the castle?"

"She has no memory of it. They knocked her out. She awoke in a ruin somewhere in the Nod. A sunbeam broke through nearby soon after, but vamps caught a couple of their group, and they scurried back into hiding."

Kassius was lying. Why? To protect the Slavas? She'd seen how he appeared to care about them. Or was his intent to go after them himself?

"Where are the rest of them, now?"

"A few more were recaptured, a few killed. The rest scattered, and she became separated from them and lost in the Nod. That's where Arturo found her."

He was lying through his teeth. Or making it up. Either way, she was grateful he hadn't implicated Grant or spilled the location of the tunnels. Although he knew about them now, which might still spell disaster. If she ever got the chance, she'd have to warn Grant.

"Leave us."

At Cristoff's command, Kassius walked away without a backward glance, joining Arturo. Shoulder to shoulder, they left her with the devil.

In the blink of an eye, Cristoff's hand was tight around her upper arm. His face inches from her own as her heart thudded in her chest.

"You're mine, sorceress. *Mine.* If you ever try to escape me again, I'll cut off your feet. Then we'll see how far you get." He shifted his hold, pulled her back against him, pushing her head to the side, and struck. His fangs sank into her neck with a fire unlike anything she'd ever suffered—as if he'd stabbed her with a tuning fork red-hot from the coals.

And she screamed.

Quinn moaned, the pain a beast inside her, devouring her with its teeth, searing her with its fire. Life had become nothing but darkness and heartache and agony as she lay chained to the floor of this unlit bare stone cell.

Two days had passed since she had seen Zack in the gladiator camp. Every time the slave arrived to force water down her throat, she asked. *Two days.* The Games were past, she knew that, too.

Zack was dead.

Pain lanced her heart, the worst pain of all. She'd failed him.

The beast roared, searing through her flesh and mind, devouring all thought, all memory of what she was or had ever been. Even in the midst of the fire, she felt a terrible coldness of the heart, the mind, the soul.

Tears slipped down her cheeks to run into her hair. She prayed for oblivion. Unconsciousness. Death.

Finally, blessedly, sleep swallowed her once more.

Arturo strode through the dark, musty dungeon deep below the castle, his hands fisted at his sides, his heart cold with an anger directed at Cristoff, at Quinn, but mostly directed at himself. He'd told himself he was washing his hands of her. There was nothing he could do for her. She was no longer his concern. Until a few minutes ago, when Kassius informed him she was being held in one of the dungeon cells. His blood had run cold.

Why had he let himself get involved with her, a human? A sorceress. The woman had caused him nothing but trouble from the moment he'd found her. If only someone else had been the one to pluck her from the greedy grasp of that out-of-control vampire.

Now she was Cristoff's prisoner, possibly their savior. Kassius had told him what happened when he'd bitten her a couple of days ago. How her magic had reached out and grabbed him, how he'd sensed a vast store of power in her, rippling in the darkness. Untapped. Possibly unreachable.

Kassius had kept that to himself, sharing it only with Arturo. Kas's loyalty to his master was not as absolute as Arturo's, but, then, it never had been.

And while Arturo's loyalty to Cristoff was solid, he would never betray his friend.

He opened the small cell door and stared in dismay at Quinn, lying unconscious on the stone floor in the dark, her face swollen and bloody. Her neck . . . *Jesus.* He fell to his knees beside her, touching her skin. She was burning up, not with fever, but with dragon fire. Cristoff had bitten her, using his unique poison to enflame the flesh until the puncture wounds were bright red and swollen to the size of a ripe plum. He'd seen Cristoff use this particular form of torture before. The pain he caused with it was excruciating, and Cristoff always fed well off that pain. But Cristoff wasn't anywhere near close enough to feed off Quinn's. He'd poisoned her for the pure satisfaction of knowing she suffered. Knowing her mind could never be cleared of the memory.

Damn him.

Fury tore through him and he flew to his feet, slamming his hand into the wall, shattering stone. He never questioned Cristoff's actions. *Never.*

He couldn't blame his master for punishing her. The sorceress had escaped them, knowing many would die if she failed to save V.C. But *this* was beyond unnecessary. Still, she'd thwarted the most powerful vampire in Vamp City. If she hadn't been needed to renew the magic, Cristoff would have killed her for that offense. If her magic proved useless, he still would.

With a shake of his head, he forced himself to harden his heart as he'd done all too many times over the centuries. How many times had he looked away? How many times had he turned a blind eye or a deaf ear to the torture, to the barbarity? Too many to count, and he would continue to do so because he was a vampire. An Emora. This is what they were.

And he was loyal to his kind, to his kovena. Above all, to his master.

Quinn Lennox, like so many before her, could not be his concern.

But as he turned toward the door, she stirred, the low sound of misery in her throat damning him.

He couldn't help her. She was suffering as Cristoff wanted her to, and he must leave her the way he'd found her.

Golden lashes fluttered up, her brows drawn in terrible pain above green eyes swimming in agony.

Her fear poured forth, sinking into his pores, sliding down his throat, easing his terrible hunger. A fear he both craved and detested. He didn't want her fear. Not hers.

The darkness. He could see perfectly well despite the lack of light, but with her human eyes, she could not. All she knew was that someone was in there with her.

"It is me, *cara*. Let me find a light." He lit the oil lamp that had been left in the corner for her, a lamp she'd probably not even known was there.

He turned to find her watching him as her fear slowly began to fade. In her eyes, he saw no damnation, no hatred, no bitterness. Nothing but a terrible emptiness. And an unbearable pain that killed something inside of him.

All his reasoning fell away as the sheer need to relieve her suffering slew his better judgment. Kneeling beside her, he gathered her into his arms, aching at the sound of her agony as he moved her that small amount. Dipping his head, he bit into her wound, sucking out the poison, which could not hurt him, as he drank a small amount of her blood. His feeding on her should alleviate some of her pain and promote the healing of her other wounds.

He couldn't think about the anger, the betrayal, he'd see in Cristoff's eyes when his master realized what his *loyal one* had done. The only thing that mattered at this moment was Quinn.

As the horrible tension in her body slowly eased, he drew back from the sweetness of her blood before he stole too much and found her gazing at him with confused, weary eyes.

"Vampire?"

He brushed her damp hair back from her face. "Sleep, *cara*. You are safe."

Her eyes softened with a pain of a different kind. "Please don't make me believe in you again. It hurts too much when you betray me."

Her words sliced him open. "I have warned you over and over against trusting me."

"And yet I keep doing it anyway."

"Don't." His muscles bunched to push her

away, to rise and leave her there. But before he could lower her back to the stone floor, her eyes drifted closed, and she slept again.

He stared at her throat, at the slowly healing wound. Never had he gone against Cristoff's wishes. Never. His master would not be pleased. But what was done was done.

He settled on the floor, pulling Quinn firmly onto his lap, tucking her head against his neck. For a long, long time, he sat like that, stroking her hair and back, feeling her warm breath against his throat and listening to her heart beat. It would take time for the poison to fully leave her system, but, little by little, she melted against him, and he knew that the worst of the pain was gone.

He pressed his cheek to her sunlit hair and wondered what in the hell he was going to do.

CHAPTER EIGHTEEN

Quinn woke, blinking her eyes against the soft lamplight. She was alone in the small cell, feeling almost human again. Her neck still burned though nothing like before. She'd dreamed Arturo had come and taken the worst of the pain. Had it been a dream?

She pushed herself up, looking around clearly for the first time. Her cell was small, and bare, the floor and walls stone, the door heavy wood slats. This place made her first cell look like a room at the Ritz. On the floor below one wall lay a smattering of dust and stone fragments. In the wall above was a divot the size of a man's fist.

Shoving her hair off her face, she leaned back against the wall, still hurting, trying to remember . . .

Memory returned like a fist to her heart, and she doubled over against a pain a dozen times worse than what she'd felt before.

Zack.

She didn't cry. She had no tears left, just a cold, dead numbness. For minutes, maybe hours, she sat like that, struggling to breathe through the pain.

A key rattled in the lock, her door swinging open, but she didn't get up. There was nothing they could do to her that would be worse than what they'd already done. Killing her brother.

It was Arturo who came through the door, a tray in his hand, the smell of food wafting in with him. She hadn't thought to see him again. She didn't want to see him now.

Without a word, he placed the tray on the floor, then turned to her, a pensive look on his face. With a frown, he squatted in front of her and reached for her neck.

"Don't." She jerked back.

His fingers stroked her jaw instead. "I'll not hurt you, Quinn. Let me take more of the poison."

She was about to say no when her mind caught the implication of that last word. "Poison?"

"Dragon fire virtually immobilizes a human with pain. Few vamps possess it. Cristoff secretes it through his fangs when he wants to. I took most of it while you slept, but it's not gone. I need to take the rest.

She stared at him, at this male who'd never hurt her with his touch yet had slain her over and over with his actions. Even as she hated him, she trusted him not to hurt her physically. And she was tired of the pain.

His knuckles stroked her cheek. "My fangs will bring you no pain, *cara*, not even where it already hurts." With gentle fingers, he brushed the hair from her shoulder, then dipped his face to her neck, and she let him. His mouth closed around the flaming wound, but true to his word for once, his bite did not hurt. She reached for him, her hands stroking his shoulders, her instinct to hold on and not let go. But then she remembered who he was . . . Cristoff's snake . . . and dropped her hands to her thighs.

Slowly, the fire ebbed, and a rush of pleasure took its place on the next draw of blood. She fought that rising tide, gripping the vampire's head to dislodge him.

"Don't. No more."

He lifted his head, his breath warm on her cheek. "Let me bring you pleasure."

"No. I don't want that. I don't want anything from you."

He turned her to face him, licking the blood off his lips. "You're still hurting," he said softly.

She jerked away from his touch, spearing him with her hatred.

His jaw hardened, and he turned and picked up the tray from the floor. "You need to eat."

"I'm not hungry." But her stomach rumbled, making a liar out of her. She'd eaten nothing in days.

Arturo set the tray on her lap, then sat across from her, his long legs brushing hers, barely able to stretch out in the cramped space. Dispassionately, she eyed the meal—a roll, a bowl of pasta with some kind of cream sauce, and a chicken thigh. She picked up the mug of beer and took a long, cold sip that tasted far too good going down and only exacerbated her hunger.

Picking up her fork, she twirled a length of pasta on it, then put the bite in her mouth. The food melted on her tongue, and she took another bite, and another, until most of the meal was gone.

Finally, as she picked up the soft roll and dug her thumbs in to tear off a piece, Arturo spoke. "Tell me about Zack."

Her brother's name on the traitor's lips was like a punch in the gut. It left her gasping. "Why?"

"Because I want to know. Because he was important to you."

She stared at him, still struggling to breathe.

"Because I'm sorry," he added softly.

Her eyes teared as she fought back the slug of grief. "He was all I had."

"Tell me, *cara*."

She ate the roll slowly, sinking within her memories, not wanting to share Zack with this man who could have saved him. Yet she desperately needed to talk about him with someone. And for better or worse, Arturo was it.

"My mom died when I was two," she began. "My dad remarried a year later. Angela and I hated one another on sight. She didn't like that I was the daughter of the woman who'd been the love of my dad's life. But more than that, I think I scared her. Weird things happen to me sometimes. I think it was worse when I was little."

"You had less control."

"I've never been able to control them."

"What kinds of weird things?"

"I don't know. Random things that only happened once. The flowers changing colors or the cat barking like a dog. Or the car horn suddenly playing the tune to 'Row, Row, Row Your Boat.'"

Arturo smiled softly. "And those scared her?"

"By themselves, probably not. But every now and then, my eyes changed."

He nodded. "They glow as if a light has been turned on behind the irises."

She blinked. "How do you know that?"

"It happened when you were trying to fight off those Traders near the gladiator camp."

"That's why you got so mad."

"Glowing eyes are the mark of great power. Neither Grant nor Sheridan's eyes have ever glowed. But their father's did."

"And Cristoff knows," she said dully.

"As a matter of fact, he does not."

She looked at him with surprise. "You didn't tell him?"

"I have not told him, not yet. I'll decide when and if to do so when the time is right." Of course he would. "So your stepmother was afraid of your eyes?"

"And the fact that I pushed her against the wall after she spanked me when I was six."

"You were strong."

"I pushed her without touching her."

He watched her with interest. "You had power."

"I did. Then. I've tried to call it since I got here, and it's deserted me."

"Your father? Did he protect you from this woman who disliked you?"

"He threatened to send me away if I ever hurt her again."

"I'm sorry."

Quinn shrugged. She'd long ago lost respect for the man who should have been her champion and instead only ever backed her enemy. "When I was five, Zack was born, and as much as I hated Angela, I loved that baby. As he got older, he followed me everywhere. It drove Angela crazy. She'd send me to the corner to punish me, and he'd join me there. She'd spank me, and he'd come put his arms around my waist." The tears started to slide down her cheeks until she couldn't go on. "He loved me, Vampire. He's the only one who ever did." Sobs caught in her throat, the grief rushing up in a crushing wave until she was drowning beneath the weight of it.

The tray left her lap, and a strong arm went around her shoulders, a rough cheek brushing her hair. And she needed that arm, she needed that cheek. She needed to believe someone cared, even a little, that she was dying inside.

The tears refused to abate this time, and she cried until her head ached, until she felt sick to her stomach, until she could barely breathe and didn't want to anymore. Finally, the sobs turned to hiccups, and the storm passed, leaving wreckage in its wake. With a shuddering sigh, she pressed her wet face against the vampire's shoulder, accepting the comfort he offered, needing it badly.

His hand was in her hair, stroking, soothing. "He was always there for you," he said quietly.

She nodded against his shoulder. "Always. We grew up in Pennsylvania, but I moved to the D.C. suburbs after school and never went back. Zack chose his college based on proximity to me. When he got into G.W., I moved into the city and rented an apartment. We've been living together for three years. I thought it was going to kill me when he moved to California next spring to take a job out there." Now he'd never go. "Lily would have gone with him."

"His girlfriend?"

"She would have been eventually. They've been best friends for three years, and she's in love with him, but he was too clueless to see it. Sooner or later, he'd have figured out what Lily and I already knew. That they were perfect together. She's the reason I'm here. She went missing. Zack and I were looking for her when I saw your world. He reached into the sunbeam to pick up a pen he recognized as hers. I grabbed him. The magic grabbed us both and sucked us in."

He stroked her hair, over and over, as she leaned against him, absorbing his strength. As usual, she was finding it hard to hold on to her hatred of him. He'd told her from the beginning he couldn't save Zack. That it was impossible. And in the end, he hadn't even tried. But he hadn't lied about that, at least.

He might be seriously lacking, as friends went, but he was the only one she had.

She sat up and wiped her face, then reached for her beer and downed it quickly, wishing she had a couple more.

Arturo stood, lifted the tray, then looked down at her for several moments, his expression pensive. Without another word, he turned and left, leaving her alone and trapped but without pain. And with a heart ever-so-slightly lighter for his having asked about Zack, then actually listened when she told him.

As long as she lived, Zack lived inside of her.

However short a time that might be.

With the pain gone and her hunger satisfied, Quinn's natural restlessness quickly reasserted itself. Pacing was out of the question since the entire cell was barely five feet by five feet. Instead, she did push-ups against the wall and a few dozen squats.

What would happen now? How badly would the shit hit the fan when Cristoff discovered her free of pain again, his dragon poison out of her system? Maybe he'd think it had just worn off. She was, after all, a sorcerer with a few quirks that seemed to surprise them all.

She was doing more wall push-ups when the door swung open behind her, stilling her heart until she saw Arturo. He closed the door behind him, his gaze grabbing hers, his expression strained and tense. "Do you trust me?" he demanded without preamble.

"No."

The tension left his face, his eyes crinkling with silent laughter as a smile lifted his mouth. "Smart girl." But the humor fled as quickly as it appeared. "I need you to trust me, now, *cara*. I am setting you free and risking both our lives in the process. Cristoff can never know it was me who freed you this time."

She stared at him, afraid to believe him. Afraid to leave. "He threatened to cut off my feet if I ever tried to escape him again."

Arturo's grim expression told her he thought Cristoff would probably do it, too. "I won't let that happen."

Could she trust him this time? Did she have a choice? If Cristoff kept her full of dragon fire, feet wouldn't matter. She'd be in too much pain to move, let alone walk.

"Where are you taking me?"

"To my house, for now. Where he'll not hurt you."

Something inside her melted, just a little. "Thank you."

"Kassius will come for you while I attend this evening's banquet. Do as Kassius says."

Her stomach fluttered with excitement and nerves. "I will."

He gripped the back of her head and kissed her, a soft brush of cool lips, warming her from the inside out. Pulling back, he watched her with fathomless eyes. "I want you in my bed. I will *have* you in my bed. But your screams will be of pleasure, not pain."

He left as abruptly as he'd come, leaving her

wondering just what he wanted from her. Sex, certainly. Was that all? Was he risking the wrath of his vampire master to have her to himself for a little while longer? She supposed it wouldn't be the first time a man had risked everything for sex.

If he got her out of here, if he saved her from Cristoff, she'd never say no to him again.

At least, not until the ground began to shake and she once more found a way to escape Vamp City through a sunbeam. Once and for all.

CHAPTER NINETEEN

Kassius entered her tiny cell, a big black bag over one broad shoulder. He closed the door behind him, watching Quinn with more wariness than she watched him.

"Has Ax told you the plan?"

"Only that he's getting me out of here and that I'm supposed to trust you." She wrinkled her nose. Something did *not* smell good.

"Is trusting me going to be a problem?"

"You're a wolf."

Surprise lit his eyes. "How do you know that?"

"I saw it when you bit me."

He studied her for a moment, his expression enigmatic. "I was born a werewolf. Caught by the Romans. Turned into a vampire."

"So you're both."

"A werevamp. We're not common, but I'm far from unique." He frowned. "Having seen what you did, you still don't fear me."

"I trust you." She shrugged. "As much as I trust any vamp." Which was the truth. There was something about this male that she liked, though *why*, she wasn't entirely sure. Instinct, she supposed.

For all the good her instincts had done her lately.

Besides, Arturo trusted him completely. Which really shouldn't be a rousing recommendation but somehow was. "So what's the plan?"

"To get you out of the castle without Cristoff's knowing we're involved." He pulled the bag off his shoulder.

"Is that what I think it is?"

A smile lit his eyes. "What do you think it is?"

"A body bag." No wonder it smelled bad.

"Then, yes. It is. And since it's imperative you act like a boneless corpse, I'm going to have to knock you out. I won't hit you any harder than I have to."

Quinn's eyes went wide as she took a deep breath and wondered if she was being a fool yet again for trusting vampires. What the hell. She didn't have a lot to lose at this point. "Okay. Shoot."

A flicker of admiration crossed his features a moment before the lights went out.

The smell hit her first, before she was even fully awake, a horrendous stench of decomposing meat. The bouncing vehicle and roar of the Jeep's engine brought it all flooding back. Kassius. The body bag. *Eeuw.*

You're safe, cara. *Be still.* Arturo's calming voice slid through her mind. *Just a few more minutes. We're almost there.*

She struggled to breathe through her mouth, trying not to think of where she was, of what had been in the bag before her. Instead, she remembered why she was in the bag. Cristoff. *Zack.*

Grief sucker punched her all over again, stealing what breath she'd managed to pull into her lungs. The pain was almost too much to bear. She wondered if this would happen every time she woke, this remembering. This agony.

Finally, the Jeep came to a halt. A moment later, she felt herself being lifted and slung over a shoulder. *Boneless*, Kassius had said. She did her best impression of a dead body as Arturo carried her up a couple of steps, then across a wooden floor, finally depositing her on something nice and soft. The sofa? Huh. If it were her sofa, she sure as heck wouldn't want a body bag on it. Certainly not one that smelled like this one. But she had to appreciate the soft landing.

She heard the zipper slide, then fresh air was rushing into her lungs. Arturo's hands slid beneath her arms, and he lifted her up and out as if she were a toddler and not a full-grown woman. They were in a living room, as she'd suspected— an old-fashioned, if decidedly masculine room, with dark wood paneling, heavy draperies, and bookshelves lining two of the walls.

Lamplight flickered over his face as he gripped her chin, tilting her head this way and that. "He didn't hit you too hard?"

"No, I'm fine. Other than the smell that probably singed off my nose hairs."

"I shall have a talk with Kassius about using

cleaner body bags in future." At his deadpan expression, she almost smiled. Warmth and concern lit his eyes, and he stroked her jaw. "You are safe here."

She nodded, then pulled herself out of her misery and focused on him, lifting her hand to touch his jaw in return. He stilled, then leaned ever so slightly into her touch. "Thank you for getting me out of there."

His fingers slid into her hair, and he dipped his head, brushing his lips against hers. The kiss felt nice, stealing a measure of her grief, if only for a moment. She wanted more. She wanted to forget. Pulling back, she slid her hands to cup the back of his neck. "I must smell like death."

A smile lit his eyes. "You smell like sunshine, *cara*. You could never smell bad to me." Then he pulled her fully into his arms and kissed her with a fierce, drugging hunger as if he understood her need to forget. His mouth opened over hers, his tongue sweeping inside to lay claim, to plunder and dance and taste. She kissed him back, lost in the heady passion, her body heating, trembling. The terrible ache in her chest eased, and she was filled with gratitude. In that moment, it didn't matter that he was a vampire. Or that he was partly to blame for her loss. He was heat and light and life, and she needed that, needed him.

His mouth left hers, trailing kisses across her jaw, down her throat. Then he pulled back and took her hand. "Come." As he led her to the stairs, she knew where they were going. To the bedroom.

To have sex. And she was ready for it, ready to lose herself in passion and forget everything else.

His hand tight around hers, he ushered her up the stairs and to the bedroom . . . her bedroom. Opening the door, he released her hand and stood back for her to enter.

As she stepped into the room, she faltered. There was someone on the bed. *Curly red hair.* The blood drained from her face and she swayed. *Zack.* He'd brought her the body.

"He's alive, *cara*," the vampire said quietly behind her.

Alive. The tears started to roll, and she took a tentative step, then another. She reached for her brother's bare shoulder slowly, her hand touching warm, vibrant, *living* flesh. "Zack." The word came out on a sob.

Her brother moved suddenly, and she jerked back as he rolled over. He blinked sleepily. "Quinn." The word croaked in his sleep-roughened voice. Then, unaccountably, he rolled back over, giving her his back.

She sat on the bed beside him, struggling against the tears that refused to cease, her mind stunned, her heart soaring. *Zack was alive!*

He wore faded, worn black pants of some kind and nothing else, his torso and feet bare, lash marks crisscrossing his back every which way, making her ache. She reached for him, her fingers in his mop of red hair.

"Go away, Quinn," he muttered with an edge of temper that was so unlike her brother. His rejection stung, but it barely penetrated her euphoric relief.

Arturo's hand landed lightly on her shoulder. "Come, *cara*. Let him sleep."

The last thing she wanted to do was leave Zack when she'd just found him again. When she'd thought he was *dead.* But he clearly wanted to be alone, and she'd give him anything. *Anything.* Even that.

She turned away, and Arturo curled his arm around her shoulder as he walked her out the door, closing it behind them. She opened her mouth to speak, but he put a finger to his lips and led her into the room across the hall, closing the door behind him.

This room was decorated similarly to the one she'd been staying in, though it was slightly larger, the plain wood bed mahogany instead of maple, the floral bedspread and canopy a navy blue instead of beige.

"He's been through a lot, *piccola*," he said, turning to her. "Do not take it personally."

She nodded, her emotions a wild tangle. She didn't know how to feel.

"Your brother is ashamed," Arturo said quietly.

Her gaze jerked to his. "Of *what*?"

"Of not being able to rescue the women he cares about."

"But that's ridiculous. He's just a kid!"

"He is not a kid, *cara*. He is a man. And he would have died as one in the arena had I not intervened."

"You took him from the gladiator camp?"

Arturo nodded. "I did. I'm not always the monster you believe me to be."

Quinn pulled away. "I'm not so sure about that. You also do nothing without a reason, Vampire. Why did you free him after you told me so many times to forget about him?"

He curved his arm around her waist, pulling her back against him, hip to hip. "Perhaps I wanted your gratitude."

"*Please.* If you wanted my gratitude, why did you make me think he was dead? Why did you ask me about him and let me sob with grief over him, never telling me you'd saved him?"

He looked away, which wasn't like him.

"What aren't you telling me, Vampire?"

With a sigh, he turned back to her. "Nothing, *cara.* I saved him on a whim after watching Cristoff hit you. I felt . . . guilty. But I had not yet considered betraying my master. I thought only of saving your brother, not what I was going to do with him after I did."

"And what *are* you going to do with him?"

He shrugged. "Horace could use some help, perhaps." He nudged her back against the door and nuzzled her neck. "Are you grateful?"

Her hands went reflexively to his shoulders to hold him away, though, of course, she couldn't budge him. "You know I am."

Lifting his head, he peered into her eyes, his own smoky hot. "Show me."

Quinn met that smoky gaze, her emotions

slowly untangling. She would never fully trust this man, but, dear God, he'd given her back her brother. At risk to himself. If that didn't balance the scales with his betrayals, it came damned close. Closing her eyes, she released her frustration, letting her immense joy and gratitude wash over her all over again. Then sharing it with him as she cupped his face and kissed him without reservation, holding nothing back. With a deep moan of satisfaction, he pulled her tight against him, slanting his head to kiss her back, deeply, thoroughly, his tongue sweeping into her mouth, his lips drinking of her own. Picking her up, he carried her to the bed and laid her down gently. One by one, he removed her boots and dropped them to the floor, then he pulled off his shirt.

He was beautiful, his shoulders broad, his chest well muscled, his abs hard and lean. He made quick work of her clothes, leaving only her panties. Long fingers circled her thighs, caressing, teasing. "You're mine tonight." The faintest question laced his words. He wanted her acquiescence.

And she gave it to him. "Yes."

The smile that lit his eyes was hot and dangerous and very, very male. He crawled between her legs, leaning over her to claim one breast in his mouth as his hands pulled her panties down off her hips, and his hand slid between her legs.

She came up off the bed at the marvelous feel of those cool fingers sliding against her most private flesh, stroking, entering, claiming. Lifting his head, he kissed the skin between her breasts, then took her other breast in his mouth, twirling the first nipple between his finger and thumb, weakening her body, making her hot and damp and needy.

Rising, he pulled off her panties completely, then spread her thighs and dipped his head, licking, sucking, stabbing inside her with his tongue as her fingers dove into his hair, silently begging him not to stop. When she was whimpering, rocking, crazed with need, he climbed off the bed and shucked off his pants to reveal strong legs, lean hips, and a long, thick, gorgeous penis.

When she glanced up at his face, she found him watching her with fangs elongated, his pupils stark white. She swallowed. He didn't move, just stood there watching her, waiting for her to accept him or to push him away.

This was what he was. A vampire. A man. And while she felt a thrill of fear, it was only a shadow of the real thing. A scary-movie or roller-coaster fear. A safe fear. Which was a bizarre thing to think about a vampire. But she knew in her bones, this one would never hurt her, not physically.

She held out her arms to him, and he came to her, covering her body with his longer, harder one. Brushing her hair off her shoulder, she tilted her neck, giving him access. And he took it, dipping his head and sliding his fangs into her neck as he slid that thick erection into her body.

A low moan escaped her throat as the twin

pleasures, his pull on her blood and his thrusting cock, shot her straight to orgasm.

Arturo thrust into Quinn's welcoming body, her sweet blood flooding his mouth, his pleasure mounting at an alarming rate, ripping through his senses. Warmth spread up into his body until he could swear he felt the sun on his back—not the burning, flesh-eating heat of his vampire existence, but the balmy caress he'd known for too short a time in his human youth. He smelled sunshine and summer on Quinn's flesh, in her hair, and tasted it in her blood.

Her arms curled around him, her fingernails digging into his back as she met his thrusts with low, sweet cries, her body rising for a second time, right along with his.

Despite the glorious sweetness of her blood, he forced himself to pull away from her neck before he took too much. His fangs retracting, he lifted his head, needing to see her face as he drove into her.

Lovely, her brow damp, her mouth open and gasping, she was angel and siren, sweetness and raw, carnal pleasure, and watching her nearly sent him over the edge. At his change in position, her lashes fluttered up, and she met his gaze, a smile, at once sexy as sin and sweetly delighted, lifting the corners of her mouth. How she pleased him! A well of tenderness flooded his mind and chest as she began to cry out with her climax, her body squeezing his until he leaped over that sensual cliff, flying with her straight into the warm embrace of the sun.

Slowly, they settled back to earth, and he kissed her, unwilling to be parted from her even now, loving the way she slid her fingers into his hair and held him as if she, too, didn't want to let him go. If only she were merely human. If only he could make her a simple slave and keep her, always, in his house. In his bed. But she was a sorceress, one claimed by Cristoff. There was nothing simple about Quinn Lennox. And she could quickly become an addiction he could ill afford.

With a sigh of regret, he rolled off her, pulling away, shoving his hands into his hair. The woman had been a problem since the moment she first entered Vamp City. A problem he had no idea how to solve.

Quinn was pulling on her boots when a rap on the door had Arturo striding across the room to open it. Looking at him, at that long, muscular body, once more dressed, at that devilishly handsome mouth, at those sexy eyes, only made her flush all over again with a heat that had barely begun to recede. After two orgasms, she should be replete. Boneless. Done. Instead, she felt energized. Incredible. And ready to go at it all over again.

It didn't hurt that her heart was light with the joy of Zack's rescue. Still, the sex had been outstanding. Was it always like this with vampires? Or only Arturo?

"Kassius is here, Master," the slave said, as Arturo opened the door.

"Thank you, Horace."

When she'd finished tying her bootlaces, Quinn rose and joined Arturo at the door. Instead of ushering her out, he pulled her into his arms and kissed her thoroughly one more time, as if he'd read her thoughts as she watched him walk across the room. As if he'd enjoyed the interlude as much as she had. Finally, he ushered her out of the room and down the stairs to the living room.

Kassius waited for them, his body still, yet radiating a coiled tension that had Quinn's trouble sirens blaring. "Cristoff has already discovered that the sorceress is missing," he said without preamble. "He's on a rampage, every guard ordered to search for her."

Arturo spat something she didn't catch, something that sounded a lot like an Italian curse word, then turned toward the door. "Ernesta!" The moment the Slava appeared in the doorway, he said, "Take Quinn. Darken her hair. At once!"

Quinn gaped at him. "What?"

"A disguise, *cara*," he said impatiently, waving her away. "Go!"

Her pulse skittered as she hurried down the hall after Ernesta. If Arturo and Kassius were this worried, she should be absolutely terrified. What would Cristoff do to her if he found her? And what if he found Zack? Of course, he didn't know Zack was her brother. Yet. But once he figured it out . . . She couldn't finish the thought. He wouldn't find out. But if Cristoff found her here, he'd know Arturo was involved in taking her. Would he kill his snake?

He might not kill him, but he'd probably make Arturo wish he had.

By the time she entered the kitchen, she was shaking.

Ernesta pulled her to a chair and pushed her down, then hurried out of the kitchen, returning moments later with a towel, a comb, and . . . shoe polish? Quinn closed her eyes, trying to remain calm, as Ernesta combed the thick polish through her hair, strand after strand.

"Ernesta . . . I'm sorry I hit you."

The woman didn't reply, just began to rub Quinn's blackened hair dry with the towel. Finally, the Slava pulled Quinn's hair back into a braid with quick, nimble fingers. "There. None will know you, now."

Quinn was kind of glad there were no mirrors around. She wasn't sure she wanted to see what she looked like. Would this dye job really fool anyone? Certainly not Cristoff, but perhaps someone searching for a blonde would look right past her. She could only hope.

Quinn turned to go, but Ernesta stopped her. "Wait. You need a dress." She grabbed one from a hanger in a small alcove off the kitchen, then opened the skirt as if she intended to dress Quinn right there.

Quinn looked at her doubtfully. "Shouldn't I take off my clothes first?"

"No. There is no time." With that, she lifted the dress over Quinn's head.

Okay.

"Now return to the master."

Quinn buttoned the front of the dress as she retraced her steps down the hallway. The men were still talking when she returned.

"I would prefer to take the Jeep"—Arturo glanced at her, his eyes lighting with surprise and satisfaction, before he continued—"but someone will hear the engine. We'll take the horses."

"And if we're stopped?"

"Cristoff most likely believes she's either run to find another sunbeam or been snatched by a rival kovena. It shouldn't be a problem. And if it is . . ." Arturo shrugged. "I'll think of something." He turned back to her. "Get your brother, *cara*. We're leaving. You cannot be caught here."

She'd figured that much. It was way too dangerous for Arturo though she wondered where he'd take them. The only part of his and Kassius's conversation she'd understood was the part about her having to ride another damned horse.

Lifting the awkward skirt, she hurried up the stairs to the room where she'd first found herself tied to the bed . . . was it just a week and a half ago? The room where Zack now rested.

She rapped lightly on the door, then opened it and went in when he didn't respond. He remained as she'd left him, his bare, scarred back to the door. "Zack, get up. We have to leave."

When he didn't respond, she bit down her frustration and circled the bed to find him staring morosely at the wall.

"Zack, I know you've been through hell. I get it. But a really nasty vampire is hunting us, and we have to go."

"Leave me here."

"You don't mean that."

Her easygoing brother speared her with hard, angry eyes. "You don't get it. I don't fucking care."

She stared at him, feeling bruised and hurt. But dammit . . . "Zack, get your sorry ass off that bed. We're going. *Now.*"

But her brother still didn't move.

"Is there a problem?" Arturo stood in the doorway.

"Could you take his memories of what happened?"

Zack reared up. "No."

"Zack, think about it. He can make you forget."

"I don't want to forget."

"Are you sure?"

"I said no!" He glared at her. "Will you move so I can piss in the pot?"

Quinn jumped off the bed, getting out of his way, storming out of the room. Where in the hell had her Zack gone? Because this angry, depressed man was not he.

In the hallway, Arturo touched her arm. "He is not the child he was when he arrived here. Do not expect him to be. But if he can accept what has happened, he'll be better off than he would be if he knew there were large chunks of his memory gone. Sometimes, wondering about the things you have forgotten is worse than knowing." His fingers slid into her hair, his eyes gentle and sympathetic. "He will be okay, *cara*. Give him time. It will be good for you to get him home."

She blinked. "Home?"

"I am sending both of you through the Boundary Circle. Back to the sunshine."

"But . . ." She gaped at him, then narrowed her eyes. "Why? You said yourself that if the magic isn't renewed, you'll die. Which means you've got something else up your sleeve."

He shrugged. "Grant is more powerful than he lets on. He is more powerful than you, *cara*. You will never be what Cristoff wishes, and he will punish you severely for it." He cupped her cheek, unhappiness darkening his eyes. "I never want to see you in pain like that again."

She saw truth in those eyes, heard it in his voice. Was he really saving her simply because he wanted to?

Dear God, is he really letting us go?

But they'd be leaving without Lily. If the girl was even in V.C. If she was even still alive.

Count your wins. Getting Zack home, getting them both out of Vamp City alive, was huge.

Ten minutes later, Arturo, Kassius, Quinn, and Zack were riding through the swampy White House grounds, due west. Zack rode like he knew what he was doing, though with nothing approaching the grace or strength of the two vampires. Though she'd coaxed him out of the house and into a shirt, he'd said nothing since they left the house. He sat now, riding to her right, silent and morose.

Quinn glanced left, at Arturo. This time he'd trusted her to steer the horse herself though he was riding so close that it was amazing the horses didn't run into one another. Hers and the vampire's knees kept brushing, though she couldn't say she really minded.

"Where is the Boundary Circle?" Quinn asked.

"Most of the southwest curvature falls within the Potomac and is useless unless you want to row out to it by boat. Only a small corner between Water Street and Georgetown crosses land. A point very close to the Kennedy Center."

She frowned, seeing a map of D.C. in her head. "There's a ton of land between Water Street and Georgetown."

"Not the curve I'm talking about. Not in 1870. The Tidal Basin did not exist, nor did the Mall west of the Washington Monument. It was all water, the Potomac Shallows. The shallows were eventually filled to make the land you know as the Mall west of the Washington Monument. That work was never done here. In Vamp City, it is still all water."

"So you're going to drop us at the Kennedy Center?"

"Yes." His expression grew very serious. "You should not travel far from D.C. until the magic is renewed, *cara*. Most importantly, do not let your brother. The magic is unpredictable in this state and may have laid claim to one or both of you. You could sicken if you go too far though not in a way that any doctor could cure."

"How will I know the magic has been renewed?" But she would know, wouldn't she? When she ceased to see the worlds colliding. "Never mind."

She shook her head, a question bothering her. "You said you can't leave Vamp City, now."

"That is true."

"And humans can't leave on their own."

"Also true."

"Then how are you going to free us?"

He stiffened ever so slightly, as if he hadn't given this escape plan enough thought. She probably wouldn't have noticed if their knees hadn't been a handsbreadth apart.

She looked at him sharply.

But when he met her gaze, his eyes were calm and sure. "I can push you through even if I cannot follow."

"You're sure?"

His eyes crinkled at the corners. "I am."

She wondered how he could be so certain when everyone kept saying the vampires never let humans go once they were caught. But the last thing she wanted to do was talk him out of trying. Besides, what might be true of other humans often didn't apply to her. She might succeed even where most would fail.

"Can you push other vampires through?" she asked. "Could you get Bram out of here?"

"No. The magic holds us. It has bound us to it."

"Ax," Kassius said, his voice low and urgent. "Four o'clock. Ivan and his troop."

"*Merda.*" Arturo suddenly grabbed the reins of her horse. "Fight me, *cara*. Ivan has seen you up close. There will be no deceiving him."

Quinn swung at him, understanding that they had to put on an act, to pretend he'd caught her and wasn't helping her escape. But, oh my God. Did this mean the escape was a bust? Was he going to hand them back over to these men? To Cristoff?

Her gut twisted, her neck burning, her feet tingling.

Fear, cold as steel, sliced her heart in two.

CHAPTER TWENTY

So this is it?" Quinn cried, struggling, as Arturo hauled her off her horse and onto his own, setting her in front of him, his arm clamping around her, pinning her own arms to her sides. "Are you going to give me to them?" Cristoff would torture her, fill her with dragon fire again. Maybe even carry out his threat and cut off her feet! "Kill me here, Vampire. Don't send me back. *Please*."

"Your fear is good, *cara*. Be afraid, as any escaped slave should. They will taste it."

No problem. Ice was forming in her veins so quickly, she might soon be sparkling with frost.

She glanced at Zack, who sat silently on his horse, staring at nothing. As if he'd already given up. Had he been paying attention to anything? Was the brother she knew and loved even in there anymore? Then again, if he'd kicked his horse into gear and taken off, Kassius would have gone after him and quickly taken him down in one of those vampire faster-than-the-speed-of-light moves. This way, he could potentially be passed off as a slave accompanying Arturo rather than one involved with her. The last thing, the *last thing*, she wanted was for Cristoff to figure out he was her brother.

She hazarded a glance at the approaching vampire guards, recognizing the bald Ivan. He certainly appeared to be the leader of the bunch.

Oh, this is not good.

Arturo turned his horse around and started back the way they'd come, riding straight for Ivan and company, leading her empty horse behind him as Kassius and Zack followed.

Quinn's pulse thrummed with fear, her head pounding with frustration. They'd been so close!

That weird, unnatural heat began to crawl beneath her skin again, and she wondered if her eyes were starting to glow. She swept her lashes down, hiding her eyes, at once hating her power and desperately wishing she could find a way to harness it.

"Arturo." Ivan nodded as the two parties converged. Quinn felt his gaze on her, heard him grunt as if noticing the change in her hair. "I see you've . . . *found* . . . her."

They hadn't fooled him about her identity, as they'd known they wouldn't. But his questioning tone made her doubt they'd fooled him about anything.

"I have found her. Just this moment," Arturo said smoothly, that hypnotic quality in his voice she'd heard a couple of times before. "You saw me capture her."

The suspicion slipped out of Ivan's expression.

"I saw you capture her," he repeated almost mechanically. Holy cow. Did Arturo actually have the power to affect a vampire's mind?

But a moment later, the suspicion rushed back into Ivan's eyes as he cocked his head. "I wonder, though, why you were riding toward the Boundary Circle, a friendly little foursome."

Quinn felt Arturo tense. "You are mistaken, *amico mio.* We had only just ridden upon the escaping slave."

But Ivan was no diplomat. And whatever mind games Arturo had attempted had clearly failed. "I know what I saw. And I saw you and Kassius riding toward the Boundary Circle with the sorceress and another slave, thick as thieves. Cristoff will be very interested in my story, I've no doubt."

Arturo's voice sounded in her head. *Hold on,* cara. *Then take the horses and go.*

What in the hell did he have in mind?

Suddenly, he was no longer behind her, no longer holding on to her, and she grabbed for the horse's neck, nearly slipping off his back before she managed to right herself. Out of the corner of her eye, she saw something large and round go airborne in a spray of . . . *blood.* As the thing landed on the ground in front of her, she stared in horror at Ivan's head. Her eyes went wide as vampire warfare erupted around her, flashes of movement, cries of fury and pain, splashes of blood.

Her horse spooked and began to run, with her barely half-on. *Oh, hell.*

Struggling against the awkward skirt, she

somehow managed to fling her leg astride the saddle, shoving her feet in the stirrups even as she clung to the horse's mane.

"Quinn! This way!" Zack was motioning her to follow.

A moment's thrill that Zack seemed to have snapped out of his depression gave way to frustration. She was all for following him, dammit, but how? Her shaking fingers closed around the leather reins, and she gathered them up and pulled to one side, trying to turn the animal. But the horse took the bit in its teeth and fought her.

"Fine! Go where you want to, just go!"

Zack made some kind of clicking noise with his tongue. She watched with surprise as her horse's ears perked up, then she gasped and grabbed the reins and mane as he lunged forward to follow her brother and his mount. Where in the hell had Zack learned that trick? Where'd he learn to ride, for that matter? Probably at one of those expensive summer camps Angela was always sending him to.

She caught up with Zack quickly, and, together, they raced in the direction they'd been traveling earlier, toward the fog and the Boundary Circle. Could she get herself and Zack through that barrier just as she had the sunbeams? There was only one way to find out.

Behind her, she heard the grunts and yells and occasional clang of steel that told her the battle continued to rage. *Don't die, Vampire.* He had his faults, a ton of them, but there was decency in him, and a gentleness that she never would have expected from such a dangerous creature.

As her horse flew over the soft earth, Quinn hung on for dear life, her heart pounding to the beat of the horse's hooves. Though the unpaved streets remained in this part of the city, whatever buildings had once existed were gone, replaced by thickets of dead trees. As they rode, the fog grew thicker, ghostly fingers probing around them, breaking through here and there to reveal the Potomac gleaming on the left, far closer than it should have been. At the corner where the river turned north would lie the Kennedy Center in her world. And the Boundary Circle in this. They had to reach that point of land before the vampires turned their attention to the escaped slaves. To the escaped sorceress.

Suddenly, out of nowhere, hands gripped her waist as if the fingers of mist had turned real. She cried out with surprise. The reins were ripped from her hands and her body hurled off the horse to land on something hard and narrow. A shoulder. Her forehead cracked against his backbone. "Ow."

She smelled vampire. Not Arturo, which meant she'd been caught by one of Ivan's guards! He must have flown at her on foot, no horse able to carry him as fast as he could move on his own.

Dizzily, she craned her head up to see that Zack, still mounted, was swinging around and heading back to her. What was he planning to do, *try to save her*? She shook her head at him. He needed to keep going, to run! But he continued toward her as if he meant to rescue her from a freaking *vampire*.

That tingling, useless heat began to flow up into her arms, and she pointed her palms toward her captor's butt, willing him to fall or go flying . . . preferably dropping her first. But, as before, nothing happened. Her power was useless!

If only she could reach her weapons, but they were in her pockets, beneath her dress, and her dress was firmly pinned to her thighs by her captor's arm. Maybe she could make him shift his hold enough for her to get to the stake in her pants pocket.

"Let me go!" she screamed, and began pounding his back and kicking her feet, accidentally . . . brilliantly . . . landing a direct hit to his crotch with the toe of her boot.

"Fuck!" the vamp cried out, jerking her legs around one of his hips so she couldn't kick him again, his movement grinding to a halt as he bent over in pain. Apparently, even vampires could be brought low by a swift kick to the family jewels.

Unfortunately, he didn't loosen his grip on her enough for her to lift her dress, but she spied the hilt of a knife at his hip. Vamps were too damn fast. Then again, this one was a bit preoccupied.

She went for it, amazed when she was able to snatch the blade from its sheath. With no time to hesitate, she whipped the knife out and down into the bastard's thigh. He yelled a vicious curse in some language she didn't understand and tossed her onto the ground with a bone-jarring thud.

Beneath her, she felt the vibration of pounding hooves. Through the swirling mist, she saw Zack racing toward her on horseback. She scrambled to her feet, but the vamp had already recovered and was stalking her, his fangs long, his eyes white with hunger and blazing with a fury that told her his hunger was for revenge.

Taunting heat crawled beneath her flesh.

She glanced toward Zack, who was bearing down on them, inadvertently drawing the vamp's attention to her brother. With the swish of metal, the vamp drew his sword. He'd kill Zack with one quick, careless swing!

"No!" The heat flamed inside of her, pulsing, pounding, as if trying to get out. A memory flashed, a dream of a door buckling beneath the weight of the light trying to escape, a light . . . *power* . . . she'd desperately sought to keep contained. Hidden. From Zack.

And suddenly she understood. God help her, she was the one who'd been fighting her power. Because she'd never wanted Zack to see it. She'd never wanted him to know.

Well, *fuck it.* He was going to die!

With a cry of surrender, she closed her eyes. Trembling, she released her hold on that door, on the heat that swirled inside her, lifted her hands, and poured her will into stopping the vampire who would kill her brother.

Power blasted from her fingers, sending the vampire flying a dozen feet to land hard on his back. She stared at him, stunned. Euphoric. *I did it.* But a second later, the vamp leaped to his feet.

Like hell. She knocked him down a second time. And a third. Every time he moved, she blasted him until he was pinned to the ground, struggling, shouting with fury.

She hazarded a glance at her brother and found him sitting still on his horse, staring at her as if he'd never seen her before. As if she terrified him.

Ice formed in her veins, crawling through the heat as she instinctively fought to shut that door again. To hide again. But the power was loose and wild. Out of her control. It turned on her, stinging as it had in the Focus with Grant and Sheridan when they'd tried to pull the magic. The pain ran up her arms, burning, devouring.

But her vampire victim remained as trapped by her power as she did herself.

Behind her, a man cried out in pain, then another, and the sounds of battle went silent.

A moment later, Arturo was at her side. "*Quinn.*"

"I don't know how to stop it!"

"Easy, *cara*, easy. Can you lower your hands?"

"No. It's fighting me. It's attacking me!"

She felt Arturo's strong arm go around her, his body tensing as if he shared her pain. His cheek brushed her temple. "I'll try to help you. Do not fight me."

"I won't," she gasped. "Not if I can help it." But she had no control over any of it. None. Her vision was beginning to spin, turning bright with light that wasn't there.

She felt Arturo's cool fingers close around her forearm, felt that arm drop, the connection breaking in both. But the power, once directed at the vampire, recoiled, attacking her fully instead. Quinn cried out, pain lancing her, her vision blazing white.

"Quinn, listen to me." Cool fingers gripped her face as Arturo's voice came at her from the front now. "Listen to me! You must turn it off inside, or it will kill you."

"Don't . . . know how."

"Look at me."

"I can't!" All she could see was white.

"Yes, you can," he insisted, his voice turning low, soothing, with that hypnotic tone she'd heard him use on others. "Come, *cara*, focus on me, on my voice, on my face." He released her, gripping her hands, pressing them against his cheeks as if she were a blind woman trying to see. And she was exactly that.

She pressed her hands to his face, tracing the contours of his cheekbones, his brow, his nose. As her fingers dropped to his mouth, her hands began to shake violently. Her whole body began to quake, as if preparing to implode.

But Arturo only gripped her hands with his, taking them to his mouth. "What do you see, Quinn?"

"White, just white."

"Push pass it, *piccola*. Through it. I am here, on the other side."

Trembling, Quinn fought the blindness, fought to see Arturo. At last, a shadow moved within the white. Slowly, the whiteness turned to mist, dissipating, leaving her half-blind but staring into Arturo's face.

"I did it," she gasped.

He smiled with approval. "You did. Now look deeply into my eyes, *cara*, and I will help you douse the fire."

She followed his words, staring deep into those dark eyes, feeling as if he were climbing into her through her own. Instinct had her tensing, desperation battled that instinct as she forced herself to relax, to welcome his help.

"That's a good girl. Find the source of the fire, *cara*. Can you tell me what it looks like?"

"It's . . . a door. A door I opened and can't shut."

"Then we will shut it together. Focus on the door, Quinn, on the handle. Grip that handle tight in your hand. I am behind you, with you. Together we will close it. Are you ready?"

Shaking with pain, with fear, Quinn nodded. "Yes."

"On the count of three then. One, two . . . *three!*"

Quinn poured her will into closing that door, just as she'd poured her will into opening it. But it wouldn't . . . there! It was starting to move. She could feel strength pumping into her own, Arturo's strength. She could do this!

Perspiration broke out all over her body as she concentrated, as she struggled to close that door, to shut the bright glow of power behind it once more.

"That a girl," Arturo encouraged. "You're doing it. A little more. A little more."

Slowly, together, they pushed until the door finally clicked shut, containing the power. As suddenly as it began, the vibrations fled, and the pain drained away.

With a last quaking shudder, Quinn sank against Arturo.

He gathered her close, his lips brushing her temple. "Are you all right?"

"I think so." She was still out of breath, damp with perspiration, shaken. Stunned. As Arturo stroked her hair, she pulled back to look at him. "What happened to the vampire?"

His gaze was warm and concerned as he studied her as if seeking signs of damage. "The moment you released him, Kassius killed him."

"They're all dead?"

"Yes. Neither Ivan nor his guards will carry tales to Cristoff of our hand in your escape. We need to go." He pulled away, curving his arm around her shoulder as he stepped to her side and started for the two horses that stood docilely now between Kassius's and Zack's mounts.

Her stomach clenched, and she forced herself to look up at her brother, dreading the fear and horror she'd see on his face. Instead, she found him, inexplicably, grinning at her. "That was fucking *amazing*, sis. Like something out of *X-men*."

Tears began to run down her cheeks, unbidden.

Zack's grin died, his brows lowering into a frown. "What's the matter, Quinn? Are you still in pain?"

Quinn swiped at the tears fiercely. "I never wanted you to see me like that. I never wanted you to know."

His frown deepened. "That you were a superhero?"

A watery laugh escaped her throat. "That I was so weird."

Zack gave her a brotherly roll of his eyes. "You're not *weird*, Quinn. You're my sister."

Such simple words. And the fear that she'd lived with for longer than she could remember, the fear that he, too, might turn from her in disgust, slipped away as if it had never been. She brushed the tears from her cheeks. "I love you, Zack."

Arturo squeezed her shoulder. "We need to go, *cara*. Others could come." He helped her onto her horse and mounted his own, then urged all into a gallop. As they ate up the ground, something ahead caught her eye. It almost looked like . . . a Shimmer. It had the same flowing rainbowlike colors of water mist.

She stared at it, stunned. *Of course.* The Shimmers of D.C. were the Boundary Circle of the magical Vamp City, shimmers only she could see.

When they were but a few yards from the

wall of moving color, Arturo pulled up and dismounted. Turning to her, he pulled her down and into his arms, his dark eyes intense and serious. "This is it, *tessoro*."

As she stared into his rugged, handsome face, something clenched inside her, a fist of unhappiness. She would probably never see him again. Lifting her hand, she stroked his cool cheek, allowing herself to drown in that deep gaze one last time. "You'll be okay?"

"Of course. All will be as it is meant to be." He brushed a stray lock back from her face. "You'll be safe now."

"I'll miss you, Vampire."

His mouth kicked up on one side. "Will you? I doubt that. Though I will, of a certainty, miss you." He kissed her, his cool lips moving over hers, caressing, sipping, warming. Slowly, he pulled away, then began unbuttoning the front of her dress. "You'll draw too much attention in this where you're going."

Quinn was suddenly glad she'd left her clothes on underneath and began unbuttoning the buttons from the other direction. When they were done, she stepped out of the dress.

Arturo's gaze locked on hers, regret in his eyes. "Be happy." Then he released her and took her hand. "You must be touching me to go through." Just as the Slavas had to touch her as they escaped through the sunbeam. "But I cannot follow."

As Arturo led her to the wall, Zack close behind,

the air began to crackle around her, popping and fizzing, lifting the hair on her arms.

"You feel it," Arturo said with surprise.

"I do. And I see it. I'm wondering if I could pass through on my own."

He cocked his head. "It would be a good thing to know. Try, *cara*."

"It won't hurt me if I fail?"

"No. It should not."

He released her, and she turned toward the wall. If the magic sucked her through as that first sunbeam had, she'd immediately come back for Zack if Arturo didn't send him through himself. But as she reached out to the Shimmer, her fingers encountered a rubbery surface. A split second later, she was sitting on her butt in the dirt.

Arturo chuckled. "Question answered."

Quinn rose, dusted off her pants, and met Arturo's amusement with a disgruntled look. He pulled her into his arms and kissed her thoroughly one last time, then pulled away, tenderness in his eyes. "I shall miss you, Quinn."

Feeling a rush of tenderness for him in return, she kissed his cheek. "And I you." She turned to see Kassius waiting with the horses and lifted her hand. "Thank you."

He nodded gravely.

Arturo motioned her over. "Give me your hands, both of you." When she and Zack had done so, Arturo lifted their joined hands to the front, urging them to step forward.

This time, the wall embraced her, dancing over her flesh like tiny ions, tickling coolly. And then she was through, stepping into the bright sunshine, Arturo's hand no longer in hers. Zack was beside her, squinting against the brightness as the deafening noise of their world bombarded ears grown accustomed to quiet.

"We did it," Zack breathed. "Fuck me, but we're out of there."

Quinn turned back, still able to see the Shimmer, but nothing on the other side. No one.

"Good-bye, Arturo," she said quietly, then took Zack's hand and started home.

"She believes you've freed her," Kassius commented, as they rode through the Nod a short while later, pretending to search for the sorceress like the rest of Cristoff's men.

Arturo shrugged. "She believes many things . . . that I cannot leave Vamp City, that she and her brother should stay in the area, and that I have no way to follow her if she does leave."

"You have a way to track her this time?"

"I do. I would not make that mistake twice."

"Have you told her *any* truths?"

Arturo smiled. "There was truth between us." Their bodies had spoken with profound honesty though what exactly that meant, he couldn't say.

"What did you tell her to make her believe she's no longer needed to save V.C.?"

"That Grant is more powerful than she is."

Kassius snorted. "It's a wonder your nose

doesn't grow long enough to spear your next meal from twenty paces. And I assume you failed to tell her about her brother?"

"Certainly. There was no need to alarm her. Better for her to think their lives can return to normal."

"I can't fault that. I'm still not entirely sure what I saw when I drank from her."

"We'll figure it out. When the equinox nears, I'll collect them both." He smiled. "Cristoff will praise me for finding the sorceress at last. He need never know I was responsible for her escape in the first place. Or that I've known where she was all along."

Kassius shook his head. "I thought your loyalty to him had finally begun to wane."

"Never. He's my master as he is yours."

"He's a sadistic bastard, and we both know it."

Arturo shrugged. "We are what we are." But the thought of Quinn in Cristoff's hands again, suffering his wrath, chilled him. He told himself he didn't care, that he was as heartless a bastard as his master.

But he knew his own lies too well to be fooled.

"Will you leave her to her own devices, now? Or keep an eye on her?"

A grin spread across Arturo's mouth. "I mean to keep a very close eye on her. As soon as night falls, I plan to take the Jeep through the Boundary and stay with Micah for a day or two as I catch up with my work on my computer." He turned to his friend with regret. "I wish you could accompany me."

"As do I."

Arturo's lie to Quinn had been a small one. While he and Micah and a handful of others were still able to come and go through the Boundary Circle at will, most vampires had been caught by the magic and were firmly stuck inside. Kassius, unfortunately, was one of them. As was Bram.

"I will not let anything happen to our sorceress, Kas. She will renew the magic when the time is right. Vamp City will be saved."

He'd given Quinn a reprieve.

But from the first moment she'd stepped into Vamp City, her fate had been sealed.

THE *FERAL WARRIOR* NOVELS FROM
USA TODAY BESTSELLING AUTHOR

PAMELA PALMER

*They are called Feral Warriors—an elite band of
immortals who can change shape at will. Sworn to rid
the world of evil, consumed by sorcery and seduction,
their wild natures are primed for release . . .*

DESIRE UNTAMED
978-0-06-166751-0

OBSESSION UNTAMED
978-0-06-166752-7

PASSION UNTAMED
978-0-06-166753-4

RAPTURE UNTAMED
978-0-06-179470-4

HUNGER UNTAMED
978-0-06-179471-0

ECSTASY UNTAMED
978-0-06-179473-5

RETURN TO THE HOLLOWS WITH
NEW YORK TIMES BESTSELLING AUTHOR

KIM
HARRISON

WHITE WITCH, BLACK CURSE
978-0-06-113802-7

Kick-ass bounty hunter and witch Rachel Morgan has crossed forbidden lines, taken demonic hits, and still stands. But a new predator is moving to the apex of the *Inderlander* food chain—and now Rachel's past is coming back to haunt her . . . literally.

BLACK MAGIC SANCTION
978-0-06-113804-1

Denounced and shunned by her own kind for dealing with demons and black magic, Rachel Morgan's best hope is life imprisonment—her worst, a forced lobotomy and genetic slavery. And only her enemies are strong enough to help her win her freedom.

PALE DEMON
978-0-06-113807-2

After centuries of torment, a fearsome creature walks free, craving innocent blood and souls—especially Rachel Morgan's, who'll need to embrace her demonic nature to survive.

Visit www.AuthorTracker.com for exclusive
information on your favorite HarperCollins authors.

Available wherever books are sold or please call 1-800-331-3761 to order.

HAR2 0811

Next month, don't miss these exciting new love stories only from Avon Books

Scandal Wears Satin by Loretta Chase
Struggling to keep her shop afloat in the wake of a recent family scandal, dressmaker Sophy Noirot has no time for men, especially the Earl of Longmore. But when Longmore's sister—and Sophy's best customer—runs away, everything changes as Sophy finds that desire has never slipped on so smoothly . . .

Willow Springs by Toni Blake
Amy Bright is the ultimate matchmaker . . . when it comes to everyone's love life but her own. Writing anonymous steamy love letters to handsome firefighter Logan, Amy strives to make the perfect match: for herself. Will Amy overcome her shyness and turn friendship into something more? Or will the return of a woman from Logan's past ruin everything?

How to Be a Proper Lady by Katharine Ashe
Viola Carlyle doesn't care about being proper. Suffocated by English society, Viola longs to be free. Captain Jin Seton is the object of Viola's desire. Though Jin vowed not to let Viola steal his heart, that won't stop this improper lady from trying . . .

Tarnished by Karina Cooper
Cherry St. Croix knows as much about genteel London society as she does its dark underground of vagrants and thieves. Hunting murderers by night, blending in by day, Cherry is caught between two worlds...and many men. Will she be exposed and cast out from polite London society, or will she take one risk too many and wind up dead?

At Avon Books, we know your passion for romance—once you finish one of our novels, you find yourself wanting more.

May we tempt you with . . .

- **Excerpts** from our upcoming releases.

- Entertaining **extras**, including authors' personal photo albums and book lists.

- Behind-the-scenes **scoop** on your favorite characters and series.

- **Sweepstakes** for the chance to win free books, romantic getaways, and other fun prizes.

- Writing **tips** from our authors and editors.

- **Blog** with our authors and find out why they love to write romance.

- **Exclusive content** that's not contained within the pages of our novels.

Join us at
www.avonbooks.com

AVON   *An Imprint of* HarperCollins*Publishers*
www.avonromance.com

Available wherever books are sold or please call 1-800-331-3761 to order.

FTH 1111